The Heir to Longbourn

Laurence Fleming's first novel, *A Diet of Crumbs*, was published in 1959 by the Artemis Press, selected from a competition judged by a panel that included Nancy Mitford and Angus Wilson. At Cambridge he wrote scripts for the Footlights. He is co-author, with Alan Gore, of the bestselling *The English Garden* and, with Ann Gore and Clay Perry, of *Old English Villages*. He is author of *The One Hour Garden*, which he illustrated himself; of *Roberto Burle Marx, A Portrait* and of *On Torquemada's Sofa*. He has compiled two volumes of memories from British India under the title of *Last Children of the Raj*. He lives in St Leonard's-on-Sea, East Sussex.

for Clare.

The Heir to Longbourn

Laurence Fleming.

Laurence Fleming

with lots of love.

dexter
haven
PUBLISHING

Published in 2009 by Dexter Haven Ltd
Curtain House
134–146 Curtain Road
London EC2A 3AR

Some of this work appeared in an edition published in 2003 by
Bentwyck Henry Publishers Ltd.

ISBN 978-1-903660-06-5

Front cover image courtesy of the National Portrait Gallery, *Lady
Caroline Lamb* by Eliza H. Trotter; all other images © Ken Leeder,
with thanks to the Geffrye Museum.

Typeset by Dexter Haven Associates Ltd, London
Printed in Great Britain by CPI Cox & Wyman, Reading RG1 8EX

To Ann and Alan

The reader is asked to imagine that all the novels of Jane Austen began at the same time, the summer of 1814.

I

1819

Matlock was by no means as far from Pemberley as Elizabeth had thought. As they drove into the town in the early afternoon, she found herself wondering why, in the four years of her marriage, and a four-year residence at Pemberley, she had never been there before. Her spirits rose as she looked about her. Even on this, a gloomy, grey, wet day in February, the little town exuded a considerable charm. It seemed to welcome them.

All the arrangements for their visit had been made by Mr Darcy himself, in a spirit of some alarm for her health. As she moved through the lodgings he had found for them—for his sister Georgiana was to be her companion here—she smiled to herself to see that the window hangings and chair covers were all fresh, if not new, and that the rugs on the floor, and much of the furniture, had come from the third floor at Pemberley. Her spirits rose a little further. She had never had reason to doubt the devotion of her husband, a devotion which she as completely returned; but these unspoken evidences of his continuing concern could only make her count her blessings again.

It was three months since the birth of her second daughter, but her recovery had been slow. Her doctor, at last, had suggested a change.

"I cannot recommend Buxton," said he. "It is full of busy-bodies and tattlemongers, but in Matlock you may be at peace and, if I am to be asked my opinion, the waters there are the more beneficial of the two. You will not have to endure the worst of the Pemberley weather, since Matlock is peculiarly warm; and I am also of the opinion, and have long been so, that a

1

simple change of scene may bring about the improvement that we are all so anxious to see. You cannot but benefit from Matlock."

So the decision was taken. Mr Darcy, who was to remain at Pemberley, would be able to ride over and back again quite easily in a day, since their stay was expected to last for six weeks. He escorted them to Matlock; made sure that everything was in order; kissed them both, with obvious regret; and departed before the light had quite gone.

Elizabeth and Georgiana had always been great friends, but their present particularly good understanding dated from a visit once paid to Pemberley by Elizabeth's youngest sister, Lydia. She was the wife of a certain George Wickham, son of the late Mr Darcy's steward, and their marriage, after their elopement, had only been brought about by Mr Darcy himself, with some help from Elizabeth's uncle, Edward Gardiner. Previously to this, however, Wickham had paid some considerable attention to Elizabeth; and, previously to that, had actually persuaded Georgiana to elope with him, a project only prevented at the last moment by the unexpected arrival of Mr Darcy himself.

After Lydia's much-protracted departure on that occasion, Elizabeth had said, with a small smile to Georgiana: "I am sure we are both feeling, at this moment, how extremely fortunate we are—*not* to be the wife of George Wickham."

And Georgiana had caught her breath.

"But do you *know*?" she had asked. "I thought that no one knew."

"I have always known, dearest Georgiana, and sympathised more than a little. For I, as I will tell you now, allowed my heart to stray in that direction for several weeks. It was not only caused by the flattering attention that he paid me. I think I was quite captivated by the way his hair rose so crisply from his forehead."

"And I by the wave in his side-whiskers," replied Georgiana, catching her tone. "I think I have never seen anyone else with side-whiskers just like that. I wondered at first if it could be natural and then thought of the agonies one would have to go through to induce a curl in one's side-whiskers. The risk! The danger! How steady would have to be the hand that held the curling-tongs!"

"I imagine there was more than enough vanity there for him to brave that," said Elizabeth. "But then his *eyes*—so blue and so empty. And his *smile*—so white and so empty. I often wonder how I could have been so stupid. Or so blind."

"But this is *such* a comfort, dearest Elizabeth," said Georgiana joyfully. "Until now I believed myself the only simpleton to be so taken in."

"It shall be our secret then," said Elizabeth. "And if the one of us shall ever see the other about to make some really foolish error, it will be her duty just to murmur to her—*Wickham!*"

They laughed together and their friendship, firm before, had ripened into the fullest confidence.

Georgiana had not wished to test the perils of a London season, much to the disapproval, and the disappointment, of her aunt, Lady Catherine de Bourgh.

"But I have to ask myself, in all honesty," had remarked Mr Darcy at the time, "if being presented to society by Lady Catherine would carry with it any advantage? I am inclined to think, in my more sober moments, that it would be much in the nature of a handicap."

Georgiana had remained comfortably with them at Pemberley, an enthusiastic aunt to Jane, now two, and to Anne, the new baby. She was to be with Elizabeth throughout the stay at Matlock Bath, together with the children, their nurse, two nursery maids, a wet-nurse and a lady's maid.

Elizabeth was sitting quietly by the fire in their sitting-room upstairs when Georgiana came in.

"The rooms above are quite as pretty as this," she said, "and charmingly warm. There is something very re-assuring about a coal fire and, in these tiny grates, it is certainly the only thing. But I am glad we still burn wood at Pemberley."

"I am amazed by the heat given out by this very small fire," said Elizabeth. "There are coal mines near here, I believe, but when I think of the suffering of those men in the mines, I hardly like to be so warm at their expense."

"Except that," said Georgiana, with a smile, "if we did not burn their coal, they would have no livelihood."

"True indeed," returned Elizabeth. "Merely, I wish that they could have some other livelihood and that we could have some other way of keeping warm."

"Nurse says she will bring the baby down to you at four and I have asked our landlady, whose name I have yet to discover, if we may dine at five."

"Mrs Routledge," said Elizabeth. "I believe she was once one of the housekeepers at Chatsworth."

"Then we should be in excellent hands," said Georgiana.

"I have been sitting here wondering if this is not the day my mother sets out for Bath with my sister Mary. They will have ugly weather for their journey, I fear, but perhaps the waters there may bring her as much benefit as the waters here are to bring me."

"You have never mentioned this before."

"No. With my mother it is impossible to tell if her maladies be real or imagined. This time, since her doctor is a man of great good sense, I believe he must be convinced by her complaints. And I wish her rid of them with all my heart, for her sake, and for the tranquillity that it would bring to the life of my father."

Elizabeth still fed her daughter twice a day, at ten in the morning and four in the afternoon. The wet-nurse undertook the two remaining feeds at night. This arrangement, in being for less than ten days, enabled Elizabeth to sleep the night through and she already began to feel its benevolent effects. She dined downstairs with Georgiana, both exclaiming over the excellence of the cooking; and by nine o'clock Elizabeth was in bed and perfectly ready to go to sleep.

"You look almost too comfortable," said Georgiana, smiling as she wished her goodnight. "I think we may be very happy at Matlock."

The gloom of the weather lifted on the following day. It did not rain and, while the sun did not shine, it was possible to see where it was through the blanket of cloud. At twelve o'clock, they ventured out and walked the few hundred yards to the Bath itself.

"I do not feel strong enough yet," said Elizabeth, "to go into the warm bath, which the doctor so particularly advises. For the moment I am but too happy just to drink the waters—less effort is entailed altogether."

"But I must hope you mean to do so before long, since I am determined to go myself," said Georgiana, "and I would hesitate to go alone."

"Surely you are perfectly well? What need can you have of the warm bath—or even the water-cure?"

"I am perfectly well, indeed, dear Elizabeth. But perhaps I may become perfectly better. I am persuaded that to stand up to one's neck in warm water can do one nothing but good."

"And is that what one must do? I quite thought that one lay down, submerged in a kind of coffin."

"I hope not so," said Georgiana, laughing. "I am sure one can walk around or even *float*. Are not you *consumed* with curiosity, Elizabeth? Shall we not try this very day?"

"Well, no, if you will forgive me—but perhaps tomorrow. Today I will simply endeavour to drink the one pint recommended by the doctor to begin with—and sit and watch the world go by while I am doing so."

They settled on a sofa in the Pump Room, which they occupied almost alone, and devoted themselves to that task. There was a screen to one side of them and they soon found themselves listening to a conversation which had clearly been going on behind it for some time.

"And when I ask you particularly to get cotton stockings for Bridget you buy instead this *abrasive* mixture which will certainly remove all the skin from her legs."

"I have *never* condoned your determination to spend a shilling where sixpence would do. These stockings were less than half the price of the cotton ones—and Bridget, when all is said and done, is only a servant."

The speakers were two women, the first perhaps the younger; and it was she who continued now, in a voice of cool anger: "In my house—and I repeat, in *my* house—we do not speak of anyone as being *only* a servant. They all chose to come with me, at their own suggestion, and I regard them rather as friends."

"I think you forget that I chose to accompany you myself. When servants are treated as friends their respect is lost."

"Except that, in this case, it is *you* who have forfeited their respect. Your nip-farthing, mean-spirited, penny-pinching ways are a byword in the kitchen and I now find that I have had enough of them. Bridget you have reduced to tears on more than one occasion and, when I think of the family she left behind in order to come with me, that touches me very nearly. If I am to choose between her and you, I choose her without a struggle."

"I do not understand you, Maria."

"I doubt my ability to put it more plainly."

"I hope you do not forget the sacrifice that *I* made in order to accompany you into your exile here. I left quite as much behind as Bridget."

"I think not. You left only a small house, in which you lived at your own expense, and a family—a sister's family—which included you only reluctantly. The advantages to you were plain for all to see. Bridget left her mother behind, and her brothers and sisters. While she can now spend a month with them every year, it is not the same as seeing them every week."

"You are too generous to your servants."

"I rather think that you are too grudging. But this is by no means all. Shall I *ever* forget, for instance, the mortification I felt at Ashover—when the bandages I had asked you to procure proved to be made of some inferior stuff—*not* the linen ones I had asked for—which tore when they were stretched and through which the ointments and salves soaked all too easily? That is an occasion I shall always remember."

"I was able to buy twice the number of those bandages with the money you gave me, more, as it transpired, than you needed."

"So that I now have two chests full of inferior bandages in my loft. Of what use do you imagine they are going to be?"

"They will come in handy should there ever be another such accident. I do not suppose that coalminers are particularly nice in the matter of bandages."

"I can only pray that there will never be another such accident."

"Whatever you may think, I have always had your advantage in mind, and yours only, in matters of economy. Just as I always tried to prevent the disgraceful, wasteful ways of your father's servants."

"For which I hardly think my father ever thanked you. Indeed, I am sure your interfering ways made for more ill-feeling in his house than was justified by any consequent saving of five or six shillings."

"The saving of money, even when not of necessity, can always be justified. In fact it is quite an end in itself."

"But what was the end in our case? There is no need to practise economy here. My father has been more than generous. We have lived very comfortably, independently of the contribution that you have never made."

"As to that, there was no suggestion that I should be asked for such a contribution. Your father accepted my offer to accompany you as soon as I made it. And I am sure that the economies I have insisted upon in your kitchen have more than equalled any contribution I *could* have made."

"I believe my father accepted your offer when he saw it as an excellent opportunity to rid himself not only of *one*, but of *two*, thorns in his flesh."

"I have had his interests at heart all my married life. I have *devoted* myself to them, to his family, and to you in particular. He could *not* have thought such a thing. He is too much my friend."

There was a pause. Elizabeth and Georgiana sat quite still, hardly daring to move, determinedly not looking at each other. The younger voice began again. "Enough of this. I come to the point. Your company was never of my seeking and I now wish to dispense with it."

"To *dispense* with it? What can you possibly mean? Who will share your exile with you if I go?"

"I am by now strong enough to live out my disgrace alone. Bridget gives in her notice. I cannot live without her but I think I can do so without you. You have been the source of every domestic upheaval, of all the little unhappinesses, in the house ever since we came to Derbyshire. Now I think I prefer a lonely tranquillity to the constant smoothing down of ruffled feelings that seems to be my permanent lot—and in my own house. Your presence, to be perfectly blunt, has turned my exile, as you call it, into a very positive penance."

Again there was a silence. Then the older voice said, as though recovering from a blow: "I cannot believe this. You are asking me to leave you?"

"No, I am not. About this time last year I asked you to leave me, but you have long been famous for your inability to take a hint. You insisted on accompanying me. I did not invite you. So I am not asking you to leave me. I am telling you to go."

"You could not be so cruel. I am as much a part of your life as you are of mine. I have always wanted what is best for you, have always *known* what is best for you."

"Be that as it may, we shall live more contentedly apart. My father informs me that he has taken a long lease on a furnished house for you in Buxton. He is satisfied that you may be quite comfortable, living at your own expense, if he undertakes, as he does, to pay your rent. You may spend the rest of your life saving your money and your little meannesses need affect no one but yourself. My brother has arranged everything for you. He will soon be here to escort you—he has already hired a cook and a servant girl—though I doubt they will remain with you long. Your clothes, and articles of furniture, will be sent on by the carrier, I hope tomorrow."

"And this is what I am to accept? After the years of my life that I have devoted to you? After all I have done for you? I cannot believe you so ungrateful."

There was a change of voice here. Elizabeth had marvelled before that the conversation had continued in an even, almost dispassionate, tone, as though between chance acquaintances:

but this time it was venomous, rancorous, aggrieved. It was imitated, however, when the other replied: "There can be no question of *ingratitude*. Your attentions to me were *always* what I did not like. We all disliked you as children. Now, on closer acquaintance, I dislike you even more."

There was a small pause. Then the older voice said, almost incredulously: "Disliked?"

And the younger one replied: "Disliked."

After a moment, the younger voice went on, perhaps even more coldly than before: "You bring this kind of parting on yourself. My patience is exhausted. You have worn me out. So certain was I that you would not agree to leave gracefully, that I am obliged to give you no choice. You have only to wait here for my brother. He will not be long."

There was a rustling, a creaking, as of someone rising from a chair; but, otherwise, a silence. Then the younger woman said: "When the weather is better I will come to visit you, but I do not mean that you should ever set foot in my house again."

Then, after a slight pause, the same voice said: "You may keep the stockings you have bought."

It was a form of surpassing elegance which presented itself, in backward view, to the interested gaze of Elizabeth and Georgiana, as it emerged from behind the screen. Dressed in the height of fashion, her face entirely hidden by her bonnet, a tall, graceful woman made swiftly for the door, soon turning a corner out of sight. A single sob, though whether of rage or distress it was impossible to decide, was heard from behind the screen. It was followed by a complete silence.

Elizabeth and Georgiana now felt strangely impelled to walk over to the window to see if it rained. By taking a slightly roundabout route it could appear as if they had just arrived, and not as though they might have heard the whole. The end of the conversation explained to Elizabeth why the Pump Room had been chosen for the enactment of this scene, since the hysterics and recriminations, which would doubtless have accompanied it at home, were impossible in such a public place.

It did not rain. If anything, the day was rather brighter. As they turned round they could see a gaunt, upright figure, dressed entirely in black except for the white cap beneath the bonnet, sitting as though turned to stone, a white handkerchief pressed firmly to its lips. They both inclined their heads as they passed, but this civility was not returned.

II

It took a surprisingly long time to drink four tumblers of water, as they were advised to leave a quarter of an hour between each one. They returned to their sofa without speaking and sat in silence while they sipped. There was almost no sound from beyond the screen. Only the occasional sigh, or rustle, proclaimed their neighbour still alive.

Then, quite suddenly she said aloud: "She could not, she cannot, mean it. I stand in her mother's place. She is not to be trusted alone."

And with these words still on her lips, she appeared from behind the screen and walked off, erect and determined, as though to argue further with her late companion; but, after a very few minutes, she returned to their part of the room, though not to her previous seat, and sat where she could see everyone who passed. A strong aura of discontent emanated from her. She fidgeted about with the parcels that she carried; she changed her chair with such frequency that, before long, she had become the centre of attention to everyone in the room. So fierce was her aspect, however, that she was allowed to remain in solitude.

Philosophically, Elizabeth was obliged to accept that, as she would never know any of the circumstances behind the scene that she had overheard, she would be wisest to dismiss it entirely from her mind.

"As we can never know even who they were," she said rather sadly to Georgiana, "all speculation will be perfectly useless. But if the Pump Room will provide us with such entertainment whenever we come here, my recovery, at least, will be greatly hastened."

Having drunk their water, they moved slowly through the room, which had filled considerably since their arrival. The others were mostly women, but there were several very stout men with imperfect, blotched complexions. The lady in black paid no attention to their almost too-interested examination of her and before long they arrived at the principal entrance. A young man, conspicuous for the simple elegance of his appearance, stood back to let them pass. They smiled at him. He raised his hat, and Elizabeth was particularly pleased to see that his second glance was bestowed on Georgiana, who was looking very handsome.

"I hardly think our fellow visitors are drawn from the very top of society," remarked Elizabeth, "but perhaps it is just that they are rather unwell. *That* young man scarcely seemed in need of any treatment, though I thought he walked with a slight limp."

"Yes," said Georgiana, "I thought so, too. But I hope I was mistaken. He had a very pleasant smile."

"Well, we all know the dangers of chance acquaintances at spas and watering-places. We shall probably never see him again—so I shall not trouble to say *Wickham* to you."

"To own the truth," said Georgiana, with a smile, "when I saw him first I thought that it was he. I wonder how they go on at Gibraltar."

"As it is some months before we may expect Lydia's annual letter, we can invent any tales we choose."

Then, as they both noticed that they were standing outside a pastrycook's, they went inside and spent a pleasant hour sampling the local confectionery.

They went into the warm bath the next morning, and every morning afterwards, Elizabeth being delighted to find that Georgiana was quite right; they did not have to lie in coffins. In the afternoons they drank their water, increasing the amount every day and visiting the pastrycook's on the way home. The lodgings were comfortable; their landlady's cooking even surpassed itself; and in this peaceful way the month of February was completed.

Mr Darcy came over two or three times every week, commenting on their improved looks and saying that, although he found the evenings at Pemberley very long without them, he could not grudge them to a place which seemed to do them so much good. He accompanied them once to the Pump Room, trying the water himself.

"I quite thought to see a series of interesting grimaces made by you both," he said. "I believe that is what happens at Tunbridge Wells. But you do it very nicely and—now that I taste it myself—I understand why. It seems to have no taste at all, only sparkle."

"No, you are right," said Georgiana, "but the sparkle adds a little zest. For those who tire of the tastelessness, you know, milk or cream may be added, or even," lowering her voice a little, "Syrup of Violets."

Elizabeth laughed with her and said: "It will be the culmination of our cure."

Although they returned very often to the sofa on which they had sat that first day, no conversation of comparable interest had been conducted behind the screen. Indeed, so mundane were their usual overhearings that Elizabeth sometimes wondered if she had not imagined that fierce, harsh scene. But she had not. The backward view of that serene, perfectly dressed shape as it glided away, and of that thin, black figure moving small objects from one reticule to another in hurried desperation, would remain in her memory for ever.

The first day of March brought a complete change in the weather, from grey and gloomy to clear and windy. They no longer went every day into the warm bath, so Mr Darcy, once a week, came over in the carriage and took them for an airing. It was on one of these occasions, as they returned down the road from Matlock Moor, that they overtook a solitary, limping figure, leading his horse. On Mr Darcy's signal the coachman drew up and Mr Darcy let down his window to offer his help.

"Indeed, Sir, you are almost too kind," said the dismounted rider. "My horse has cast a shoe but I believe there to be a blacksmith a little further along this road."

"There is one, certainly," returned Mr Darcy, "but a good two miles ahead of you. As you seem to have some trouble walking yourself, you must allow us to take you up. My groom will lead your horse to the smith."

This suggestion was accepted with great alacrity. The groom was instructed to wait at the blacksmith's, as it was on Mr Darcy's way home; and the young man entered the carriage, though not without some difficulty.

"It is a slight weakness of the hip," he said, to satisfy their questioning glances. "I suffered a serious fever some time ago and it has never since been quite right. When I expect to walk for any distance I take my stick—but today I thought my horse would do the walking."

"And do you live about here?" asked Mr Darcy directly, "or do you only visit us?"

There was, perhaps, a small hesitation before the reply came.

"I am on a visit, Sir, to friends in Matlock itself. I had the curiosity to ride out this way today, as I have never been in this direction before."

Elizabeth and Georgiana, seated side by side, were not able to exchange glances, though the pressure of one elbow upon another, duly returned, informed them both that their passenger had been recognised as the young man whom they had met at the door of the Pump Room on their first day. The conversation was entirely carried on between the two men and the two miles were very soon accomplished.

As he prepared to get down, the young man gave a small bow to the ladies, followed by one to Mr Darcy, to whom he said: "Thomas Bertram, Sir, of Mansfield Park. I am more obliged to you than I can say."

"Fitzwilliam Darcy," replied Mr Darcy. "I am only too glad to have been of assistance."

Mr Bertram raised his hat as they drove away and Georgiana, who was seated on that side, raised her hand to him.

"Bertram," said Mr Darcy. "Where have I heard that name before? Have we heard of Mansfield Park? I am sure it is no-where near our Mansfield and, I think, we might have expected him to be accompanied by his groom."

A very short discussion informed them that they had not heard of it, or him, before, but on that topic their conversation continued until they arrived back.

Just after they came out of the warm bath on the following day, and were seated on their accustomed sofa, they found themselves approached, not entirely to Elizabeth's surprise, by Mr Thomas Bertram. He asked their permission to sit opposite them.

"Most certainly you may," responded Elizabeth. "My husband is not with us today and we are only too anxious to hear how your adventure ended yesterday."

"My adventure, as you call it, ended most happily," he said, seating himself on the other side of a small table and with a look at Georgiana which did not escape Elizabeth. "That excellent smith put four new shoes on to my horse and I was somewhat ashamed to find that he thought it necessary to do so."

"I wonder," said Georgiana, rather hesitantly, "if a visit to the warm bath might not be of benefit to your hip? I was quite distressed yesterday to see how it pained you."

"I had not considered it," said Mr Bertram.

"We much enjoy our visits," said Elizabeth, taking up Georgiana's enthusiastic tone. "And we make the most interesting friends there, too."

"Yes," said Georgiana, smiling. "One is there because she is too fat and another because she is too thin—though I cannot see how getting so hot could *increase her weight*. But quite our favourite is Lady Something, who lives at the High Peak, but who tells us that the warm bath is the only place in Derbyshire which is comfortable in the winter."

"Then it seems a convenient way of meeting the high society of the district," said Mr Bertram, not too seriously. "Should I tell my adventurer friends?"

"Of whom I am sure you have many," said Elizabeth, in his own ironical tone. "Though I fear they may be in for a disappointment, as there are *two* warm baths. Fortune hunting," she went on, in her primmest voice, "is by no means permitted by these authorities."

"I am glad to hear it," said Mr Bertram, firmly. "But—I cannot quite forbear to ask—what is it that makes it necessary for *you* to enter the warm bath? There seems to be nothing amiss."

"Well," Georgiana, decidedly, "I hope there is not. My sister-in-law has not been quite herself since the birth of her daughter, though I am glad to find her increasing in health and spirits every day. I certainly went into the baths out of curiosity, but I have to say I never felt so well. Perhaps it is all the water we drink—you must allow me to recommend it to you. At present we succeed with only three, but our aim is to manage *four* pints a day."

Mr Bertram laughed out loud at this.

"Four pints of *water*? I cannot think you quite so cruel."

"Not at all," said Georgiana. "We have now been doing this every day for more than three weeks and can do it, if we concentrate, in less than the two hours. Is not that so, Elizabeth? And I am sure, to use the words of our doctor, that the benefit is enormous."

"I must agree," said Elizabeth. "I remember what a daunting task we thought it to begin with; but now, with so much practice, if we were *advised* to do so—I think we might at last increase our consumption to *five*—even though it take us the entire afternoon."

"Indeed we might," said Georgiana, very seriously. "And our friend from the High Peak says it is the only way to rid oneself of the follies of one's youth—to *soak* them away, you know, and then to *flush* them out."

"Did she say that?" said Elizabeth, in great amusement. "We must certainly cultivate *her* acquaintance."

"Then," said Mr Bertram, after a moment and with a pleasant smile, "you have convinced me. Where must I go to obtain my supplies? If they can indeed dissolve the foolishnesses of *my* youth, I shall be everlastingly grateful."

They told him where to go and he walked off, his limp by no means as pronounced as on the day before.

"I think this very romantic," said Georgiana, "and to have it happen in Matlock, of all unlikely places. A man with his air, and his *hair*—I think we must agree that it is *just* like Wickham's—and a *limp*, and a *past*. Even Madame d'Arblay could not have been so lavish. But unfortunately we already know who he is, which quite spoils it."

Elizabeth laughed at her and said: "And I have no doubt at all, my dearest Georgiana, that when we next see your brother he will tell us *exactly* who he is."

Mr Bertram returned with two jugs and a glass and, to their very great surprise, drank the first three tumblers without interruption, and in a remarkably short time.

"I find this water quite delicious," he then said, to their increasing astonishment. "I wonder that I never thought of it before."

If Elizabeth considered this an unusual beginning to what she now hoped would be a courtship, she kept her thought to herself. Mr Bertram and Georgiana sat opposite each other, exchanging sip for sip, she drinking first and he following, until all the water was quite finished.

He then escorted them to the pastrycook's, where they still went nearly every day, but would not come in. He hoped, however, to meet them again the next day, after he had been into the warm bath.

III

Mr Darcy arrived so early on his next visit, the day after they had met Mr Bertram at the Baths, that Elizabeth was still in her room and the baby not yet taken upstairs.

He admired his daughter, remarked that she bid fair to be a great beauty like her mother, and then settled himself in a chair by the window. Georgiana, who always sat with Elizabeth while she fed her child, was already seated by the fire.

When the nurse had gone, Mr Darcy smiled and said: "As I know quite well that you are expecting me to arrive with the information that I bring, I will not keep you any longer in suspense."

Addressing himself particularly to Georgiana, he went on: "I would have come yesterday but that Mr Bertram neglected to tell me that his father was a baronet and my *Baronetage*, I am quite surprised to discover, is more than ten years old. So you will be glad to know that Sir Thomas Bertram's title dates from 1690, from which, I think, we may deduce a comfortable, and unremarkable, Whig family living without much excitement on its estate in Northamptonshire. They married locally, except for the present lady—who came from as far away as Huntingdon—and there are four of the present family. Mr Thomas is the elder son. He has one younger brother and two younger sisters, but of them I can tell you only that none of them was married ten years ago. There is nothing in his manner, however, to indicate that he is other than a single man."

He paused, as though to receive the pleased assent of his listeners, but they did not speak. Elizabeth was happy just to listen to the sound of his voice; Georgiana, a more enigmatic expression on her face than usual, looked as though she would have liked to say something, but had decided against it.

"In short, my dearest sister," Mr Darcy went on, with a smile in his voice which did not appear upon his face, "should you choose to pay your addresses to this young man—who will be thirty-two years old in May, a most suitable age for matrimony—you will have my most enthusiastic fraternal blessing. I would judge them to be a regular country family—no London address was given, and this, I am sure, must suit you better than anything else. And you must not think that I did not observe that he could scarcely take his eyes from your face in the carriage the other day. I do not feel that I would be encouraging you to marry against your will."

"My love," said Elizabeth on a laugh, when he had finished speaking, "never before have I seen any resemblance between your aunt Catherine and yourself—but now I have to admit that you are indeed of the same blood. However," she went on more seriously, "you are perfectly right. We have had some romantic encounters in addition to the one on the high road to Matlock Moor. I do not think that Georgiana's heart is entirely untouched—she has noticed that his hair grows from his forehead in a very particular way."

"How can you, my dearest Elizabeth," said Georgiana solemnly, "betray the secrets of my heart in this wanton fashion? Certainly I take great pleasure in his company. I am sorry to find that he has an unsound hip—do we dare to hope that this is a legacy from his misspent youth?—but in every other respect I am charmed to receive permission from my respected brother to pay my addresses precisely where I would wish to pay them, or—as I think you really intend—to *receive* them gracefully if they come to be paid."

"Then," said Mr Darcy, in a satisfied voice, "there is nothing more to be said. We will *all* do our possible to attach this desirable person. Pray when," he asked, turning to smile at Georgiana, "—and where—is your next assignation?"

"I wish I could say," said Georgiana, with just a trace of sharpness in her voice, "that it was to be at the top of Masson Hill—the Heights of Abraham, you know—tonight at eleven o'clock. There is a full moon, as you may know yourselves. Any romantic attachment that could survive such an appointment would be one to be envied indeed—the wind up there would, I imagine, put an end to any mere flirtation. No," she said, with a faintly ironical smile in her brother's direction, "we have simply arranged to meet this afternoon, when we *all* come out of the warm bath, to pass the time encouraging each other to drink a great deal of water."

Mr Darcy did not smile. He inclined his head to her and said, with true sincerity: "To be perfectly serious, my dearest sister—it has given me the greatest pleasure to watch you blossom and flower with all the assistance of my loveliest Elizabeth. Now I believe you more than able to attach anyone whom you might wish to attach, and can only regret that, in this case, the result may be that you leave us to go and live a hundred miles away."

"I am by no means precisely sure where Northamptonshire is," said Georgiana, keeping her mouth perfectly prim, "but I believe it to be somewhere over *there*," pointing out of the window. "I shall endeavour to discover its exact location before too long. No doubt when you return to the library at Pemberley—?"

"*You* are right," said Mr Darcy. "It is over there. But I fear that *I* may be right about the distance."

Mr Darcy did not accompany them into the warm bath. He said he would reserve this pleasure until he came over to spend the night, an occasion which he hoped would be not too far distant. His old nurse, he said, with just the ghost of a rueful smile, would *never* agree to his riding home so soon after a visit to the warm bath.

"But I will await you," he said, "with the best seats in the room."

He was to be found there, quite at his ease, when Elizabeth and Georgiana joined him some time later.

"It is not wholly true to say," he remarked, "that all the world and his wife comes strolling by, but I have to say that I have seen more astonishing faces and figures in the last forty minutes than I would see at Pemberley in a twelvemonth. For which, I think, I must be modestly grateful. But as a *pastime*—a pastime which has absolutely specific limits, the 'constant study of mankind' is a serious, and a rewarding, diversion. And I have drunk, as you will observe, almost all of my two pints."

Elizabeth, always pleased to find him in such good spirits, said, smiling at him: "I am truly delighted that you have been so well entertained. *We* have had a *very* pleasant day. There is a new attendant at our bath, one who encourages us to bend and stretch—and, indeed, to go through all the motions of swimming."

"She prods, you know," added Georgiana, "when one is on the slab, prodding what she calls 'the affected joints'. She was rather put out to find that I had no joints that were affected. Then she said it was rare indeed to see such a beautiful girl in the warm bath and, after a closer look at my companions, you know, I could not but agree with her."

They laughed together at this and then Mr Darcy said, to Elizabeth: "But I hope that you too have no affected joints? I believe your visit here to be more in the nature of tonic?"

"As indeed it is. Our new—mentor I think I can certainly call her—seemed very pleased with me. She said I had been wise to come and that she would soon have me in full energy again and better than ever before. And I am inclined to think she may be right—I am still in quite a glow."

"You are both in quite a glow," said Mr Darcy. "In fact, you both look so extremely well that I can hardly wait to try the treatment for myself."

Elizabeth and Georgiana had started upon their third pint before Mr Bertram made his appearance. He came up to them, broadly smiling, accompanied by one of the servants in the Rooms, who carried his jugs of water. He bowed to Mr Darcy and asked if he might join them. He then sat down opposite Georgiana and, to their very great surprise, drank off four tumblers of water without saying a word.

"That is much better," he said, when he had finished. "But you did not tell me," he went on, almost accusingly to Georgiana, "how very entertaining my visit to the baths was going to be. I had expected just to lie there, you know, and perhaps think some elevated thoughts—and this, for a very short while, I did. My mind seemed more active when the rest of me was surrounded by warm water. But not at all. The moment I got out I was captured by this enormous man who called me 'm'l'd'— a most convenient appellation meaning both 'my lord' and 'my lad', though 'my lad' was certainly how he treated me— who obliged me to walk up and down in front of him for nearly five minutes, I should think. Then he put me on the table and felt all round my hip—but in the most matter-of-fact way, you know, one could not object—and *then* he said, 'There is nothing at fault with the bone. We must get the muscles strong again.'"

"So you see," he continued after a moment, smiling at them all, "I am having a celebration. If this man can do that for me— and he is so huge I could not think of arguing with him—it will be the best thing ever. And so I shall tell the old sawbones at Mansfield, who has said I would always limp."

"That would be a triumph indeed," said Georgiana. "You must visit the bath *every* day."

"Well," said Mr Bertram, with a slightly conscious smile, "that will be no hardship on my side. I rather went in as a joke— against myself, you know—but now I am very glad I did. It is an excellent way of passing the time and there is nothing to do at Mansfield in March."

"Your Mansfield is some distance from our Mansfield, I think?" said Mr Darcy.

"Oh certainly, more than a hundred miles. But I believe the first Sir Thomas came from your Mansfield—and it was he who built the house and named the Park."

The conversation now continued with each side trying to discover how long the other proposed to remain in Matlock, though no very definite conclusions were reached.

"But I am sure," said Mr Darcy, "that you will be able to honour us at dinner, in four days' time, perhaps? I shall have paid my first visit to the warm bath myself on that day—and indeed may have met you there first!"

This invitation was immediately accepted. Mr Bertram accompanied them to their front door and Mr Darcy very shortly rode off back to Pemberley.

He returned very early on the morning of the fourth day. Once more Elizabeth still fed her child but, as soon as she had been taken upstairs, he said, without preamble, smiling broadly: "I bring you a letter from your father, my love. His letters are always of the greatest interest and this one quite burns a hole in my pocket. As it was addressed to you I did not open it, though I confess my fingers itched to do so. I beg you will keep me in suspense no longer."

"I will not, indeed," said Elizabeth, smiling in her turn. "You shall open the letter yourself and read it to me while I lie here in comfort."

Mr Darcy did so and read out the following letter.

I have neglected to tell you, my dearest Lizzy, that your Mother and your sister Mary have been gone to Bath these six weeks. Not, I must hasten to add, in any frivolous frame of mind, but simply to see if your Mother cannot find some relief in the waters of that town. They are settled in lodgings in Queen Square, advised by Lady Lucas, and which appear to be so incommodious and lacking in every comfort that your Mother can only suppose that Lady Lucas must have occupied them herself upon occasion and now recommends them to her out of spite. I will admit to you, my dearest child, that her constant sighings and moanings, and heavings and flutterings, had rendered the house quite hideous to all, husband, daughters and servants. I cannot sufficiently admire Mary's heroism in offering to accompany her there. I understand there are some excellent libraries in Bath. However, the expedition has not been without permanent result. A fellow lodger in this humble building is a certain James Morland, a young clergyman without present benefice. He is of respectable family in Wiltshire, where his father is also in orders, has a sister well-married in Gloucestershire, is personable, well-mannered and neither rich nor poor. Your Mother gave her permission at once to this engagement—and you will understand that her amendment dates from precisely that moment—and I have now given mine, with only the proviso that the marriage cannot take place until a living can be found for him.

I am beset by letters from William Collins who, as heir to Longbourn, expects to be informed of what I propose to plant in every field on the estate this year. When I told him, a little mendaciously perhaps, that I intended to put *all* the lower meadows down to turnips, he wrote by return to tell me that Lady Catherine did not, could not in any circumstances, advise anyone *ever* to plant turnips. I am only astonished to find that she, his insensitive but impeccably patient patroness, has ever encountered a turnip. I do not know how she can endure his constant presence.

Let me hear from you soon.

Your loving Father.

A short silence followed this recital. Then Elizabeth said: "A chapter of sensation indeed. My sister Mary is certainly formed to be the wife of a clergyman. I hope he may be more interesting than he sounds."

After a moment, Mr Darcy said: "Yes. If you think we could support having her settled within thirty miles of Pemberley, the living of Kympton is still vacant."

"Kympton!" exclaimed Elizabeth. "Do you mean where Wickham—?"

"I do. The living that was to be kept for him should he decide to take orders."

"Should you ever have permitted him to take orders, my love?"

"In fact I can think of no one less fitted for orders than your unamiable brother-in-law. But it is a good living, with a good house, and they might be very comfortable there."

"Your kindness has no bounds at all. And yes, I think I could support her at thirty miles. We could drive over by the day in summer and in the winter they will be far too busy with their own parish to want to spend the Christmas with us."

"Spoken, my love," said Mr Darcy, still smiling, "like a true Christian. I will write to Mr Bennet as soon as I return."

IV

Elizabeth and Georgiana were some minutes before Mr Darcy in coming out of the warm bath. They had been seated, placidly on their sofa, long enough to have consumed their day's intake of water, before he joined them, wreathed in smiles.

"Now," he said, the smiles even invading his voice, "I understand your enthusiasm. I am a total, willing, convert and indeed cannot understand why, as a family, we have never come here before. For here, one can scarcely doubt, is a cure for *everything*, quite, as one might say, on one's own front doorstep."

"Perhaps," offered Elizabeth, "the Darcy joints were never in need of this kind of remedy."

"Perhaps not," said Mr Darcy. "I do not recall either my father or my mother ever complaining on that score. And I am happy to find, on the authority of the attendant there, that my own joints are in the most perfect order. It is just that, after only one visit, I find myself feeling even better than well."

"Did you happen to encounter Mr Bertram there?" asked Georgiana.

"I did not," replied Mr Darcy. "But there were some individual rooms from where, I have to say, the strangest noises proceeded. I thought it wiser not to enquire too closely."

After the customary visit to the pastrycook's they retired to change, and were all together in the sitting-room a little before five.

Mr Bertram was punctual to his engagement. As he very shortly informed them, he had taken rooms at a local inn since he had been going so regularly into the warm bath.

"It is called The Swan in Nectar," he said, "which I understand to be some kind of mediaeval feast dish, although, as the landlord himself says, there appears to be no known receipt for nectar, it must be some years since anyone ventured to prepare it."

"But I hope you are very comfortable there?" said Elizabeth. "It has quite a welcoming aspect, from the outside at least, and could hardly be better placed for visitors to the Baths."

"My man in the Baths tells me I must walk everywhere for at least a month. My kind friends look after my poor horse for me—I cannot quite bring myself to send him back to Mansfield—as my giant mentor tells me he thinks that getting on to my horse too soon—after the fever went, you know—must have been part of the trouble."

"You are fortunate to be in the hands of one who seems to know so much," observed Georgiana.

"I am," said Mr Bertram, "as I have been the first to acknowledge to him. He says, however, that the local surgeons do not approve of his methods—perhaps he succeeds too often where they fail."

"At all events," said Mr Darcy, "we can each of us say conscientiously—that we have never seen you look so well."

The dinner was beyond reproach. As they waited for the second course, Mr Darcy brought the conversation round to Mansfield Park.

"It is," said Mr Bertram without any immodesty, "in one of the finest parts of Northamptonshire, which I, of course, have been reared to think the finest county in England. It has a rich, friable soil, though I am surprised to hear myself say so." He looked round at them with an almost apologetic smile. "But I promise to trouble you no further with more recondite agricultural niceties."

"But I am a great gardener myself," said Georgiana quickly. "Perhaps, if you have time before you return, you might come to Pemberley to see the flower garden that I have made there, though at this time of the year, you know—"

"With all the pleasure in the world," said Mr Bertram, obliging her not to finish her sentence. "I hear a great deal about Pemberley."

"And do you have brothers and sisters?" pursued Elizabeth, hoping she did not sound *too* inquisitive. "Do perhaps some of them still live with your father?"

Mr Bertram paused momentarily before he said: "My father is not an easy, or a sociable, man. Any talent in that direction that his children have is inherited from my mother. Though I must in all honesty say that no one could have been kinder or more considerate than he was, when my life was, in fact, despaired of. Though perhaps, between ourselves, I might remark that I agreed with myself to recover as quickly as possible, because I lacked the courage to do anything else."

"Then," said Georgiana firmly, "we owe him quite a debt of gratitude, stern and unbending though he be."

"Stern and unbending," repeated Mr Bertram. "I think you are right. His manners must be softened a little to be acceptable and he visits very little in the neighbourhood. My brother Edmund, who is in orders, frequently remonstrates with him about this."

"And have you only the one brother?" asked Elizabeth directly.

"One brother and two—two sisters," said Mr Bertram, as though something had interrupted his train of thought. "My sister Julia lives in London, quite poised on the *edge* of society, as her husband is by no means as rich as she would like. But she seems to keep up with all the latest kicks of fashion."

As no one spoke immediately, and there was a kind of silent requirement for him to continue, he very shortly added, in a slightly constrained voice: "My other sister—made a bad marriage and is no longer welcome at Mansfield."

"I am grieved to hear it," said Elizabeth and Mr Darcy at once, and together.

"I believe that family ties are always worth preserving under any provocation," said Mr Darcy.

"And in every family nest one cuckoo is always to be found," said Elizabeth. "My own youngest sister fills that role in our family but, entirely owing to the generosity of *my* husband," she went on, smiling at Mr Darcy, "*her* husband is at present stationed at Gibraltar—so we may most truly say that out of sight is out of mind."

"I have small wish to leave England," said Mr Bertram slowly. "My recent experiences outside Northamptonshire—in London and Newmarket to be precise—have not encouraged me to stray any further."

"I hope you do not include Derbyshire in these strictures," said Mr Darcy pleasantly. "We would like to think your stay among us, however foreign it may seem, is more than agreeable to you."

"And you would be perfectly correct," said Mr Bertram, equally pleasantly. "I find myself very much at home among you."

Elizabeth and Georgiana withdrew when the second course was finished, Elizabeth receiving a compliment from Mr Bertram upon the dinner.

"Yes," she said, very calmly. "We are most fortunate in our lodgings."

The gentlemen did not keep them waiting long. The tea and coffee had hardly been brought in before they joined them.

Mr Bertram, coming in first, went immediately up to Georgiana, possessed himself of her hand, kissed it and said: "I have your respected brother's permission to attempt to capture your heart. I must hope you will allow me to try."

"I will allow you to try, Mr Bertram," said Georgiana, suddenly transformed into a great beauty. "I will even give you my best wishes for your success."

The evening passed effortlessly in happy conversation, and Mr Bertram left shortly after nine o'clock. As they prepared for bed, Mr Darcy said to Elizabeth: "I wonder if we ever made such a radiant couple *before* we were betrothed? I rather doubt it. I recall that our engagement aroused nothing but astonishment in all our nearest relations."

"It did, my love, but I cannot help observing that the result of that engagement has brought nothing but the warmest contentment. Do we know of any other couple as comfortable as ourselves? I could instance my sister Jane, perhaps—but she, you know, is constantly beset by her husband's sisters. Whereas

I am deeply appreciative of mine. I cannot feel anything but confidence in this marriage. I believe they will deal extremely well together."

An unusual courtship began on the following day. In the mornings they walked, accompanied by Georgiana's footman, or by Mr Bertram's groom. They scaled the Heights of Abraham and, on the other side of the river, the High Tor. They visited the Great Rutland Cavern, only very lately opened to the public.

"Never," said Georgiana to Elizabeth, "could I have imagined such a thing. The different colours, the amazing shapes—I would have been very frightened alone. But he held my hand—it was quite dark so no one could see—and the comfort I derived from that you could hardly believe. I am *quite sure*, dearest Elizabeth. I am so fortunate to be so certain."

In the afternoons they attended the warm baths and sat together drinking their pints of water as though it were the most natural, and the most amusing, thing in the world. Elizabeth rejoiced inwardly to see the glow in Georgiana's eyes, and the gradual disappearance of Mr Bertram's limp; and felt that, had her visit to Matlock had no other consequence, it would have been more than fully justified.

But her own health had by now mended entirely. Her baby thrived; her energy had returned; it was time to go back to Pemberley. As March showed every promise of going out like a lamb, she mentioned to Mr Darcy, on his next visit, that she would like to come home within the week.

"I can hardly wait for that, my love," he said, kissing her hand. "And you may bring Mr Bertram with you. I wish to know him even better."

They returned to Pemberley five days later.

With the nursemaids and babies they filled the carriage completely. Mr Darcy and Mr Bertram rode beside them. A second carriage, sent from Pemberley, followed them, with footmen, all their luggage and the remarkable number of objects that had been casually acquired during their stay.

They took a kind farewell of Mrs Routledge, promising to come to her again should they ever return to Matlock, which seemed to Elizabeth, in view of the excellent results, to be a very agreeable probability. So, while she left with regret, she also harboured the pleasant thought that Matlock was less than thirty miles from Pemberley.

It was a particularly brilliant spring day, early in April. There was bright sun and a sharp wind. The pussy-willow was in bloom and there were primroses under the hedges. The first sight of the house caused, as always, a little lift in Elizabeth's heart and the welcome they received could not have been warmer had they been absent for a twelvemonth.

Mr Bertram did not stay with them long. Having been shown Georgiana's flower garden and having accompanied her on several brisk walks—for it was no weather for dawdling—he formally proposed to her in her most favourite spot, a rustic seat on the edge of the high woods. He was formally accepted; and no one seeing them, as they returned from this particular expedition, could doubt their happiness or the pleasure that each felt in the other's company.

He was to travel post, leaving his groom to follow with the horses.

"Because my man at Matlock tells me I must take up riding again only very slowly. A different set of muscles is involved, he says. And if I have one ambition to fulfil more pressing than another, it is to walk down the aisle with you, my dearest Georgiana, without the slightest vestige of a limp."

He bade them all a most affectionate farewell, and Elizabeth was slightly surprised to realise, as he waved to them when the carriage started to move, that she had not before noticed how extremely good-looking he was.

That night Mr Darcy said: "I do not think any brother could ever have sanctioned any marriage so thankfully, and so confidently, as I have this one. What pleases me especially is that he has never asked the size of Georgiana's dowry. Possibly he was informed of it at The Swan in Nectar, but if so his informant could hardly have been precisely correct. What I more particularly hope is that he himself is rich enough for it to be a matter of indifference."

V

A flurry of letters followed Elizabeth's return. There was a letter from Mr Bennet to Mr Darcy, thanking him for his generosity in the matter of the living of Kympton; a letter from Mr Morland to Mr Darcy, accepting it in simple, gentleman-like terms; and a letter from Mary to Elizabeth, saying how much she looked forward to living near her, but that her mother would not hear of a May wedding.

> "You might as well be married in green as in May," she says, so we propose our union for the first week of June. I will not ask you to be present, with your small baby, and we have every prospect of seeing one another frequently thereafter; but Mr Morland asks me to request the presence of Mr Darcy, if he would be so kind. He hopes, too, that his sister, Catherine Tilney, and her husband will be able to be there.

The immediate focus of their lives thus shifted, from Georgiana to Mary. They all drove over to Kympton, on the first fine day, and found there a handsome, substantial parsonage, dating from the time of William and Mary.

"In far better order than I had dared to hope," remarked Mr Darcy. "The previous incumbent died here early last year at a great age. Very often old people and their houses go down to the grave together."

Georgiana admired the possibilities in the garden and Elizabeth the aspect of the principal rooms. Certain repairs and improvements were put in hand immediately—for Mr Darcy's steward had come with them—and Elizabeth found herself thinking, as so often before, how much her family owed to Mr Darcy—a captaincy for Lydia's husband and now a living for Mary's—and wondering if she could ever possibly make him as happy as he made her. His generosity did not even stop there.

"We will settle them in," he said to her, "and then see what they particularly need by way of a wedding gift."

Over the next few weeks, they paid several visits to Kympton. Elizabeth re-engaged the gardener, but the former housekeeper was nowhere to be found. There was some furniture in the house—"I must suppose it to belong to the living," said Mr Darcy—and Elizabeth supplemented it with various pieces they had had with them at Matlock and some others from the third floor at Pemberley. With the curtains washed and re-hung, fresh counterpanes on the beds and some new covers on the chairs, the house looked more than just welcoming.

"It looks extremely desirable," said Georgiana. "I should not at all mind living here with someone I loved very much. I hope the Mansfield Cottage that Sir Thomas Bertram is contriving for us may be as pleasant."

"That I am sure it will," returned Elizabeth. "And you have performed a miracle in the garden. My sister Mary's lot should be a comfortable one."

"You say very little about her," said Georgiana, a smile lurking in her eyes. "One could be forgiven for thinking that you did not *really* want her to live so close to you."

"One could," said Elizabeth, actually laughing. "She is the one of my sisters that I know least well, number three of five. The two eldest and the two youngest were closest to each other and Mary, I think, very often felt left out. She would take refuge in a book, so her accomplishments are of no mean order. She will be perfectly able to write her husband's sermons for him, should he fail to do so himself. She is a considerable performer on both the harpsichord and the forte-piano, though she may find the primitive pipe organ in this church beyond her skills. I think well enough of her determination, however, to be sure that she will oblige it to respond to her wishes if that is what her husband requires."

"She is very brave to leave her family so completely because her husband's living is so far off," said Georgiana, with just a trace of nervousness in her voice, "though I suppose that is what you did yourself."

They were sitting on the one seat in the garden, which was placed under some trees at the far end of the small lawn which lay between the house and the glebe fields. Elizabeth put her hand on Georgiana's arm.

"I hope you are still quite happy at the prospect of also having to do so?" she said, very softly. "I can only say that, from the moment I first arrived at Pemberley, I have never had a second's alarm or discomfort. Certainly, I am an exceptionally fortunate wife as your brother, I am sure, is quite an exceptional man—but so, from my careful observation of him, is your Thomas."

"I am concerned that we should have to live so close to Sir Thomas. There is the prospect of having to see him *every day*!" exclaimed Georgiana.

"Well," said Elizabeth, smiling, "if it is of any comfort to you, your brother thinks that Sir Thomas is painted in undeservedly dark colours by his elder son. All his letters express only the greatest delight at the thought of you as a daughter-in-law."

"I can hardly wait to hear what that aforesaid brother will have to say when he comes back from London tomorrow. Sir Thomas himself will be at the lawyer's, so we shall at least have a first-hand account."

"I believe you can have nothing to fear from such a father-in-law," said Elizabeth. "If your reservations were about your husband I would be the more concerned. I have only the one friend who married simply in order to be married. She is the wife of my father's heir, and my greatest childhood friend. But even she, I am reasonably certain, very often forgets her husband's existence. And no one, you know, who has seen you and Mr Bertram together could doubt your affection for each other."

"No, you are right," said Georgiana cordially. "It is just that, sometimes, in the middle of the night, I find myself reflecting that I am *also* marrying his family—of whom I know nothing."

"Then I think you have nothing to be afraid of. A brother in orders, a sister on the edge of fashion and another sister never to be seen, a husband who loves you and a house in the finest part of Northamptonshire! Truly no one could describe that as anything much short of the ideal."

"Yes, indeed," said Georgiana, putting her hand on Elizabeth's arm in her turn. "I am being very foolish. I just hope they will respect my wish to spend the whole month of June for the last time at Pemberley."

"As far as that goes," said Elizabeth, turning a little towards her, "you are welcome to spend the month of June at Pemberley *every* year. Indeed I think we might regard that as a regular engagement from this moment."

Mr Darcy came back from London in high good humour.

"I can only say, my dearest Georgiana, that Sir Thomas has taken me quite by surprise. The spirit of your fortune is to be yours—I suspect he is a man who spends nothing unnecessarily—so you may be the best-dressed woman in Northamptonshire if you choose. I collect, however, from the small gossip I was able to have with their attorney, that Lady Bertram may offer some little competition there. He described her as one of the most beautiful women he had ever seen—but added that she was also one of the least energetic."

"Now that," said Georgiana, a sparkle in her eye, "I am *very* glad to hear. It must mean that she will not be for ever in my cottage telling me that my sheets are imperfectly aired."

"I think you to be more than safe on that score," said Mr Darcy with a laugh. "In fact I rather imagine that it will be you who must visit her a little more often than you might like. But the work on your cottage is already in hand. It is a very pretty farmhouse, I understand, which is to have a bow-fronted wing planted on both sides—so that in plan the building will be an H. Sir Thomas seems very pleased with it as an idea and Mr Thomas goes every day to hurry them on."

This information left Georgiana in quite a glow and she returned to the agreeable task of assembling the clothes she was to take with her with much more enthusiasm.

Mr Darcy left them again on the last day of May, to travel to Longbourn for Mary's wedding. He was to convey the bridal couple to Kympton and Elizabeth and Georgiana were to meet them there, two days later, in time for a late breakfast.

They arrived in plenty of time, bringing with them all the food and some provisions to be left behind, and two servants to assist the cook and the maid-of-all-work whom Elizabeth had already engaged. Knowing as little as she did about her sister, she thought it best to err on the side of parsimony and to do too little rather than too much.

The Parsonage looked well, clean, shining and scrubbed. In the garden, too, there was no sign of the year of neglect. Nevertheless, as the moment approached, Elizabeth found herself wondering if she had, in truth, done what Mary would have wished.

But her fears were quite unnecessary. Scarcely had the carriage stopped, and the steps been let down, than Mary was out and exclaiming: "What a truly beautiful house. Mr Darcy had prepared me for something special but I had no notion it could be so handsome. Dearest Elizabeth, how pleased I am to see you again and," without any apparent irony, "how good of you to come and welcome me to my home."

Mr Morland followed her, a very straight-forward, upright man, better-dressed and better-looking than Elizabeth had expected. He kissed her hand, thanked her for her good offices on his behalf and he and Mary both shook hands with Georgiana. From Mr Darcy she received not only an especial hug but also a kiss upon her cheek. He was looking particularly pleased.

After they had eaten, Elizabeth took Mary over the house.

"I did not like to do too much," she said. "I only hope I have not done too little. But you will wish to make the house your own in the matter of hangings and ornaments. Here is only the essential furniture; but I hope you have your own things to add to it."

"Oh yes, they follow us by carrier, some things of Mr Morland's as well."

She took Elizabeth by both hands.

"I am so happy I can hardly believe it. And this Parsonage exceeds my highest expectations."

"Certainly, my dear Mary, I have *never* seen you look so well and I hope you will be truly happy here. When you have had time to look around you, you must let us know what you and Mr Morland would like us to give you as a wedding present. But now—as we are alone—how are my mother and father?"

"My father is well, as always. He sends his best love and will write. My mother's spirits are unequal, as always. One does not know what to expect, though I am sincere in thinking our stay in Bath did her only good. She says rather too often how surprised she is that I should marry before Kitty—she was always disappointed when she came back unwed from Pemberley, you know, or from the Bingleys'. But Kitty bears it very well."

"Perhaps Bath is the place to get husbands."

"Lydia always thought it was Brighton, if I remember."

"So the less said about *that* the better!"

They laughed together and went downstairs again, very pleased with one another.

It was a new Mary. As they drove away, Elizabeth said as much to Mr Darcy.

"Probably we have never seen her as she really is, away from her pretty sisters and my father's critical tongue, and my mother's rather-too-often expressed despair at her chances of finding a husband."

"I remember her first," said Mr Darcy, "on the occasion of that ball, when your father informed her, and the assembled company, that she had delighted them long enough."

"Oh, do not recall that evening," said Elizabeth, with a shudder. "I do not remember another so replete with miseries. Tell me, instead, how you find Mr Morland."

"Sensible, pleasant, a charming latent sense of humour. Having expressed his gratitude for my generosity once, he did not mention it again; and I am much mistaken if we have not inadvertently supplied the village of Kympton with an irreproachable parish priest."

"And my mother? Did you get a glimpse of her?"

"I did. She was in high good humour all the time, rather more silent than I remembered her. And, in spite of myself, I have to say, that I thought her grown very stout."

"Stout? There was a tendency there, I suppose. Nevertheless, *I* have to say—that I am very surprised. I hope there may be nothing more alarming."

"I must hope so, too. I think not."

"Was there anyone of interest at the wedding?"

"On the bridegroom's side only his sister and her husband, Mr Henry Tilney, he a very upstanding, handsome man, she rather bustling, but with kindness written all over her face. I understood him to be from a family in Gloucestershire of large and famous property, while she and her brother are two of a family of ten. I do not think," he added, smiling at her, "that your sister's marriage has done her family any harm."

"It would appear not. I hope the Lucases were suitably impressed with Mr Henry Tilney—not to mention Mr Morland himself."

"I only bowed to Lady Lucas," remarked Mr Darcy with some satisfaction. "I thought her looking rather sour."

"As well she might," said Elizabeth, "since it was she who recommended the lodging in Queen Square to my mother. If she had imagined there to be a wedding in the result I am sure she would have held her tongue. Is Maria married yet?"

"That I could not tell you. I bowed also to Mr and Mrs Philips, to the Gouldings of Haye Park and to the present occupants of Netherfield. I am glad to say that most of my time was spent in conversation with Mr Henry Tilney, whom I liked very much. His family appears to be in something of a turmoil, since his father's second wife, his widow I should say, some thirty years his junior, refuses to leave the family seat at Northanger. His brother, an Army man, had returned after many years' service abroad to find his stepmother immovably resident. They spend their time avoiding one another—I fancy the Abbey—it is actually an Abbey—is large enough and diverse enough to render this quite easy. But Mr Henry Tilney and his wife find the situation so unpleasant that they have ceased to visit."

"He will not be the first man to find himself in such a position, I am sure," returned Elizabeth. "One can only wish them a happy issue out of all their afflictions. But what memories those other names bring back! I believe Sophia Goulding married into the Army a year or two ago and is no longer in this country. Her mother will not like that."

She turned to her sister-in-law.

"Forgive all this Longbourn gossip, dearest Georgiana. I will bring it to an end. And now that Mary is safely settled we can begin to prepare for the next marriage in the family—and make sure it is one that everyone will remember."

VI

It was forty-two years since there had been a marriage from Pemberley, the bride being Mr Darcy's aunt Dorothea, his father's sister. As she had married slightly beneath her, a man of very indifferent property from Lincolnshire, the rejoicings had been kept to a minimum.

"I do remember the occasion," said Mrs Reynolds, house-keeper at Pemberley, "but there can be nothing to compare with this one. Miss Dorothea was no beauty, as I recall—and I *do* recall. I might be fifteen at the time. And her husband, when he appeared we could do nothing but gasp. A large man, very badly put together, in a coat that must have belonged to his grandfather. The winds of Louth took her off a little more than two years later."

"Then," said Elizabeth, by no means dashed by this small history, "as there are no precedents to follow, let us see how many we can set. I must have the marriages of my own daughters in mind."

"Certainly, madam," said Mrs Reynolds, her whole person seeming to smile, "and you will have the assistance of every soul at Pemberley."

The wedding was agreed for the second week in July, by which time the haymaking should be finished, and the harvest some way off. The ceremony would take place at eleven in the morning, followed by a breakfast, in the saloon for the family and neighbours, on the North Lawn for the whole village. Elizabeth had already begun to pray for good weather.

As the preparations for her wedding became more and more visible, and as they appeared to occupy more and more people, Georgiana rather diffidently remarked to Elizabeth that she wondered if so much trouble could be justified when the occasion would be over on the inside of a day.

"My love, my *dearest* Georgiana," fervently replied Elizabeth, "for once you must submit to being of great importance to us all. It is forty years since your aunt was married. It will be another twenty before your nieces are. Here is a magnificent opportunity to spread a deal of happiness and we must seize it with both hands. Pemberley goes *en fête* very rarely, you know. I wish it did so more often, but there are not enough Miss Darcys in the world for it to be able to do so more than once or twice in a lifetime. The enthusiasm of Mrs Reynolds, and the steward, and the butler and the gardeners, quite warms my heart; and, to equal them on my side, I have only to ensure that the bride herself will enjoy her wedding as much as they are going to do. I hope you will *assist* me here?"

There were to be no more doubts or hesitations. After a discussion, in which Mr Darcy did not join, as to whether the bride should be married in white, as was increasingly the fashion, or not, the preparations continued without interruption. A dressmaker and two seamstresses arrived from Chesterfield and took over most of the third floor. Elizabeth was amused, and pleased, to see how Georgiana blossomed in the warmth of all the compliments she was presumably being paid upstairs.

"But only after she had ascertained," said Georgiana, with a touch of acid in her voice, "that my bridegroom is four or five inches taller than I am. I am quite large, I know, and Mrs Dunkely is quite short. But you will be glad to hear that I am precisely the right height for the fashions of this season, that my feet are surprisingly small and that my colouring will be admirably set off by all the silks that she happens to have in stock."

"I am delighted indeed to hear all this," said Elizabeth, laughing. "What did she decide about the wedding dress?"

"A very pale cream satin," said Georgiana, "under yards and yards of the most beautiful lace that Mrs Reynolds produced from somewhere. When Mrs Dunkely saw it she was rendered quite speechless, you know, and I really believe that, had she been alone, she would have accorded it a full Court Courtesy."

Elizabeth, recalling the slight air of bitter-sweetness which had attended her own wedding, was determined that there should be only smiles at Georgiana's. She and her elder sister Jane had been married in a single ceremony at Longbourn, Jane to Mr Darcy's greatest friend, Charles Bingley. The expression of mingled pride and regret on her father's face as he walked them up the aisle—pride in their beauty, regret at their impending departure—she could never quite forget; or the fact that, when he put her hand into Mr Darcy's, he could not quite restrain a tear. As she got into the chaise to leave for Pemberley, his last words to her were: "I will come to see you very soon, my Lizzy. There will be no one to talk to here." And these words had remained with her ever since.

But there was no father in the present case. Elizabeth had accepted the role of the bride's mother with equanimity and enthusiasm, and was only prevented by Georgiana from allowing Mrs Dunkely to make her an imposing robe more suitable for a dowager.

"Dearest Elizabeth, please to recall that you are my *sister*— and one whom I believe I love more than any that could have been provided by my own parents, whom I scarcely remember. If anyone is to take the place of bride's mother, it must be Mrs Reynolds, who has known me all my life and who has always been a pillar of strength to me. I should have thought of that before—unless, of course, Aunt Catherine chooses to grace us with her presence. You will be my *bridesmaid*, that is to say my *attendant*, in this pink satin with more of this magnificent lace, and Mrs Reynolds may have the dark blue silk, which will suit her very well."

Elizabeth smiled and agreed, secretly delighted that the silent, diffident girl she had first encountered should have turned into this decided, but not too decided, young woman more than able to express her own opinions.

"I think Miss Darcy is right, Mrs Dunkely," she said. "My dress should be in similar style to the bride's but not, I think, with quite so much lace."

The question of Lady Catherine de Bourgh, whether or not she was to be present, was very shortly settled by Mr Darcy himself.

"You will be relieved to know, my dearest sister," he said to Georgiana and Elizabeth one morning, "that our cousin Anne cannot face the journey in this heat and Lady Catherine does not choose to come alone. So I think," he went on, with just the slightest twinkle in his eye, "that joy may now continue unconfined."

"And I may ask Mrs Reynolds to stand in place of the bride's mother?" asked Georgiana, a trace of the old hesitancy in her voice.

There was a silence. Elizabeth realised that this was a notion that had not previously occurred to Mr Darcy and she awaited his answer with great interest. After a moment he said, very cordially and actually smiling: "Yes, a most graceful gesture indeed. I must compliment you on it. I cannot think that any of our neighbours would take such a thing amiss and, in fact, in most cases they would find it perfectly appropriate. And perhaps we have been here long enough to be able to set a precedent. She will agree? And you will make her a present of her dress?"

"She will agree," said Georgiana, smiling in her turn, "and I will make her a present of her dress."

The Pemberley family were a little disappointed that, of the Mansfield family, only the bridegroom and his brother were able to be present. Elizabeth had hoped to see the most beautiful woman in Northamptonshire—even if, as her arithmetic told her, she must be approaching fifty—but then recollected that she was also the laziest. Sir Thomas would not leave his wife and Fanny, Edmund's wife, would not leave her infant daughter, who was particularly delicate. The two Mr Bertrams were to stay with Mr Thomas's friends in Matlock.

Mr Darcy had rather thought that Mr Edmund Bertram, who was in orders, would wish to assist at the marriage ceremony, but he preferred simply to support his brother.

"Then perhaps," said Georgiana, "we might ask Mr Morland to come instead. What do you think, Elizabeth?"

"I think that would be a most graceful gesture, indeed," replied Elizabeth, a little archly, "and I must compliment you on it. He would be delighted and Mary would at last see Pemberley."

These were, in fact, Mary's first words to Elizabeth as the Morlands arrived in the afternoon the day before the wedding.

"I have heard a deal about it," Mary went on, "as you may imagine, but nothing to prepare me for the actuality. My sister Catherine's powers of depiction may most kindly be described as confused—she offered me a pale water-colour drawing of this magnificent painting. But I am delighted to see you look so well," she said, her voice a little lower than usual, "and you must be the first to know that I believe myself to be breeding."

Elizabeth, astounded into silence by this new sister, who bore only the slightest resemblance to the sister she remembered, kissed her on the cheek and murmured her pleasure.

"I am like one of our old gowns," continued Mary, "which became as new when they were turned. You may remember how tedious we used to find it—I do not recall, in fact, that we ever completed such a task by ourselves. But now I am of *value*, dearest Lizzy, of value to my husband. The house is charming, the garden very pretty, and all this in the space of less than six months. I have brought with me the new gown in which I was married, to wear at the wedding tomorrow. Then you will see what I mean."

"I can see it already, dear Mary, old gown or new gown, and I am but too happy to assume, from your words and your appearance, that everything at Kympton is as you wish it."

"Everything except the organ in the church," said Mary, smiling. "The hymns I am obliged to play with two fingers, in octaves, you know, and the psalms and canticles I cannot manage at all. The voices in the village are so excellent, indeed, that it quite grieves me to be unable to give them the support that they deserve."

Elizabeth stored this remark at the back of her mind, wondering how much one of the new organs would cost; but, before her remotest conjectures could take shape the Bingleys were announced, and she hastened forward to greet them.

It was almost nine months since she had seen her sister Jane, a longer separation than usual. Both had given birth to a second daughter in November but, with Elizabeth's visit to Matlock and the Bingleys' visit to London in April, no earlier meeting had been possible.

"But," said Jane, "how you *bloom*! I was quite nervous when I heard you were going to Matlock and for the *cure*—but I think you look better than ever. I long to see your baby, and the bride, and—but can this really be Mary?" she asked, in a sudden aside. "I hope I can hide my amazement."

"No need," said Elizabeth at once. "It is a new Mary, who will be only too pleased to receive your compliments."

The evening passed tranquilly. The three sisters included Georgiana in their family talk, the news about the improvements to the Bingleys' house and estate being almost as interesting to her as it was to Elizabeth; the three brothers-in-law, after dinner, went to inspect the many arrangements for the next day; and they all, by common consent, went very early to bed.

Activity began with the sunrise. The gentlemen breakfasted in Mr Darcy's book-room, the ladies in the nursery. Jane, Elizabeth and Mary, fully dressed themselves, went to assist the bride, but found their help unnecessary. A triumphant Mrs Dunkely oversaw the whole and no one attempted to hide their enthusiasm for the dress, or their admiration of the bride, though there might be a little silence just at first.

"My dear, dear Georgiana," said Elizabeth at last. "How beautiful—how *radiant*—you look."

"I hope," said Jane, going to her and kissing her cheek, "that you may always look as happy and serene."

"And I," said Mary, following her, "must wish you the joy and contentment that a truly happy marriage can give."

Georgiana could only smile and nod; but then, finding her voice, she turned to Mrs Dunkely and said: "I believe there will be room for you in the carriage with my sisters and Mr Bingley, but your two assistants must make haste if they hope to see me arrive. That is to say," she added, with a smile, "if you are quite satisfied with the appearance of Mrs Darcy?"

"I am indeed, madam," said Mrs Dunkely, with almost a curtsey, "and I would wish to say that it has been a pleasure and a privilege both to work for you two ladies."

Left alone with Georgiana, Elizabeth could think of nothing to say.

"You need not speak, dearest Elizabeth," said Georgiana, as though reading her mind. "I have arrived at a point in my life that I never thought to see. Much indeed I owe to you and this must be the moment to acknowledge that. Thank you—for your constant help and support, for teaching me not to be afraid and for patiently showing me how to go on."

They exchanged a kiss and Elizabeth said: "It was not as difficult as you seem to think. The material was of the finest and I must just express the hope that you will *always* do justice to yourself. Mr Tom Bertram is a most fortunate young man."

They went downstairs together. Mr Darcy and Mrs Reynolds stood at the bottom and the hall was filled with those who had to stay behind, to prepare the feast that was to follow the marriage. A murmur of appreciation greeted their appearance, and this gradually swelled into an expression of good luck and good wishes. They entered the carriage together, quietly smiling.

It was a particularly agreeable day, the sun high, screened occasionally by lazy clouds. Little knots of people stood along the short mile to the church and they arrived there at exactly five past eleven by Mr Darcy's watch. There was a crowd in the churchyard, to indicate that the church was filled to capacity, and Elizabeth was pleased to see two fiddlers there, to accompany those who stood outside.

While the Vicar of Pemberley performed the marriage, the rest of the service was read by Mr Morland, in a very fine voice and with great sincerity. The two Mr Bertrams looked handsome and tall and Elizabeth was delighted to see, as she followed the bridal pair down the aisle, that there was no trace of a limp in the walk of the bridegroom.

The fare at the breakfast was of a superb excellence. Mr Bingley proposed the health of the bride and bridegroom. A little later, Georgiana introduced her husband to everyone present, all of whom she knew by name. At five o'clock precisely they left on the first brief stage of their journey to the Lake District; and at half-past five the dancing began.

Elizabeth had fully expected to open the dancing with Mr Edmund Bertram, but he shortly accosted her, excusing himself.

"I have promised Tom's friends to be home tonight, to tell them about it, and at once. I hope you may forgive me."

Elizabeth expressed herself disappointed, offering to house him for the night, but it was to no avail; and he shortly took his solitary way back to Matlock.

"His friends," said Mr Darcy to her afterwards, by no means pleased, "must either be very beguiling—or very powerful. I have been asking around among my acquaintance here as to who these mysterious friends may be, but I can in no way discover who they are or anyone who knows them."

It was the only shadow on the day. The dancing continued into the dawn.

VII

Letters from Georgiana were eagerly awaited, but they were eagerly awaited for some time. A note was received from Keswick to say that they had journeyed there without incident; that the weather continued fine and warm; and that their accommodations were infinitely better than she could have imagined. She finished by saying that she could never expect a happier day than her wedding day, and sent love to them and heartfelt thanks to everyone at Pemberley who had contributed towards that happiness.

> I will write from Mansfield when I get there, dearest Elizabeth. I am too happy and too lazy to send you more than a brief assurance of my continued existence. This is a honeymoon indeed. Mansfield will be the reality.

Elizabeth compelled herself not to be alarmed by the formal tone of this letter. It had, perhaps, been written with someone looking over her shoulder, although she thought too well of Tom Bertram to do more than suspect this.

Georgiana's situation was by no means similar to her own. She had married the master of the house, had taken her place at once as its mistress, displacing a much-relieved Georgiana, who was only too happy to abdicate. But Georgiana herself was now faced with a pompous Sir Thomas, a lackadaisical Lady Bertram, a totally unknown sister-in-law and, indeed, a house which quite possibly had not yet been built. Elizabeth stifled the misgivings awakened by the letter. Mansfield, formidable reality indeed, was possibly looming already.

The letter, when at last it came, was long and addressed to Elizabeth. She took it up to her own sitting-room to read in peace and solitude.

Here I am, dearest Elizabeth, sitting in the one room in the house which is not occupied by painters, carpenters, glaziers or plasterers, namely—my own bedroom! The work is all done by men from the estate and I am thankful to say that at least the *roof* is on—both roofs I should say as there are two new wings. I am sorry that things should be so little advanced and glad at the same time, since I shall now be able to choose the wallpapers and colours that I want—at the moment the Head Carpenter does exactly as he likes since Tom and Sir Thomas are in constant disagreement and to please one is to offend the other. However, I do not mean to weary you with our domestic details because, as we dine at the Great House *every day* (our own primitive kitchen being unable to do more than provide us with a most excellent breakfast, which we eat upstairs) I have to tell you all about *them*! Sir Thomas, I have to say, is much misrepresented. He is a tall, very upright man, not as handsome as his sons and with a set of principles that I am sure no one else could possibly live up to. He is kindness itself to me, referring to me far more often than I would wish, but I already see myself as peace-keeper between him and his heir, which I do not at all relish. Lady Bertram is much as I expected, handsome, indolent and rather plump, speaking rarely but, when she does so, the whole household pays attention. She seems to have no notion at all of the state of *our* house. To get her there would be the work of a lifetime, since she will only travel by carriage and there is no road at the moment across the park. She would have to go round by the high road, a distance of seven miles! So, much as I esteem her, I feel quite *safe* from her. But there is a third person there whom no one had thought to mention before, a niece of Lady Bertram, Miss Susan Price. I cannot imagine that house without her. She is kind, patient, conciliatory and never at a loss. It is she who tells me how to go on, to speak to Dick Jackson the carpenter rather than to his father if I want something done in a hurry, and to admire the work of the principal plasterer—whose work is even beyond the amazing— and encourage him in all his wildest flights of fancy. He decorates the ceiling of what will be our drawing-room in what he calls "country style". He began with a *dead* pheasant in one corner, which I could not bear, so asked him to replace it with a live one. And this he thought an excellent idea, so we now have a duck in one corner, a hen in another and, I suppose, a *goose* in the fourth—perhaps it will be a partridge. And all connected with floral garlands, climbing vines, hops, roses, blackberries, lilies, peonies, tulips, poppies and bryony—but *no* animals. The birds will all be sitting on their nests, with the young ones in the undergrowth. I am entranced. Susan Price, if you can keep a great secret, has contrived to enter into an understanding with a young naval lieutenant, a friend of her brother's. How she has succeeded in this I cannot at all conceive since her whole life is spent in the drawing-room at the Great House doing Lady Bertram's embroidery for her. Her sister Fanny I hardly see. She has a second daughter nine months old in a very poorly way and so cannot leave her. I do not believe marriages between cousins are wise and only hope the little girl may not prove to be too delicate for this world. I find myself quite worn out with penning this missive so will close. Be assured I am as well and as happy as it is possible to be and receive all the love that can be spared from Tom, both to you and my respected brother!

Your loving sister, Georgiana.

There was enough in this letter to put Elizabeth's anxious thoughts entirely to flight and she showed it to Mr Darcy. He read it, smiling most of the way through, finishing actually on a chuckle.

"That final sentiment is a compliment to you, as you may not be aware," he said. "Georgiana could never support the idea of Anne de Bourgh as a sister-in-law, although she scarcely knew her. I only hope that her marriage may be as happy, and as pleasurable in every way, as my own."

"I no longer have any doubt about it," said Elizabeth, smiling back. "If I ever had one, it was on the ground that Mr Tom Bertram seemed to be hiding something from us. But, whatever it was, or whatever it *is*, it cannot concern Georgiana so long as she continues in domestic happiness at Mansfield—where, I think, she is even more highly valued than her letter suggests."

"It is a responsibility," said Mr Darcy, after a moment, "a dire responsibility, sanctioning a marriage. I am only too thankful to think it must be almost twenty years before we are obliged to find a husband for Jane."

"If my instincts are worth anything at all," said Elizabeth, in reply, "we may be perfectly certain that our elder daughter will take care of that matter herself."

Georgiana's wedding remained the chief topic of conversation throughout August. September passed quietly and October took Elizabeth and Mr Darcy to Longbourn, an annual engagement which Elizabeth valued, and enjoyed, a little more each year.

As a little girl, she had much disliked the month of October. It promised nothing more than the grey months of November to March, interrupted only by the occasional ball at Meryton. Her favourite walks grew muddier and more and more impassable until, by February, she was confined to their own small park near the house. But, since her marriage, the glooms of October had been dissipated. Her life at Pemberley was as different as possible from her life at Longbourn. At present that life was centred round her two daughters, but she had once been with Mr Darcy to his house in Brook Street. She had found this to be so large, so dark and so depressing that she had recoiled from spending any time in it; but, at the back of her mind, the intention lay hidden, to let the light into that house.

They travelled with their own horses for the first stage, and they slept one night on the road. The weather was fine, and the highway so much improved, that they arrived some two hours before they were expected. Her sister Catherine greeted them at the door.

"Dearest Lizzy," she said, as they exchanged a kiss, "how glad I am to see you. My father will be quite vexed, as he went out only ten minutes ago to see his agent, thinking he would be back before you arrived. And my mother, too," she added, with the smallest smile, "will not be pleased, as she had hoped to be down to receive you. But I am glad to think your journey must have been a good one."

Leaving Mr Darcy to wait for her father in his book-room, Elizabeth went upstairs alone with Catherine.

"As it is a year since you saw her," said Catherine carefully, "I think you must expect a change in my mother."

Elizabeth, at first sight, was quite shocked. Catherine's calm words had not prepared her for the appearance of her mother. She sat, in her wrapper, in a chair by the window, accompanied only by her housekeeper. Her hair had been done, but it was everywhere streaked with grey, much more so than Elizabeth remembered. Her face seemed rounder, but more lined. There were dark shadows beneath her eyes and the area between her chin and her neck was much fuller. But it was her mother's pose that secretly alarmed her. She sat quite still, her hands crossed upon her lap, as if motion had become impossible. She turned her head, however, as her daughters came closer to her.

"Oh my dear child," she said at once to Elizabeth, "how sad I am to hear that your second baby is a girl, and Jane's as well. I hope you may not take after your mother and produce nothing but females, not but what females are quite essential in any gentleman's family, but Mr Darcy and Mr Bingley must have heirs. I am glad to hear, too, that your sister Mary is in the family way. Perhaps she will have more luck."

Elizabeth, after exchanging a glance and a smile with Mrs Hill, kissed her mother on the cheek.

"Perhaps she may indeed," she said. "I believe Mr Morland has four brothers and five sisters. And Jane and I, you know, Mama, are by no means in our dotage."

"But it is such an unlucky start," returned Mrs Bennet. "However, I do not mean to say that you are not looking very well and I would like to think you benefited from the waters of Matlock more than I did from those of Bath."

"I think I did benefit, indeed. I am sure I have never been so well, but I believe it to be the waters that I drank, rather than those in which I bathed, that brought this about."

"A very handsome twill, Lizzy, more than ten shillings the yard, I suppose. I did not drink the water at Bath. One sip was enough. Something seemed to have died in it. And your bonnet is very becoming."

"I am glad to hear you say so. We found two milliners in Chesterfield to make Georgiana's bonnets, quite in competition with each other. So we had not a single disappointment."

"I hope Georgiana may be quite happy?"

"From her letters, she is so. But I share your hope."

"Mr Bennet says the estate at Mansfield must be worth eight thousand a year."

"I believe so. There is also extensive property in the West Indies."

"Slave money," said Mrs Bennet, nodding her head a little. "My brother Gardiner says it is to be avoided at all times as it brings only misfortune."

"I hope you have some good news of my uncle and aunt?"

But there was no answer. Looking more closely, Elizabeth realised that her mother had fallen asleep on the instant. She turned in dismay to Mrs Hill.

"Do not be alarmed," said Mrs Hill, in a low, re-assuring voice. "It often happens thus. You will find that she will wake quite soon and be unaware that she has been asleep."

"Has she been like this for long?"

"I would say—perhaps three weeks," said Mrs Hill.

"Yes," said Catherine, "and in those three weeks we have been obliged to have her dresses let out, though it is only in her wrapper that she feels comfortable."

"Has the doctor nothing to suggest?" asked Elizabeth. "That is to say—I suppose you have consulted him?"

"We have, madam," said Mrs Hill, very quietly and very quickly. "He is at his wits' end."

"He advises only that she should drink a great deal," said Catherine, "but my mother can find nothing that she truly fancies. Lady Lucas has recommended everything you can think of, but of course my mother will accept no suggestion of hers."

"Has she suggested a syrup of lemons?" enquired Elizabeth, after a moment. "I would suspect perhaps not, being of too saving a turn of mind to think of it."

"I believe not," said Mrs Hill.

"I also believe not," said Catherine.

"I will see what I can do," said Elizabeth.

"They are both quite well," said Mrs Bennet. "My brother proposes a journey to India which I cannot like, but once he has made up his mind about a thing there is no altering it."

"I was sorry not to see them at Pemberley this summer," said Elizabeth, as calmly as possible, "but perhaps next year we may be more lucky."

"My sister Gardiner wore an embroidered shawl from India, from some coast or somewhere as I recall, and also a dress of silk from there, very fine indeed and easy to work she said, quite half the price of the French or Italian silks. Some tea they brought as well but it is all finished. I thought it would settle my nerves but it did not do so and I am getting fatter and fatter. If I get any larger I shall not be able to get out of my chair. Lizzy, my dear child, what am I to do?"

Elizabeth, who had almost never been appealed to before by her mother, was silenced. She took the hand that clutched her sleeve and stroked it gently.

"What we must do, my dear Mama, is to find something that you like to drink. If Mrs Hill were to make you a syrup of lemons, would you try to take a little?"

"I am sure there is not a lemon in the house," said Mrs Bennet.

"That is easily remedied," said Elizabeth. "I will drive this moment to Meryton and purchase every lemon in the town. And Mrs Hill has an excellent receipt. When Jane and I were full of the measles I remember it was our greatest treat."

"If only it were the measles," said Mrs Bennet, the tears beginning to flow. "I can find nothing that I want to eat or drink. Every mouthful is a penance. I am sure I do not know what is to become of me."

"Then let us try the lemons, Mama, as you have not done so already."

"I can bear nothing sweet, nothing sour, and nothing hot and nothing cold, and nothing plain and nothing flavoured. I eat nothing and drink nothing and yet every day I am larger. Is not this very strange? There is a contradiction here. Lady Lucas gets thinner and thinner and yet, as everyone here can witness, her appetite is second to none in the neighbourhood. I have seen her eat more than her whole family put together and one may be sure that any remedy she recommends is in truth a cure for something else. But no—she has never mentioned lemons. Pray, dearest Lizzy, go at once and buy some lemons. I only hope that you can find some."

Elizabeth did not hesitate to obey this instruction. She and Catherine set off at once for Meryton, where they had the good fortune to discover two gross of lemons still in their wooden barrels. The greengrocer, whom they had known for many years, looked a little aghast, as they were buying his entire stock; but he said, as he put them in the carriage: "I hope with all my heart that they may do the lady good."

Elizabeth smiled and thanked him, before saying, in an undertone to Catherine: "And if they do not, which I hope may not be the case, I will take them back with me to Pemberley."

But the news, from later in the evening, was good. After much experimentation, a drink was evolved which was neither sweet nor sour, neither hot nor cold and neither tasteless nor too fully flavoured. Mrs Hill reported with satisfaction that Mrs Bennet seemed to be pleased; and Elizabeth, with the memory of Matlock behind her, recommended that she take a tumbler every hour and sip it very slowly.

VIII

The Darcys' arrival at Longbourn seemed to lift the air of gloom which had hung over it and Elizabeth was only too happy to be aware of this. Mr Darcy and Mr Bennet had always had much to discuss where the use of their land was concerned and they remained now in the book-room, either engaged in rational argument or in independent reading. Elizabeth took her turn in sitting with her mother who continued, much to Elizabeth's surprise, to sip her lemonade every hour upon the hour, and whose colour, if Elizabeth did not imagine it, seemed to be somewhat improved.

The twenty-eighth of October dawned fair and clear and Elizabeth and Mr Darcy set off for their annual walk to Oakham Mount. Their way led principally through little-frequented lanes and they spoke seldom, commenting only on the weight of berries on the hawthorn or the bright colour of the leaves on the field maple. Elizabeth's hand tightened on Mr Darcy's arm as the stile came into view, and her heart began to beat a little faster.

He helped her up on to the stile and waited while she settled herself. Then he took off his hat, caught her left hand in his and put his right foot on the step of the stile.

Looking up at her he said: "Miss Bennet, my very dearest Elizabeth, you know, I think, how much I both love and admire you. Let me now, in all humility, ask you to become my wife. You must allow me to offer you my hand—my heart—my mind."

Elizabeth's own heart always moved when she heard these words, repeated as they were each year. Taking his hand in both of hers she said, in a voice from which the tremble was only just removed: "Your hand I accept. Your heart—I will *keep*. Your mind I must hope to share. And, in return, for what they are worth, you must allow me to give you mine."

"You have relieved me, and my mind, of an almost intolerable burden."

Their little ceremony usually ended here, but Mr Darcy did not move.

"I have to thank you, my love," he said, "for my second beautiful daughter."

"I shall hope, my love," returned Elizabeth, "one day to give you a beautiful son."

"We will think about that only when *I* am convinced that you are perfectly strong again."

Elizabeth nodded, not quite smiling.

"And I have to thank you, too, for your loving kindness to my sister."

"Oh indeed," said Elizabeth impulsively, "I have only one sister whom I love more than yours and it gave me, always, the greatest pleasure. I must hope that she will be as happy as you have made me."

"I think there can be no doubt of that."

He stood back as he spoke and helped her up, so that she was standing on the step of the stile. Here, five years before, they had exchanged their first kiss and here, today, they exchanged it again.

They had not reached Oakham Mount on that occasion, and neither did they reach it today. They turned back quietly to Longbourn.

"The view your mother recommended must wait another year," said Mr Darcy. "Though, by Derbyshire standards, Oakham Mount is little more than a hillock. But your father's fields are in excellent heart and their soil is richer than anything we have at Pemberley."

"I have hardly spoken to my father. How do you find him with all this upset in the house?"

"Ironical, perhaps. Disengaged. He seems surprised by the change in your sister Catherine. His feelings for your mother I have never wholly understood and he has never referred to them now."

"They remain a mystery to me, too," said Elizabeth. "Now that I know what a marriage should be, my knowledge of theirs makes it seem stranger than ever."

"No one's marriage," said Mr Darcy emphatically, "is as happy as ours. That day, this day, five years ago was a milestone in both our lives. The shell my childhood had built around me began to crack in good earnest, and then to disappear. And you, if I am not very much mistaken, had begun to feel confined at Longbourn."

"I had indeed," said Elizabeth, "although I did not know it then."

Her principal task in the domestic life of Longbourn proved to be the daily reception of Lady Lucas, who walked up from her own house and came in through the garden, entering unannounced. She was occasionally to be found actually wandering through the house by herself. As her visits always occurred around midday, the butler began to station himself by the garden door at that time, bringing her to Elizabeth in the morning-room.

Lady Lucas was the mother of Elizabeth's greatest childhood friend Charlotte, now married to the Reverend William Collins, a distant cousin of Mr Bennet's and heir to the Longbourn property. He was incumbent of Hunsford, a living in the gift of Lady Catherine de Bourgh, Mr Darcy's maternal aunt; and he was well-known both to him and to Elizabeth for his all-too-frequently-expressed gratitude and for the length of his sermons.

While life at Hunsford was by no means an enlivening topic of conversation, it could always be reverted to in the event of an awkward silence. Today, however, there was no need.

"I heard from Charlotte this morning," said Lady Lucas abruptly. "She is in the family way once more."

"I am happy to hear it," said Elizabeth untruthfully. "I hope she is quite pleased herself?"

"She does not expressly say so, but I think there can be no doubt. She dotes on the children she already has. We must hope that this one may be a boy."

"And what has Lady Catherine to say about this?"

"Charlotte does not tell me, but she is in general an advocate of large families. There may be a trace of envy, perhaps. She has only the one child, who remains an invalid upstairs."

"It is certainly strange that Lady Catherine, so large and so healthy herself, should have produced such an insignificant daughter."

"Charlotte says that, on the occasions when she can be persuaded to speak, she has a very interesting turn of phrase."

"I am thankful to hear it. I often feel a pang for Charlotte, condemned to converse only with her husband and Lady Catherine."

After a moment, Lady Lucas said, sharply and as though offended: "She has a friend in Mrs Jenkinson, the daughter's companion. They sometimes drive out together. The countryside round Hunsford is charming."

"Yes," said Elizabeth, ignoring her tone. "I have very often thought so."

"But—your mother?" asked Lady Lucas, returning the attack. "I have not come here to talk about Charlotte."

"She seems more comfortable, more cheerful in herself," said Elizabeth. "She moves around her room more easily. The doctor is delighted with her new progress and I think I am not allowing my judgment to be coloured by my wishes."

"I am only too happy to hear it," said Lady Lucas. "She cannot be an easy patient."

"No, she is not," agreed Elizabeth. "But we are blessed by the presence of Mrs Hill, and my sister Catherine, too, is proving both kind and understanding."

"I hope she may be perfectly well before the winter sets in. Sir William thinks it may be a cold one as the hawthorn is so heavy."

"I hope so, too," said Elizabeth. "Her complexion is improved and, indeed, she has become a different person since our arrival last week."

She went with Lady Lucas to the garden door and waited to return her wave. It was only while she did so that the reason for Lady Lucas's frequent visits occurred to her and she wondered why she had been so stupid as not to think of it before. In the event of her mother's death, a possibility she had not previously entertained, her father could marry again and Charlotte might no longer have the Longbourn property in prospect.

Returning Lady Lucas's wave mechanically, she went back to the morning-room, the turmoil of her feelings a conflicting mixture which she did not choose to examine.

They stayed a further week at Longbourn. Elizabeth, fully satisfied by her mother's progress, was anxious to return to her children, as there seemed to be nothing more that she could usefully do. She arranged for a continued supply of lemons from Meryton and was considerably re-assured when Catherine said to her: "I think you may leave us now with a clear conscience. My mother is firmly on the mend and we hope that, by Christmas at least, she will have returned to her usual size."

"I hope this is also the opinion of Mrs Hill."

"It is," replied Catherine. "She has known my mother better than any of us—that is to say, since we grew up—and she says every day that the diet of lemonade could not be more beneficial. I think," she added, with a smile, "that you may safely return to your children."

Elizabeth's leave-taking of her mother was more affecting than usual. Torn between tears and smiles, Mrs Bennet could only say: "Oh my dear child, how sad I am that you are settled so far off. Sometimes I must regret my success in finding husbands for you all but Catherine is a great comfort to me still. Your idea about the lemons has had the best results and that bonnet is the smartest I have ever seen. Pray give my regards to Mr Darcy and tell him how disappointed I am not to have seen him but he will understand I could not receive him in my bedroom. I wonder when we shall meet again, my dearest Lizzy. Not until after Christmas, I fear, but at least I am sure we *shall* meet again which I by no means believed when you first arrived. Your visit has done me the greatest good and I can only give thanks that you have turned out to be so sensible. You see me here in very good hands and I trust you will not travel very far after dark. There can be no occasion to do so although the nights are drawing in and we must do what we can to prevent my brother going to India. Why must he go himself? My dear Hill promises me that my weight is going down and I hope to be into dresses and down to your father before the end of the week. I have become quite tired of the paper in this room and will mention to your father, as I must have done a dozen times, that I would like it changed, with leaves, you know, and birds, not flowers. These garlands are too like wreaths. Tell Jane she must write to me soon and I hope she is as beautiful as ever. It is time, too, she came to visit me."

Elizabeth, considerably restored by this effusion, which was very much in her mother's usual manner, kissed her and said simply: "I am delighted to find that you are indeed upon the mend and I will certainly give Jane your messages, though I cannot be certain that she can come before Christmas. We are spending the Christmas in our own houses this year, as Mr Bingley's sisters and Mr Hurst are to be with Jane, but I hope we may manage to see something of them, and of Mary and Mr Morland, around the time of the New Year."

"I was glad to find that Mr Morland was so much richer than we thought. The first time we saw him Mary had begun to do her hair in a new way and I quite felt it was the working of Providence. You must thank Mr Darcy again for his generosity to Mary—and to Lydia. My dearest Lizzy, what would we all do without him? It quite distresses me to think how much I disliked him to begin with but he was so tall and so proud and he did not wish to dance with you."

"He is the kindest man in the world," said Elizabeth calmly, "and the best husband. I yield to no one on that point. And now, Mama, I must begone."

She kissed her again, squeezed her hand, and offered her own to Mrs Hill, merely exchanging a smile with her. The carriage waited below and they were off in a very few minutes. Mr Bennet came to the door but, as she waved to him out of the window, Elizabeth thought she had never seen him looking so alone and so deserted, though he had Catherine beside him and the butler behind.

"I have hardly had two words with my father in all this time. I hope you have found him quite conversible?"

"As indeed I always do," replied Mr Darcy. "Your father is a man quite able to surmount the kind of problem that commonly confronts us all and the illness of a wife seems to be considered one of these. He has faith in the doctor, in the attentions of Mrs Hill and in the fact that Mrs Bennet has had attacks of this kind for some years. 'Her nerves are my very old friends,' he told me. 'I must hope that my Lizzy will leave her more cheerful.'"

"I, too, must hope that his Lizzy did that," said Elizabeth. "I truly believe her to be improving and can only trust that I am right."

The time before Christmas passed very quickly. A letter from Catherine three weeks after they returned to Pemberley brought nothing but good news. Her mother's weight had returned to normal; she was cheerful and moving easily; she was strong enough to receive Lady Lucas herself and hoped to be able to see any callers who might come to Longbourn to wish them the compliments of the season.

Elizabeth was entirely persuaded by this letter. With all thoughts of Longbourn behind her, she put her energies into preparing for the large party which usually took place at Pemberley on Boxing Day. She was joined for this by her sister Jane, who came alone, leaving her husband to entertain his two sisters and his brother-in-law.

"They grow more and more disagreeable each year," said Jane to Elizabeth. "Caroline does nothing but disparage every change we have made and Louisa agrees with everything she says. Mr Hurst does nothing but eat while complaining about the cooking and, in every way, I could *not* endure it. So I am most happy to be here. But your Boxing Day party gets larger and larger. Surely all these people cannot be tenants?"

"Most of them, I promise you. I know there was a new purchase of land near Cutthorpe. I must suppose all the strangers to be from there."

The snow fell in the first week of the New Year and lay until the end of January. Jane was safely at home before the first fall and it was reported that the countryside was deeply covered as far south as Leicester. Elizabeth enjoyed the feeling of siege that the snowdrifts gave her; the great task of each day was to keep everybody warm; and only one path was clear as far as the village. But the mails were delayed and it was not until the second day of February that an express came through. It was addressed to her.

> I grieve to inform you, my dearest Lizzy, that your Mother died peacefully, this afternoon, suddenly but without a struggle. Her funeral I propose for this day week, by which time I hope you may both be with me. I have expressed separately to the Bingleys and to Kympton, but need hardly tell you that you will be the most welcome of all.
>
> I am, as always,
> Your loving Father.

It was dated two days previously.

Elizabeth's one wish was to share this at once with Mr Darcy and she wondered where he was. But he had heard of the arrival of the express and, looking up, she saw him coming towards her. In silence, she handed him the letter.

IX

It was a little less than two hours before they entered the carriage, with the intention of getting to Ashbourne that evening, drawn by four of their own strongest horses. A detour to Kympton was necessary, in case Mr Morland, or indeed Mary herself, should wish to accompany them; but, much to Elizabeth's relief, for Mary was very near her time, neither of them wished to do so.

"I believe Mrs Bennet will understand that I can be of more use here to Mary than I could, any longer, be to her," said Mr Morland.

Elizabeth found Mary perfectly calm and philosophical. "We must all die," she said, "and I cannot pretend that my mother's life gave her any pleasure. I only hope that Catherine may not find the burden of my father's grief too much for her to carry. Pray give them both my best love and take this letter to my father."

The snow began to disappear after they had crossed the Trent on the following day; and it was soon after their second change of horses that Mr Darcy said: "You are very, very silent, my love."

"I am," said Elizabeth. "I am aware that I am. But I am so disgusted by my thoughts that I cannot bear to share them."

"Perhaps, should you choose to do so, they would appear less disgusting."

"I fear not," said Elizabeth, with a sigh. "But I will say two things. The first is that I am trying to grieve for my mother; and the second is that I cannot endure the thought of Mr Collins in that house."

For a long minute, Mr Darcy did not speak. Then, taking her hand, he said: "Your mother and I never ventured beyond politeness, after, that is to say, she had judged me worthy to marry her least favourite daughter. But I will mourn her sincerely as I owe so much of my own happiness to that daughter. Whatever her faults, I cannot but acknowledge a great debt. And as far as Mr Collins is concerned, the less you think of him the better."

"Just at present he occupies my thoughts entirely—and *most* unpleasantly."

There was a pause, a long one. Then Mr Darcy said, carefully, consideringly: "It must have been an anxious time, for your father and for Catherine. Do you think they both might benefit from a change of air?"

"I cannot recall that my father ever had a holiday, unless you include his visits to us, and to Jane. I must suppose that I take your meaning correctly?"

"Perhaps he has sat for too long in his book-room?"

"It has been his sanctum—his refuge—for as long as I can remember. Like those books on his top shelves, he has become quite *dusty*."

"He must be in mourning for a year," said Mr Darcy thoughtfully. "Do you think we should invite him once more to Pemberley."

"There is not enough society for him there," said Elizabeth, almost too quickly. "I do not mean that as a complaint, my love, but I would wish to show him around a little. And his mourning will at least oblige him to buy some new clothes—if he has any at all it must be mourning for his father, nearly thirty years ago. No one has died in the family since then."

"It will be best if he goes away as soon as possible after the funeral, before he has had time to settle in again."

"Would you dislike it if I went with him to Bath—by myself? And with Catherine, of course. I know your aversion to Bath too well to ask for your company."

"My aversion to Bath could be conquered, if circumstances were to demand it. In fact, though I would hesitate to admit it to anyone else, I believe I am now *old* enough to go to Bath. Have we any acquaintance there?"

"No, but my aunt Gardiner has. A school friend, a Mrs Frankland, is now resident there. When she heard that my mother had gone to Queen Square, my aunt wrote to me that, if we were ever to go to Bath ourselves, she would write to Mrs Frankland for advice."

"A school friend of Mrs Gardiner is one in whose judgment I would be more than willing to trust," said Mr Darcy.

A certain stillness seemed to invest the scene as they drove up to Longbourn, in the late afternoon of the following day. The blinds were down, or the curtains were drawn, on every window in the house. They were received by the butler, clearly on the look-out for them, who said, as he handed her down: "I am most truly glad to see you, Miss Elizabeth. Mrs Hill and I are become a little alarmed for the master, who will neither eat nor drink. He bade me bring you to him as soon as you arrived."

Elizabeth was gratefully conscious of the presence of Mr Darcy behind her. As they entered the hall, as the butler finished speaking, he said: "Go with him, my love. I can need no guidance, or assistance, in this house."

The butler led the way and opened the door to the book-room for her.

"Miss Elizabeth, sir," he said.

Mr Bennet was seated in his accustomed chair by the side of an excellent fire. It was the only source of light in the room. He rose as she entered and kissed her.

"I am glad you are come, my dearest child," he said. "One should not sit alone in the firelight."

"Perhaps I could send for some candles?"

"In a moment. I have been consumed by some unsettling thoughts and it is easier to communicate them where the light is not too strong."

Elizabeth sat down on the other side of the fire.

"Your mother," went on Mr Bennet, "as I must suppose you to know, was a lasting disappointment to me; but today I have wondered, and for the first time, if I were not a disappointment to her. Had I been kinder to her, less critical, more appreciative, she might have been less foolish, less concerned with only the more mundane things of this life. I think I must blame myself there," he added, after a short silence. "Certainly I must do so for never having thought of it before."

Elizabeth tried to collect her thoughts. She paused for a moment before saying: "I am sure that my mother never understood you, Father, any more than she ever understood me. But I think she was not unhappy. She had a wide acquaintance and a comfortable home. She was an excellent housekeeper herself and her interests hardly extended beyond her house and her family. I cannot imagine her sharing *your* interests or being absorbed in any life other than her own. You must not blame yourself too much."

"Do not sympathise too deeply, Lizzy. The feeling will pass off soon enough. We had exhausted every topic of conversation by the time you were born, since when we have scarcely discussed anything more profound than the time of day, unless some family crisis intervened. Now I have to wonder if her nerves were a source of real pain rather than the figment of imagination that I always thought them."

"And yet it was surprising how obligingly they healed when any crisis that brought them on was over. But you surely do not think her recent illness was of nervous origin?"

"Who can say? The doctor, or doctors towards the end, had nothing to suggest. I try to convince myself that it is a merciful release and not only for her. But this must go no further, Lizzy."

"It shall not. I might say two words to my husband."

"You may say what you like to him. He remains a haven of good sense and intelligence in an increasingly idiotic world."

"Then I will send for some candles and ask him to come in at the same time."

She found the butler hovering in the hall and asked him for the candles.

"At once," he said. "I have them here. And Mr Darcy is in the morning-room, Miss Elizabeth. There is a good fire in there."

She found him standing in front of that fire, gazing down into it. As she came in, he looked up and said only: "Well?"

"My father is in some distress, my love, as was to be expected. Not, however, at the prospect of his return to single life, but rather as he blames himself for his treatment of my mother. And there, I have to say, I must at times agree with him, though in general I thought him admirably patient with her—certainly when we were present. How they went on when they were alone I do not choose to conjecture."

"Unadvisable, I think," he replied, a smile lurking in his voice. "When my own mother died I was obliged to admit, to myself, how little, how very little, I knew of her as a person; and when my father died, some years later, I had to face that same fact again. He was a fountain of generosity, a source of encouragement, a repository of knowledge which never failed—but I had no idea about him as himself. I could not, at eighteen on my mother's death, offer him my sympathy and he did not seem to expect it. He was a man who stood very much on his dignity and who would mourn alone. I envy your closeness to your father."

"He is asking for you now. Pray give him all the comfort that you can."

Having left him at the door of the book-room, Elizabeth turned to go upstairs to take off her bonnet; but, as she did so, the unmistakable sounds of a carriage arriving were to be heard.

"Miss Jane, I apprehend," said the butler with satisfaction. "Now my master will be more comfortable."

He was right. Within two minutes Jane came into the hall, greeted the butler and then, seeing Elizabeth behind him, exclaimed: "Oh my dearest Lizzy, how glad I am to see you. I hope my poor father is not too cast down? What a journey we have had!"

They embraced, as closely as their bonnets would permit, and remained within that embrace for a short minute.

"I am so pleased to see you again," said Jane, a little uncertainly, "and to be here again, even on such a sombre occasion. But I must go to my father. I must suppose that I know where to find him?"

"Indeed, yes," said Elizabeth, recovering her own voice with some difficulty. "You will find Mr Darcy with him."

She then turned to welcome Mr Bingley and received his accustomed affectionate hug.

"We are shaken quite to pieces," he said. "One of my wilder friends informed me that the fastest way south was by the North Road and we took his advice—from Grantham to Stevenage. He was perfectly correct. We are here at least four hours earlier than if we had travelled by our usual route, but I think I never realised before how many bones I have in my body."

"You must be worn out indeed. Perhaps," said Elizabeth, turning to the butler, "you would take the ingredients of a punch to my father in his library? And ask Mrs Hill to send some tea upstairs to my sister's room. I must go to her at once. At what time is our dinner to be?"

"Mrs Hill hoped you would all be here in time to dine at six, Miss Elizabeth. I trust that will be in order?"

"Most certainly it will. One can always rely on Mrs Hill. But pray hint to her that, if my judgment does not err, all her travellers are fasting."

Elizabeth waited in the hall until Jane joined her. Mr Bingley went to Mr Bennet in the library. Jane and Elizabeth went up the stairs together.

X

They found Catherine alone, tranquilly sewing a seam on one of her new mourning dresses by the light of a great many working candles.

"I knew you were both here," she said as they entered, "but I did not come down. I hoped you would come up to me here."

She put her sewing aside and gave each of them a kiss.

"You look well," said Jane, "so far as one can tell by candle-light. I feared the last few weeks to have been too much for you, but I hope not."

"I have asked Hill to send up some tea," said Elizabeth.

They sat down together, Jane on the sofa beside Catherine, Elizabeth on a chair opposite them. A silence fell, not uncomfortable, until Elizabeth found the courage to say: "Dearest Kitty, we have to know, and perhaps it is best and easiest for us to know at once. As we are at the moment quite alone, just tell us quietly how my mother died and then we need not ask again."

"Oh," said Catherine, putting a handkerchief to her eye, "it was so—so *disappointing*—and at the end so distressing. There was nothing one could do."

Then, taking a deep breath, she went on. "It was so—so *satisfying* to see her improve each day after you left. The lemon-ade seemed to work like magic. She regained her usual size, her usual spirits even, and was able to go down at Christmas time. But then she continued to lose weight. She grew thin and began to return her food. We tried everything the doctors recommended, but she could keep nothing down—that is to say, she could take chicken broth and gruel if they were very finely sieved—but not even a lightly boiled egg. The doctors could not help. The surgeon came from Hertford at the request of our doctor from Meryton, and they would have consulted from

London had the time permitted. But she—she *disappeared* so fast—" said Catherine, suddenly bursting into tears.

"Calm yourself, dearest Kitty," said Jane, in her kindest voice and taking her by the hand. "Much better to tell us *all* about it."

"When you say she *disappeared*," said Elizabeth in astonishment, "what could you mean by that?"

"It was just as I said," said Catherine, mopping her eyes and controlling her voice with a strong effort. "Each day there was less of her to see. She was not a small woman, but by the end she made scarcely a mound under her covers—she seemed hardly to be there. She spoke not a word for two days before she died. I fear she was in some pain as she could not even take the medicine the doctors had left. And then, one afternoon, when we were alone, I saw her eyes fixed on mine and I put my ear down on her face. 'Remember,' she said, 'remember how much I loved you all. You were my pride—my joy.' And the next moment—she was dead."

There could be no reserves after such a disclosure. They sat for some minutes, their hands held, sobbing quietly into their handkerchiefs, Elizabeth herself suddenly more aware than she had been before of the nature of the event and how irreversible it was. At last Jane said: "My poor Mother. I hope she did not suffer very much. I think we did not always appreciate her as we should."

"Amen to that," said Elizabeth. "I must admit to being one of the chief defaulters there. But tell us, Kitty dear, where is she now?"

"In the chancel of the church. The doctor, not knowing why she died, recommended that she be taken at once from the house. One of the grooms makes sure there are always candles lit about her and I have put some sprigs of myrtle on her—on the coffin. There are no flowers to be found, you know, at this time of year—not even a snowdrop, because I have looked."

"You have done everything as you should," said Jane. "I am sad that we could not have been here to help you, but you must let us do so now."

"Oh," said Catherine, "while you are here everything will be quite easy; but I dread being alone with my father."

This aspect of the matter had not presented itself to Elizabeth before; but she said, a little more cheerfully than she actually felt: "If you can keep a secret, dearest Kitty, and if I can persuade him to come, we mean to take you and my father off to Bath, for the first few months of his mourning, at least."

"But that would be almost *too* much pleasure," said Catherine, beginning to cry again. "I have wished to go to Bath ever since Mary came back. She spoke so well of it, you know, even if she did spend all her time going to the library."

"I have a letter from her for my father," said Elizabeth, "which I must not forget to give him. I think she may be a mother before the end of next week."

Much to Elizabeth's relief, the tea was now brought in; and, on this rather happier note, their anxious conversation ended, skilfully guided by Jane, and by herself, into calmer waters, as, for instance, what was to be procured in Meryton by way of mourning apparel.

They dined at the large square table in the morning-room, and Elizabeth was happy to see her father, encouraged by his two sons-in-law, make an excellent meal.

Mrs Bennet was buried, two days later, in the afternoon. Mr Bennet went alone in his own carriage, followed by his brothers-in-law and his sons-in-law in Mr Gardiner's. The ladies remained behind, engaging in spasmodic talk, refreshed by many cups of tea.

Elizabeth had never had very much to say to her aunt Philips, her mother's sister, finding her a little too overwhelmingly good-humoured to make rational conversation a possibility; but with her aunt Gardiner, wife of her mother's brother, she had always been on the best of excellent terms. She found the opportunity to take her aside and, as they stood together, looking down on the garden, dim and damp in the February gloom, she said, very quietly: "I mean to take my father away from here at the earliest possible moment, my dear aunt. I think of going to Bath and wonder now if your friend Mrs Frankland might still be able to help us?"

"Indeed, yes," said Mrs Gardiner, after a second's thought. "I think that an unimpeachable proposal and I will write to her the instant I get home. She lives with a sister-in-law, a Lady Alicia whom I have never met, and they are quite leaders of a particular set in Bath. They are widows. Their husbands were brothers, both lost in the wars against the French. I could not recommend you to more charming people—and I must *commend* your courage in intending it. But do you think he will consent?"

"I hope so, very much," replied Elizabeth. "I believe that, if Jane or I were to suggest it to him, as being of benefit to Catherine, he might consider it. But if Mrs Gardiner were to mention it to him, as being of benefit to *himself*, I believe he would consider it very kindly."

"I must suppose," said Mrs Gardiner, with a smile, "that I shall sit next to him at dinner?"

"I must suppose so, too," said Elizabeth, returning her smile.

"But take care, Lizzy," went on Mrs Gardiner. "It is late in the season to be looking for lodgings. I hope you may not find yourselves in the finest rooms in Bath, at a rent of extortionate size, there being nothing else to be found."

"My father would not dislike that," said Elizabeth, smiling again. "It is to be Mr Darcy's party."

"You are greatly blessed in your husband," said Mrs Gardiner. "But in all honesty I must say that he is greatly blessed in his wife. Your scheme has all my blessings and Mr Gardiner's as well, I am sure, were he to be informed of it."

"Does he still intend to go to India?"

Mrs Gardiner's face fell a little.

"I fear so. He is quite sure that there are great fortunes to be made there and purposes to leave towards the end of April. It is a journey of six weeks and more, across the desert from Alexandria, but otherwise by sea. I must admire his energy, since his intention is only to benefit his family; but I could wish that energy to be expended just as profitably elsewhere."

"I can only commiserate with you, my dear aunt, most sincerely," said Elizabeth. "But let us be practical. While he is away you must come to us at Pemberley. Georgiana is promised for the month of June. May I engage for your presence as well?"

"You may indeed, and with my warmest thanks. I had been wondering how those long months were to be filled. I fancy he cannot return much before Christmas."

The dinner was served soon after the gentlemen returned. The conversation was general, constant, but conducted with a certain air of restraint. Elizabeth, seated beside Mr Gardiner and opposite Mr Philips, found herself closely questioned about Matlock by the one and about her housekeeping arrangements at Pemberley by the other.

When the tea and coffee were brought in to the drawing-room upstairs, Mr Bennet came over to Elizabeth and said: "I have to thank you, my dearest child, for your kind invitation to Bath, conveyed to me at second-hand by Mrs Gardiner and at first-hand by your excellent husband. As I collect that all the arrangements are to be made by him, and that I have nothing to do but be present, I accept it with all my heart. It is more than thirty years since I went to Bath but I daresay it is much the same."

"If I were to have the good luck to find a house for three months from the beginning of March, could you be ready by then?"

"So I would think. There are no further formalities attached to your mother's death and I believe I shall be wise to absent myself from the prolonged condolences of my neighbours."

"May Jane and I also arrange with Mrs Hill to have new curtains in this room while you are away? And, if you would not dislike it too much, some new paper in my mother's bedroom? She would have done it herself, you know, had she been able."

"You must do what you think best," said Mr Bennet, after a short silence. "I have some thoughts of moving into that room myself."

The party broke up early. The Gardiners and Philipses returned to Meryton and Mr Bennet retired to his book-room. The remaining five drew closer to the fire, and it was Jane who spoke first. With a glance at her husband, and then at Mr Darcy, she said: "I hope you mean to tell us now, and in the greatest possible detail, how it all went off. I trust the church was quite full?"

"It was," replied Mr Bingley, "as full as it could possibly be, and not only with your father's neighbours, so far as we could judge. There were all his tenants, one had to suppose, but also a great many labourers and workmen, all in their best clothes, but with a black cravat or armband. One could not but be impressed, both with how many there were and with their civil behaviour. And at the end of the service, your father stood at the door of the church and shook hands with them all."

"He appeared to know every one of them by name," added Mr Darcy, "which astonished us both. We, who have only seen him in his book-room, or at covert, could not have known him to be such an excellent landlord, or so fully acquainted with everyone in his employ. We think we must congratulate you on your father."

"Oh, I am glad," said Elizabeth, in a glow. "My father does always know what should be done but is not always in a mood to do it."

"But what had the parson to say?" pursued Jane. "He was no friend to my mother on account of her having taken in one of his servant girls, dismissed when she got with child. She told him very roundly that if he didn't know who his neighbour was, she most certainly did. She comes and sews for us still."

Mr Darcy and Mr Bingley exchanged a look and smiled at each other.

"That would explain much," said Mr Bingley. "He gave us quite a long speech, about her generosity and her willingness to help in time of trouble. He also informed the congregation that the soup to be had from the back door at Longbourn was some of the best in the country."

"Your father looked up when he said that," said Mr Darcy. "We thought perhaps that that was news to him."

"My mother never troubled him with details of that kind," said Catherine. "She took great pride in her housekeeping—but you may well be right."

"And the—actual burial?" ventured Elizabeth. "It must have been extremely damp."

"Dank and dripping," said Mr Darcy, "but it was all done with the greatest respect and expedition. The Bennets are buried in a gloomy corner of the churchyard—one could not help feeling sympathy for your mother."

"Your father sprinkled the earth, and your uncles, and then, at your father's request, the two of us, on your behalf you understand," went on Mr Bingley. "I do not think that any respectful detail was omitted. She ended her life with honour."

"Indeed she did," corroborated Mr Darcy. "There was no fault to be found. The whole congregation attended the graveside."

"I should like to plant rosemary there," said Jane, "but in that dark corner, as you say, I fear it would not flourish."

"Did you recognise anyone?" asked Elizabeth. "Sir William Lucas, I suppose?"

"Sir William Lucas and a son or two," said Mr Bingley. "And another, much younger Sir William, whose name I did not catch."

"Goulding," said Jane, "the new baronet at Haye Park. His father died quite lately."

"But no sign of Mr Collins?" asked Elizabeth, in spite of herself.

"Did you expect him?" asked Jane, in surprise.

"I know my father did not mean to tell him," said Elizabeth, "until the funeral was over. But the Lucases might have done so."

"There was no sign of Mr Collins," said Mr Darcy.

"We particularly looked, you know," said Mr Bingley, "so that we could avoid him. If he had been there, he would have wanted to sit with us, or at least take part in the service."

"No doubt there will be an aggrieved letter from him before long," said Elizabeth. "But at least we are spared his actual presence at this time."

"Let us hope," said Catherine, "that his visit of sympathy will take place after we have left for Bath."

"Another reason for making all possible haste," said Elizabeth. "I have asked my father if he could be ready by the first of March. Could you be so yourself, Kitty?"

"Oh certainly, and on such an incentive—even before."

"Then," said Elizabeth to Mr Darcy, "our way is clear. All our dependence must now be on Mrs Frankland."

XI

They stayed only another three days at Longbourn. Jane and Elizabeth received callers and answered letters of condolence, but the flow of these soon dried up and Elizabeth, especially, began to wish to be at home again.

"The thought of my visit to Bath has given me quite a new view of life," said Mr Bennet to her one morning. "And you, I think, must hasten back as your arrangements must be more intricate than ours. Your presence has given me the greatest comfort—even greater, perhaps, for the fact that I shall shortly see you every day for three months. So do not linger here, my dearest child. I hope I am strong enough to come through the next two weeks without you."

If they did not linger at Longbourn, Mrs Gardiner did not linger in her correspondence. They had not been at home five days before an express arrived, addressed to Mr Darcy from Mrs Frankland, informing him that an excellent house in Upper Camden Place had unexpectedly become available until the end of May, and asking his consent to her securing it on his behalf. The express containing this consent was sent off by return and Elizabeth began the considerable task of preparing her family for an absence of three months.

But the next day brought a civil note from Mr Morland, announcing that Mary had been safely delivered of a handsome boy, and assuring them that both mother and child were quite well.

Elizabeth, only too conscious of the fact that she could forget about Mary for days, if not weeks, together, drove over to Kympton by herself, to find Mary in high bloom, and by no means insensible of the fact that she had produced the first grandson for Mr Bennet.

"I am quite proud to be the first in this respect," she said, "as I am not at all accustomed to being first in any respect in our family. But, my dear Lizzy, what a struggle, what a *battle*—it makes one think of one's mother with an even higher regard. What was God thinking of when he designed this process? Not even my dear Mr Morland can answer that question. What do you think yourself?"

"I have not *thought* very deeply on the subject at all, I confess," replied Elizabeth. "As I can see no alternative, I fear we have no choice but to accept things as they are. But your remark about my mother is extremely *apropos*. How would it be if her daughters joined together to place a new organ to her memory in your church?"

"Oh my dear Lizzy," said Mary, her face suddenly illuminated, "what a brilliant notion indeed. It would keep her memory alive as long as it is played and would, if nothing else, crown the pinnacle of comfort that I have created for myself here at Kympton. But have you mentioned it to anyone else?"

"No," said Elizabeth, "I have not, for it only occurred to me this minute. But it *is* a brilliant notion and I will certainly write to Jane and speak to Kitty. Lydia, in her retreat at Gibraltar, might as well be living on the moon, but I will mention it to her when I write. And I will put the matter in hand before we leave for Bath."

"How I wish I could come with you, but you will write to me, and I think it very wise of you to go there with my father. How did he seem to be?"

"Cast down, certainly, as one would expect. I hardly know how to answer, indeed; but I am sure that, both for him and for Kitty, a complete change of place and air is what is required at the moment."

The journey to Bath was accomplished without incident, or upset. They travelled in three carriages. Two were to return to Pemberley. Their own four horses were to follow at their own good pace, since Mr Darcy wished to ride every day and hoped that Mr Bennet would join him.

The Longbourn family arrived about an hour after they had done so themselves, and a very joyous reunion took place. They were delighted to see each other again, delighted by the size and style of the house, delighted by the ease of the journey, even by the state of the weather. At their first dinner together, Elizabeth flattered herself that she could detect a small rise in her father's spirits.

To her great pleasure, Lady Alicia and Mrs Frankland called on them the next afternoon. Elizabeth was sitting upstairs with Catherine when their cards were brought in.

"This is the truest *civility*," said Elizabeth. "I acquit them entirely of *curiosity*."

The sounds on the stairs dissolved into two low, musical voices admiring the ceiling; and the two ladies entered the room together. They were both in deep mourning, but a certain smiling warmth seemed to accompany them.

"I am Mrs Frankland," said the shorter of the two, "and I am only too delighted to welcome you to Bath."

Smiles, courtesies, passed, the covert examination on both sides resolving itself into the pleased approval of all parties. Their two guests smiled even more broadly and Elizabeth and Catherine smiled back.

"It is a most charming surprise," said Lady Alicia, "to welcome two beautiful young women, especially at this time of the year. It quite gives one confidence that the spring will arrive."

She seated herself by the fire, but Mrs Frankland walked over to the window.

"I have never been in this room before," she said, "but it has the reputation of having the best view in Bath. And now that I see it myself I have to agree—and to say how glad I am that it is to be yours for the next three months."

"We come in particular to ask you to dine on the day after tomorrow," said Lady Alicia. "We have already engaged your near neighbours, the Elliots—to whom, in a sense, you owe your presence in this house—and I believe it would give us great pleasure to bring you all together."

"Lady Elliot just happened to be with me when your aunt's letter arrived," said Mrs Frankland. "And I happened to mention its contents to her. And she just happened to know that the prospective tenants for this house had cried off, as her house-keeper had happened to talk to its owner, who happened to come out of the house when she happened to be passing. And so I wrote at once to your husband."

Elizabeth had to smile at this.

"Clearly our visit here was ordained by Providence," she said. "And I must thank you indeed, as the agent of that Providence, for your swift and decisive action. We are quite delighted with this house."

"Well," said Lady Alicia, "I believe we shall all benefit. Sir Walter Elliot is particularly severe on the subject of the female residents of Bath. None of them, he thinks, is quite as handsome as himself. So I look forward to confounding him."

"And I," said Elizabeth, "look forward to meeting him. I will enter my husband in the lists against him. We shall be delighted to accept your invitation."

"It is rather a long story," said Lady Alicia, "but quite an interesting one. Bath, in fact, is divided between those who speak to Lady Elliot and those who do not."

"What *can* she have done," asked Elizabeth in astonishment, "to cause such a deep division of opinion?"

"All she did," said Mrs Frankland, in a very matter-of-fact voice, "was to marry Sir Walter."

"Which was regarded by many as being a *mésalliance*. An ugly word," said Lady Alicia reflectively. "So many French things are ugly. But she was a perfectly respectable girl, the daughter of an attorney, and her name was Isabella Thorpe."

"Only she had no fortune," added Mrs Frankland, "and she came from Putney."

"Whereas Sir Walter had already spent his fortune and had come to Bath to retrench."

"He was a widower of many years' standing, you understand, with two married daughters, of three."

"Then," said Catherine, speaking for the first time, "I think we must at least admire her courage."

"Yes," said Lady Alicia, smiling approvingly at her, "we must. But Sir Walter's great friend Lady Russell took vast exception to the marriage and in fact quitted Bath as a result. And Sir Walter's eldest daughter was still single at the time and actually living in the house. So to begin with poor Sir Walter was obliged to have breakfast with his daughter and dinner with his wife, since the two ladies would not speak."

"I think one must sympathise with him there," remarked Elizabeth. "Indeed I can hardly imagine a more comfortless situation."

"However, it did not last long," continued Mrs Frankland calmly. "Within the year the daughter received an offer from old General Tilney and she went off to live with him at Northanger Abbey."

"Northanger Abbey!" exclaimed Elizabeth.

"Where he very soon lost his temper with one of the stable-boys," said Lady Alicia imperturbably, "and was carried off in an apoplexy."

"So she remains there, firmly ensconced, despite the return of Colonel Tilney from many years of soldiering abroad, and with whom she has quarrelled entirely. Over, we are led to believe, the family jewels."

Elizabeth and Catherine glanced at each other while this conversation continued. When Mrs Frankland had finished speaking, Elizabeth said: "I think we must declare an interest here."

"Our sister Mary," said Catherine, "is married to the brother of Mrs *Henry* Tilney. I believe he has the living of Woodston."

"Ah," said Lady Alicia, "Mr *Henry* Tilney. That is *quite* another matter. He is a charming man with more sense than one would expect in such a family. I think we have not met his wife. How small a world it is, indeed," she went on, smiling. "The connection will do you no harm with Sir Walter, who pretends to dislike complete strangers."

"So we will just tell you," said Mrs Frankland, "that Mrs *General* Tilney considers that she has the right to wear *all* the family jewels for the rest of her life, but that *Colonel* Tilney does not agree. I thought I ought to inform you of it," she added, with a beguiling smile, "so that you will know what *not* to mention!"

They all smiled understandingly at this, and Lady Alicia rose.

"Until the day after tomorrow, then," she said. "We dine at six, but I hope you will arrive a little before that."

They attended their visitors downstairs.

"We are fortunate," said Elizabeth to Catherine, as they climbed the stairs again, "to be in Bath under such excellent auspices. No one, I think, could possibly dislike such charming women. I must write at once to my aunt."

XII

The ladies lived in Laura Place, right at the bottom of the hill, in a large house standing by itself. The drawing-room, on the first floor, occupied the width of the house at the back.

Lady Alicia and Mrs Frankland rose to greet them. Elizabeth introduced her father and her husband, and then their whole party was presented to Sir Walter and Lady Elliot.

Sir Walter was very tall and upright. His bow was the merest sketch caused, Elizabeth somewhat irreverently suspected, by the presence of a corset. The height of his neckcloth prevented any movement from side to side. His gaze was direct, but empty; and his face was curiously unlined, giving rise to the idea that the brain behind it had never been very much used.

Lady Elliot was quite different. She seemed to flow towards them. She returned their curtsey with a smile and remarked at once how pleasant it was, at that time of the year, to meet someone in Bath with a little youth and sparkle.

"As my dear Sir Walter will tell you, we find ourselves deserted in October by everyone under the age of forty. But I am sad to see your mourning so deep. Your mother, Mrs Frankland tells me?"

"Yes," said Elizabeth quietly. "Only last month."

"Then we must not expect too much gaiety from you. For my part, I think the private parties about Bath are to be preferred to anything that can occur in public. I hope there is no one amongst you who *needs* to take the waters?"

"No, indeed there is not. My father is perfectly healthy, but my mother's illness was a long one and I felt he would benefit from the change."

Mr Bennet was standing next to Sir Walter, conversing in a somewhat desultory way. Beside Sir Walter, in his immaculate immovability, he looked both worn and shabby. He was, at Elizabeth's guess, the younger by perhaps ten years; but now, even in the gentle candlelight, he seemed the older of the two. Elizabeth, who had secretly been forming several resolves, felt some of those resolves hardening within her.

She was placed between Mrs Frankland and Lady Elliot at a new, round dining table.

"It proved impossible on this occasion," said Mrs Frankland to her, "to avoid three women together, unless we put relatives next to each other. There are very few loose men in Bath and we thought, too, with your mourning being so recent, that two strangers would be enough. I do not consider myself a stranger at all, you know. I have been acquainted with you ever since Mrs Gardiner became your aunt."

"She is a person one can hardly love too much," said Elizabeth sincerely. "Her kindness and her common sense have stood me in good stead more than once. Where was the school that you attended together?"

"Oh, it was here in Bath. Perhaps that is why I found it so easy to settle here again. When we were widowed it was quite a puzzle to know where to choose. My dear Alicia thought of returning to Ireland, but I am only too thankful that we did not."

"Your widowhood is of recent date?" asked Elizabeth gently. "I cannot but observe how sombre is our party—only Lady Elliot in colours."

A shadow passed over Mrs Frankland's face, but it was soon gone.

"Our husbands fell together at Talavera," she said quietly. "A most fearful battle now more than ten years ago. Alicia and I were in Portugal at that time, sharing a house in Lisbon. We both remember it as a most pleasant adventure—until its end. But we shall continue in mourning," she finished, on a rather defiant note, "until the Corsican Monster is taken for his sins and consigned, as we both do most sincerely trust, to the hottest and remotest region of the great inferno."

Elizabeth, slightly at a loss, said only: "It cannot be long now. He has been for five years on St Helena. One might have thought that such a man would die from despair in the tedium of such a place."

"It is a thought," said Mrs Frankland, summoning a smile. "No punishment can be too great for him. He has caused the death of many a good man and all for nothing. He has not advanced his country in any direction, not by a single iota. It is in more confusion than it has ever been. But let us find a pleasanter topic. I hope that Bath will do all that you wish for your father?"

"I hope so, too," replied Elizabeth. "I have the greatest hopes of it and we have begun so well."

"We must do what we can to see that those hopes are not disappointed."

Elizabeth spoke little to Lady Elliot while they dined. The conversation was very often general and, when it was not, Elizabeth was delighted to find that Lady Elliot turned to Mr Bennet, on her other side, and seemed to entertain him even to occasional laughter. But when they had returned to the drawing-room, she came to sit beside her, on a sofa, and began their discourse in a very direct way.

"It is quite a treat to have you and your sister to talk to, and indeed to look at, among all the grey heads. I hope you like walking? I walk a great deal in Bath. Sir Walter has no carriage and there are some very pretty walks at our end of the town. Should it ever happen not to be raining, that is to say. Sometimes it does not. But how very pretty you both are. I cannot discern the smallest resemblance between you and yet you are undoubtedly sisters."

Lady Elliot paused for a moment but Elizabeth could think of nothing to say. Lady Elliot was playing with the single gold chain that she wore round her neck, on the end of which was a diamond of considerable size set among a number of smaller ones. It had a habit of disappearing when the chain was lengthened and Elizabeth became quite mesmerised by the performance of this stone, having the greatest difficulty in attending to Lady Elliot's words.

"Usually," continued that lady, "older men are married for their money, but I married Sir Walter for his position. It was quite a romance in its way. We had both just suffered a disappointment in love. We were both, as the vulgar phrase has it, on the *rebound*, I from Mr Morland and then from Captain Tilney—and Sir Walter from a very injudicious admiration of a Mrs Clay, who ran off, you know, with a much younger cousin of Sir Walter's, the heir to the baronetcy no less. So he was in a mood to confound him, as you might say. Or, indeed, for a trifle of revenge. In fact, almost his first words to me were— 'You seem quite formed to be a mother.'"

"I cannot believe," said Elizabeth, stifling her astonishment, "that anyone could be so rude to someone he had never met before."

"Well, I did not find it so," replied Lady Elliot calmly. "It was a very hot day. We were at a luncheon in somebody's garden and we were both, I am sure, quite bursting with strawberries and champagne. So Sir Walter went on to tell me how he required an heir and how I seemed to be quite fit for the purpose, though he did not precisely phrase it in that way. So I murmured something about his age and he told me he was quite able in every way—and indeed the evidence was there for *all* to see, Sir Walter wearing his clothes very snug."

Elizabeth hoped only that she did not look as amazed as she felt. The diamond re-appeared and her attention was entirely held.

"Well, the next day he called at my mother's and informed her that he thought he had proposed to her daughter on the previous day. So I was sent for and I said that I did not regard it as a serious proposal and would certainly not hold him to it. "But, my dear young lady, it was a very serious proposal and I am come today to re-new it," said Sir Walter, his words quite engraved upon my mind. So, I thought, I have everything to gain. Sir Walter cannot live a great deal longer, so I shall either be the widow of a baronet or, if I have good luck, the mother of one, so we compounded on the spot. And now, as I am sure you have been told, the baronetcy has three heirs, the Elliot fortunes have been recovered and within two years we shall return to the ancestral mansion."

"Then I must congratulate you on all three counts."

"Except that, as I keep asking myself, what am I to do for the next forty years?"

"I am sure you will find much to employ your time at the ancestral mansion," said Elizabeth, hiding her smile. "Life in the country is full of event. Is it far from here?"

"Some forty miles, I believe. I have never been there. It is let to a rich old admiral who has entirely repaired the roof, so it is no longer damp—or falling down."

"Your lot seems to have been cast in very pleasant places," said Elizabeth, "and your sons will be companions to you as they grow up."

"Indeed I hope so. But one cannot be always in the nursery."

"One thing I must ask you, if I did not mis-hear. The Mr Morland that you mentioned?"

"Certainly. The Reverend James, recently married to some girl he met in Queen Square whose family have supplied him with a living."

Elizabeth's astonishment was now quite plain to see.

"I think I have to tell you that that girl is my sister Mary. My mother was quite misinformed about the situation in Queen Square and their lodgings, Mary told me, were the most un-comfortable she had ever been in."

There was a very decided pause.

"And is she as pretty as you and your sister?" demanded Lady Elliot.

"I think handsome is more the word for Mary," said Elizabeth, after a moment.

"And is purple still his favourite colour?"

"That, I am afraid, I cannot tell you."

"What a small world it is, to be sure," said Lady Elliot reminiscently. "I had a narrow escape there—to be the wife of a country clergyman would be an even worse fate than to be the wife of an ancient baronet. I suppose I shall have to take up embroidery in the end."

The diamond re-appeared. Lady Elliot smiled and seemed to subside. The gentlemen entered the room. As she sank back into the cushions, Lady Elliot said: "I like your father very much, you know. He needs only a lick of paint to be quite as good as new."

And Elizabeth had to admit that, while it was not quite how she would have phrased it herself, the opinion expressed was exactly her own.

The party now re-arranged itself. Elizabeth gave up her seat on the sofa to her father, who was warmly welcomed by Lady Elliot. Catherine and Mr Darcy sat on either side of Sir Walter, assisting each other to assist him to maintain a flow of somewhat repetitive conversation. Elizabeth found herself seated most happily between her hostesses.

"I like your menfolk exceedingly, Mrs Darcy," began Lady Alicia. "We were overjoyed to receive Mrs Gardiner's letter, as company in Bath is thin in the winter. But to find that your party consists of two highly intelligent men and two charmingly pretty young women was a heavenly dispensation we could *not* have expected."

"I will try to accept your flattering words with the modesty that is by no means their due," said Elizabeth, laughing. "No one, I am sure, could have been more kindly received in a strange town than we have been, though my father tells me he was here thirty years ago, immediately before his marriage, I must suppose."

"Appearances can be deceptive," remarked Mrs Frankland. "We had expected Mr Bennet to be much older. Mrs Gardiner always mentioned him as being considerably senior to herself."

"My father is not yet fifty," said Elizabeth, with a glance to make sure that he could not hear. "He married—against the wishes of all his advisors, as I understand—three weeks after his twenty-first birthday. My mother was only just sixteen at the time but she, I rather think, married with the goodwill and good wishes of all her family."

"The usual pattern of evening parties here is for the card tables to be brought in after the tea and coffee. But we thought that Mr Bennet would prefer this first evening to be a quiet one," said Mrs Frankland.

"My father is no card player, certainly," said Elizabeth. "That is to say, Whist is a favourite abomination of his. But if you can persuade him—and you must allow me to return your compliments as best I may—to play at Commerce, or Speculation, you will have all my admiration and support. By which I would be understood to mean that I regard your powers of persuasion as *immense!*"

Her remark was received with acclamation by both her hearers.

"You begin to make us out," said Lady Alicia. "We like to see people happy whatever their circumstances—and your father is quite a Cinderella."

"And you, of course, must be his Fairy Godmothers," said Elizabeth. "I see no reason why a person should not have two."

"Our role precisely," said Mrs Frankland. "It is a pleasure to reach agreement so soon."

The evening did not last long after the tea and coffee were taken out. At twenty-five past nine, by the clock on the chimneypiece, Sir Walter rose.

"Lady Elliot," he said.

Lady Elliot completed what she had been saying to Mr Bennet, but then acknowledged him.

"Sir Walter," she said.

"I believe we must trespass no longer on the kindness of our hostesses."

"For shame, Sir Walter," said Lady Alicia pleasantly. "To use the word 'trespass' in such a context is to make us both a stranger."

"You must forgive him, Lady Alicia," said Lady Elliot swiftly. "He meant, I think, that the evening had passed almost too quickly and delightfully—and wished to upbraid me for not noticing the time."

"You are fortunate, Sir Walter, to have at your side an interpreter of such skill," said Lady Alicia, broadly smiling. "I am but too happy to accept that meaning of your words."

"That clock," said Mrs Frankland, in an aside to Elizabeth, "came back with us from Portugal. I believe it to be Spanish and the Spanish, you know, have no notion of the time. It is always ten minutes slow." Then, catching her eye, and with her most delightful smile, she added: "It prolongs the trespass a little, you know, much to our advantage."

Elizabeth smiled back and found herself contemplating the next three months with the greatest possible confidence.

XIII

There was a short silence in the carriage as they drove away. Then Mr Bennet said: "I confess myself a little disappointed after all. I was expecting a serious eccentric in Sir Walter. Instead I find him, if not exactly commonplace, at least too set in his ways and opinions to be at all amusing. His wife, however, is quite another matter—something interesting will probably happen there. But if Sir Walter is *not* the vainest man in the kingdom, we must have grave fears for the future of the nation."

"And yet you seemed well enough entertained by him before we sat down to dinner," said Catherine.

"Indeed. He favoured me with his comments on the age, height, rank and fortune of every male resident of Bath."

"He was kind enough," said Mr Darcy, "to ask for the name of my tailor."

"Did he so?" said Mr Bennet, rather sharply. "He merely gave *me* the name of *his*."

"Well, my dear Father," said Elizabeth, "one cannot quite blame him, after all. You have been wearing the coat you have on since long before my marriage."

"True, my dear child. Though I think I would rather have Darcy's tailor than Sir Walter's. And what is this Gowland that he talks about?"

"It is a kind of cream, Papa," said Catherine, after a moment. "It is supposed to prevent wrinkles."

"And do you tell me that Sir Walter uses it himself?"

"I thought," said Mr Darcy, not very kindly, "that his face looked rather fossilised than wrinkled."

"What age do you suppose him to be?"

"Not above sixty, I fancy," said Mr Darcy, "and his wife would be about thirty."

"Then," said Mr Bennet to Catherine, "you may procure some of this magic substance for me. But you are forbidden to ask if I use it or not. And Sir Walter, you may be glad to hear, *also* gave me the name of his barber."

"I will do so, Papa," said Catherine graciously, "and I shall certainly *not* tell Sir Walter."

"Lady Elliot does interest me, however," went on Mr Bennet. "Her single-minded pursuit of unadorned self-interest has landed her very comfortably, quite early in life. Now she looks about her for new sources of entertainment. I think that, if I were the wife of Mr Darcy, for instance, I should mount a constant guard upon him."

"No need, Sir, I assure you," returned Mr Darcy. "He is perfectly able to mount a constant guard upon himself."

"She appeared quite astonished to find that I had heard of Putney," said Mr Bennet. "I see no reason why it should not be a very pleasant place."

"And had you heard of it, Papa?" asked Catherine.

"I had. In the days of my youth it acquired a certain transient fame. There was a writer, a Mary Wollstonecraft who, wishing to end her life, went, for this purpose to Battersea Bridge. But the crowd on that bridge was so dense that she could by no means approach the railing—so she took a boat and *rowed herself to Putney*—where the bridge was less crowded and she was able to throw herself off it."

"I hope she did *not* succeed in drowning herself," said Catherine.

"No, my dear, she did not. She was picked up by passing watermen—I must suppose at once since clothes at that time were very heavy—and lived to write more books, to be married and to give birth to a daughter."

"It is difficult to believe," said Mr Darcy. "It must be the best part of two miles from Battersea to Putney by water."

"She was a very strong woman," said Mr Bennet, "and very tenacious. I have some of her works at Longbourn but rather fear that I may not have read them."

"You are quite sure, my dear Father, that you are not inventing the whole?"

"I *am* sure, my dear Lizzy, but remain highly flattered that you should think me so clever."

"I was always used to think you very clever. But I hope you did not tell Lady Elliot how it was that you came to have heard of Putney?"

"I did not. I told her only that I believed it to be some two miles up river from Battersea and she agreed with me."

"She must be a breath of fresh air in the Elliot family," remarked Catherine. "The Elliots, whose whole history Sir Walter kindly gave us, seem to have lived in the same place for centuries without doing very much to the purpose."

"Very well said indeed," said Mr Darcy, laughing. "My own thought exactly. They took much without giving anything back. Sir Walter has a great sense of his own dignity, coupled with a great sense of his own indignity at being unable to occupy his own house just at present. Whatever the reasons for that, you may be sure that Sir Walter does not hold himself responsible."

"I should imagine that he is himself the sole source of all his own problems," said Mr Bennet. "But you, my dear Catherine, must watch your tongue lest you turn out to be too much a daughter of your father—a thing that would give *me* a great deal of pleasure."

"I will do my best, Papa," said Catherine demurely, "to heed your excellent advice."

Elizabeth was particularly pleased with the very good understanding between the members of her party which this conversation seemed to suggest. Her one great wish, in the present instance, was that they should enjoy their visit to Bath; and a state of great comfort at home was the first requirement for this.

Lady Elliot called on Elizabeth the following morning and sat with her for twenty minutes, regretting deeply that the weather prevented her from proposing that they walk out together; but in the course of their conversation an understanding was clearly reached. Lady Elliot did not give dinners. Lady Elliot, indeed, did not entertain at all. While Sir Walter and his lady were only too happy to grace the table of anyone who chose to invite them, this invitation was most unlikely ever to be returned. The most that Mrs Darcy and her family could expect, said Lady Elliot in almost as many words, would be an evening party with cards and perhaps some music.

"We sometimes give one on the occasion of Sir Walter's birthday—the first of March, you know, but we did not do so this year—and one on the occasion of my own, at the beginning of October."

Consulting her feelings soon after Lady Elliot had left, Elizabeth found herself openly relieved at the prospect of *not* dining with the Elliots. It did not prevent a certain gloom, however, at the thought that she should invite the Elliots to dine with them; but, remembering that they could always be diluted by the presence of Lady Alicia and Mrs Frankland, her spirits revived a little.

A pleasant pattern was quickly established. Mr Bennet and Mr Darcy rode out every morning, rain or shine, and Elizabeth and Catherine accompanied the children and their nursemaids on their daily walk, whenever the weather was fine. Discovering that morning calls were no longer the fashion in Bath, they very often ended their afternoon expeditions to the shops with a call in Laura Place, where they were always very enthusiastically received.

By the end of the third week in March, with some change in the weather, Mr Bennet began to talk of a visit to London in quest of some new clothes. Mr Darcy gladly offered to accompany him and they set off, in their own carriage but with post horses all the way. They left early, to make the fullest use of the daylight, and Elizabeth and Catherine found themselves, soon after their own breakfast, seated together in the drawing-room upstairs, wondering what to do with the day.

They had scarcely taken up their sewing, however, when Mr Collins was shown into the room.

He followed the butler immediately, as though uncertain of his welcome, and Elizabeth had just presence of mind enough to reflect that, had they brought with them the butler from Longbourn, instead of their own butler from Pemberley, Mr Collins would certainly have been denied. He was quite unknown at Pemberley.

But she rose at his entrance and said, in an astonished voice: "Mr Collins! And to what do we owe—?"

"Miss Elizabeth, Miss Catherine," said Mr Collins, ignoring this greeting with a solemn bow to each. "I trust I do not intrude upon your valuable time?"

"I hope there is nothing amiss at Hunsford?" said Elizabeth, searching her mind for a reason for this visitation.

"There is nothing amiss at Hunsford. Lady Catherine and her amiable daughter, Mrs Collins and her children, all enjoy the best of health."

"I am more than happy to hear it."

Elizabeth now indicated a chair to Mr Collins, but he declined it. Catherine came to join her on a small sofa so that they faced Mr Collins, whenever he happened to be stationary, together. After pacing the room for some time, he stopped in front of them and said: "You can be at no loss, I think, Mrs Darcy, Miss Bennet, to account for my visit here."

"You are mistaken, Mr Collins," said Elizabeth at once. "I cannot account for it at all."

"We remain entirely in the dark," said Catherine.

"I am surprised," said Mr Collins, and continued his pacing through the room. At last he stopped before one of the windows and said: "It is a fine view, indeed."

Elizabeth sat silent, determined to offer him no encouragement to prolong his visit; but her knowledge of Mr Collins was sufficient to inform her that it would take more than a hint to remove him.

"I think the butler must have told you, Mr Collins," she said, as coldly as she could, "that my father and Mr Darcy left this morning for London."

"He did," replied Mr Collins, "and I can hardly express the sense of shock, of shame even, that his information gave me."

"Pray explain yourself, Mr Collins."

"I will most certainly do so," said Mr Collins in a heavy voice. "I have come here to do so."

Elizabeth felt Catherine's hand steal into hers and she clasped it warmly.

"About three weeks ago," began Mr Collins, "I received a letter from your amiable parent, to the effect that his wife, your honoured mother, had recently died after an illness unexpectedly short. It further informed me that the nature of her malady demanded a swift burial and that, in fact, her funeral obsequies had already been performed."

"That is perfectly correct, Mr Collins," said Catherine. "My mother's death took us completely by surprise. The several doctors who were consulted could offer us no reason. You may rest assured that every possible remedy was tried, but to no avail. I was present all the time at her bedside."

"I have no doubt of that," said Mr Collins. "Although Mrs Bennet's illness was of long standing, its precise nature was never understood. But I accuse no one of neglect."

"I am glad to hear that," said Catherine very shortly. "I do not believe that anyone in England could have saved her."

"You mistake me, Miss Bennet. You miss my point. Which is this. As the heir to your father's estate, I would expect to be informed at once of such an occurrence, so that I could be on hand to offer support *before*, rather than *after*, the funeral had taken place."

Elizabeth gave Catherine's hand a squeeze.

"You may be quite sure, Mr Collins," she said coolly, "that if my father had wished you to be present, he would have made it very plain."

"I do not recall that my mother ever expressed a wish to see you before she died," remarked Catherine, almost absently.

"Nevertheless, whatever the circumstances, I regard it as my duty to be present at such a time and it is certainly your father's duty to keep me informed of all such eventualities," said Mr Collins peevishly. "I consider him to be completely at fault."

He took a few paces through the room before turning to face them again.

"But it is not only that," he said, "not only that at all. I gave myself the trouble of a journey to Longbourn only to find that your father, a grieving widower of less than a month's duration, had left there for Bath, of all frivolous localities, and that the house was actually in process of new decoration. There are to be new curtains, which I understand are to be *yellow*, of all inappropriate shades, in the drawing-room, new paper in the room where Mrs Bennet died—it was as though all memory of your mother were to be expunged. It was all too soon, Mrs Darcy, Miss Bennet. A year's deep mourning, in closed solitude at Longbourn, would have been suitable. But to be gallivanting off to London, in all the present circumstances, is by no means the action of a person worthy of respect."

"I think you forget yourself," said Elizabeth angrily. "The memory of the mother of five daughters cannot possibly be expunged so long as those daughters are alive; and the changes at Longbourn have been under consideration for a long time. My mother wished to bring them about herself and would certainly have done so. We thought it best to have them made while my father was away."

"But to come to *Bath*, Mrs Darcy, a place known for its thoughtless frivolities and which can offer him no opportunity for serious reflection on the permanence of the event which has recently overwhelmed him—who can have made such a decision?"

"In choosing Bath, Mr Collins," said Elizabeth coldly, "I thought only of the benefit to my father's health and spirits. We live very quietly here."

"And very well," retorted Mr Collins. "I am astonished to think that the estate at Longbourn can support the expense of such a residence as this."

Elizabeth was by now too angry to speak, and did not do so. It was Catherine who said, and in a voice which Elizabeth had never heard before: "You may be quite easy, Mr Collins. It is the estate at Pemberley that supports us here."

"And not content with coming to Bath," continued Mr Collins, in royal rage and as though Catherine had not spoken, "he must needs go jaunting off to London before he has been here a week. Pray, what is the reason for that?"

"The reason for that," said Elizabeth, with an edge to her voice which she made no attempt to conceal, "is that my father is urgently in need of some new clothes. The last person to die in his family was his father, some thirty years ago. He has gone to purchase his mourning which, as you have said yourself, is liable to last for a year. I presume you have no objection to that?"

"I should have thought it possible to purchase mourning a little nearer home," said Mr Collins sullenly. "At his age there can be no requirement to be at the height of the mode. But none of this alters the fact that at no time have I been consulted. As the heir to his estate it is my right to be closely consulted about everything that appertains to that estate. The changes in the house at Longbourn are costly and unnecessary. This visit to Bath is costly and unnecessary. The visit to London is extremely costly and entirely unnecessary. I can hardly express my sense of outrage sufficiently."

Elizabeth stood up, and Catherine with her.

"You appear to be under some misapprehension, Mr Collins," she said very politely. "It is my *mother* who has died, not my father. Until that event occurs you have no right whatever to concern yourself in what goes on at Longbourn, unless my father specifically invites you to do so. He has been his own master for a great many years and he is most unlikely to require any assistance, or brook any interference, from you or from anyone else."

Mr Collins appeared to register this remark. He turned a little and faced them directly.

"None of this alters the fact that I *should have been* both informed and consulted. Like it or not, I am heir to your father's property and its management nearly concerns me. As to his present thoughtless, unsuitable, *unChristian* behaviour, I have no words to describe it. His every action seems to insult the dead."

Elizabeth rang the bell.

"You will understand, Mr Collins," she said, with as much steel in her voice as she could muster, "that, in the absence of my husband and my father, I cannot receive you in this house, or offer you accommodation here. I did not invite your visit and I have now no choice but to request you to leave us, and at once."

"I shall certainly do so, Mrs Darcy. There is clearly no point in remaining."

When the butler came in, Elizabeth said: "You may show Mr Collins out. If he should call again, we shall not be at home."

Mr Collins favoured them with a look of malevolence entirely inappropriate to a man of his cloth. As he went through the door he said deliberately, and very loudly: "You may rest quite easy. I shall make no attempt to re-enter these unhallowed portals."

And Elizabeth and Catherine, suddenly released, turned to each other and smiled.

"Good-bye, Mr Collins," they said together; and Elizabeth added, in a lower voice: "I am but too thankful that my father was not here."

XIV

The discussion, and re-discussion, of this extraordinary event occupied the entire conversation of Elizabeth and Catherine for the next few days. A particular agony lay in the fact that they could discuss it with no one else. It stayed at the back of their minds during visits to Laura Place, and during a visit paid by Lady Alicia and Mrs Frankland to them. It was all they wished to talk about during their own meals, but the presence of the servants forbade it. When, therefore, more than a week later, Mr Bennet and Mr Darcy returned from London, they found themselves welcomed with a warmth which aroused the comments of them both.

"My dear," said Mr Bennet, "I had not thought you would be so very lonely."

"My love," said Mr Darcy, "I had not dreamed that we had been so long away."

"Not that, not that at all," said Elizabeth, very decidedly. "We are simply unable to contain ourselves any longer. We have news which no one else can share."

"I hope no disaster?" said Mr Darcy, quickly.

"Of a kind, perhaps," said Catherine, smiling. "We have sustained a visit from Mr Collins."

"From Mr Collins!" exclaimed Mr Bennet. "Pray, what had he to say?"

The answer to this question took Elizabeth and Catherine, in joint effort, the best part of half-an-hour to achieve. They were interrupted only by the occasional explosive comment from their hearers, an "incredible impertinence" from Mr Darcy and an "insolent dog" from Mr Bennet. "Why is he to be the arbiter of my behaviour?"

But by the end of the recital they were all in a state of such high amusement that the whole episode was simply laughed away.

"Mr Collins has been a source of entertainment ever since he came into our lives," said Mr Bennet admiringly. "I would not be without his acquaintance for a fortune. I regret only that I was not here to receive him, but you seem to have disposed of him very skilfully."

"Perhaps you could now enlighten us, Papa, as to how it comes about that Mr Collins *is* your heir?" said Catherine.

Mr Bennet paused for a moment and then said: "We must go back to the time of my great-grandfather. He received the property from a childless maternal uncle, who had it from his wife—I do not even recall his name, or hers. The proviso was that it was to descend through the male heirs of his nephew— my great-grandfather himself, that is to say—as it has done. But, in default of male heirs in that line, it was to revert to the male heirs of my great-grandfather's sister, by her marriage to a certain William Collins of Churston Ferrers in the county of Devon, a small country gentleman of whom I know nothing."

"A cruel, heedless arrangement," said Mr Darcy musingly. "I am glad it is not the case with us."

"But, at present," remarked Elizabeth, "Mr Collins has nothing but daughters. So what is to happen then?"

Mr Bennet paused again.

"A lawsuit would ensue," he said thoughtfully. "The family of the eldest son of my eldest daughter would claim against the eldest son of the eldest daughter of Mr Collins. The whole estate would quite certainly have to be sold to pay the costs of such an action, and there would be an end of the matter."

He then added: "It must be a source of some regret that none of us would be there to see it. Surely an amusement of the first class, an enjoyment for all."

"I don't understand you, Papa," said Catherine. "How could anyone *enjoy* such a sad procession of events?"

"Only such old cynics as myself, perhaps," responded Mr Bennet. "Any operation of the Vanity of Human Wishes must be a pleasure to observe. What did my great-grandfather's maternal uncle hope to achieve by his entail? He would have been wiser to leave the property at the disposal of those who occupied it."

Elizabeth was sufficiently disturbed by this manifestation of Mr Bennet's continuing black mood for her to suggest to him that they take a walk together one morning, instead of his accustomed ride. She found a willing accomplice in Mr Darcy, whose small, sudden indisposition gave grounds for his cancellation of their ride some three days later; and Elizabeth was able to claim her father's company for a walk round the upper reaches of the town. They made their way towards a secluded glade on the edge of a little wood, where Elizabeth had been several times with Catherine and the children.

"I take this very kindly in you, my dear child," said Mr Bennet, as they entered this glade, "and also in your excellent husband, whose disorder is of so infinitesimal a nature as to be visible only to himself."

"I hope," said Elizabeth, hiding her smile, "that I may always be aware when you have something disagreeable on your mind."

"I hope so, too," said Mr Bennet. "It is a luxury indeed to have someone with whom to share one's moods, a luxury I never achieved with your mother. At the same time I find myself—beset, I think, is the right word—haunted is altogether too dramatic and I do not in any case believe in ghosts—I find myself beset by the memory of something I once said to her."

"Then pray tell me what it is," said Elizabeth very softly. "We are alone and I am the soul of discretion."

After a moment, and several thoughtful paces, Mr Bennet said: "It was, I think, one afternoon, when we were all together, and I brought our conversation to a close by saying 'Let us flatter ourselves that I may be the survivor.' I did not mean it unkindly, or even wholly seriously, but now that I *am* that survivor I find myself concerned that I may have wounded her when all I intended was to silence her, or to put her fears to flight."

"Of course, I remember it well," said Elizabeth immediately. "My mother was in one of her highest flights of fancy, imagining herself and her five unmarried daughters being turned from the house by Mr and Mrs Collins before—I think these were her words—you were cold in your grave. And was not my uncle present? I seem to recall that she finished with a plea for help from him."

"I believe she did," said Mr Bennet, "and on Mr Collins's recent performance here, I think she was not so greatly mistaken. I have not had the opportunity to say to you how excellently you dealt with him, for I have had the complete history from your butler, who was privy to the whole. And you are not to think," he went on, "that I am in the habit of gossiping with your servants for I most certainly am not; but the occasion seemed to concern us all and I could think of no other way of finding out the truth."

"In retrospect," said Elizabeth, "I think you would have been proud of us. There is a strength in Catherine that I had not previously observed. I am only relieved that he did not remain in Bath until your return, *haunting* our threshold every day."

"A substantial spectre he would have been indeed," returned Mr Bennet without a smile. "I, too, am relieved. But can you, my dear Lizzy, remove from my mind the feeling of guilt that I cannot but have over that remark? Could she have felt that I was wishing her away?"

"No, my dear father, she could not. My mother was not a woman of the greatest sensibility. I doubt that she ever saw beneath the surface of any remark and that one, I am sure, soon disappeared from her consciousness. If her house was in order, if her daughters were elegantly dressed, if her dinners were satisfactorily superior to Lady Lucas's, she was content. And if she had a wish, deeply buried in her heart, it would have been that she should end her life at Longbourn."

"Kind, kind Lizzy," said Mr Bennet with a heartfelt sigh, "almost you put my mind to rest. At least, if that were her wish, it has been granted to her."

"You are not to think," said Elizabeth, in a little burst of courage, "that I am entirely without knowledge of your married life. Since I have had the good fortune to marry a man with whom I am able to share everything, and who consults me on almost every point, I am the more able to form a clear picture of a marriage where this is *not* the case. My mother's intelligence was by no means of the first rate, but no one could fault the kindness of her heart however indirectly it showed itself. It is some years now since I came to realise what inroads her flutterings must have made upon the peace of *your* mind—why so much time was spent alone in your book-room."

Elizabeth's hand was on Mr Bennet's right arm. He put his other hand on hers and said, in a voice rather deeper than usual: "I am glad to have had this talk with you, my dearest child. I think you know me better than I think."

They walked on for some moments in silence after this remark, until they reached the end of the glade; where, finding a seat that was surprisingly dry, they sat down, the length of the glade opening before them.

Their attention was held by two rather elegant people, a man in uniform and a woman with an umbrella, or a parasol, going through the pantomime of meeting unexpectedly. After a very short while, they linked arms and set off down the glade; but, observing, as they could not fail to do, Mr Bennet and Elizabeth observing them, they turned abruptly to their left and disappeared into the wood.

"And did you think that that was Lady Elliot?" asked Mr Bennet.

"I did," said Elizabeth, "but it was certainly not Sir Walter."

"A very handsome younger man," remarked Mr Bennet musingly. "If I am not greatly mistaken, Lady Elliot is quite ready to throw over the traces and gallop off. It is often the case with such marriages and Sir Walter, for all his self-importance and fastidiousness, can only strike the unbiased onlooker as being extremely dull."

"What makes you say that of Lady Elliot?"

"While she conversed very charmingly with me at that dinner party, she hardly moved her eyes from contemplation of your very handsome husband."

"He *is* very handsome indeed," said Elizabeth, in a sudden glow. "I think so every day—and he looks better now than ever. I cannot decide why I did not think so when first we met."

"Darcy is shy," said Mr Bennet. "Or, I should say, Darcy *was* shy—his excellent wife has cured him of that. And in those days Bingley's more appealing manners eclipsed him completely. But I truly think, despite my admiration for Bingley's easygoing charm, that you have much the better bargain. I like your husband more and more."

It was not weather to remain seated for long. They got up and began to walk gently back.

"You have quite put my mind at rest," said Mr Bennet. "I can only be most grateful for that."

They returned home to find that Mr Darcy's indisposition had disappeared and he was well enough to ride out that afternoon with Mr Bennet.

Elizabeth and Catherine had already decided to pay a call in Laura Place that day. They found themselves welcomed with even more than the usual enthusiasm.

"Because we have a new neighbour," said Mrs Frankland at once. "We do not always call on the occupants of number 8, who seem to change with most remarkable regularity, but there was something about the carriage which brought them and about the quantities of elegant baggage which accompanied them. Alicia and I decided we would risk it this time, especially as we discovered it was let only for six months. We left our cards two days ago and so we are in constant expectation of having them returned. All we know is that it is a Mrs Grant and her sister, Miss Crawford."

As she finished speaking the butler came in, carrying a small tray with some cards on it.

"Pray ask her to come up," said Lady Alicia, to whom he presented it. "I am sorry to find that she is alone."

Within two minutes the butler returned.

"Miss Crawford, my lady," he said; and a very decided figure, neither short nor tall, but dressed with every consideration for the latest mode, was shown by him into the room.

Lady Alicia performed her introductions. Smiles and courtesies passed but, before they had a chance to sit down again, Miss Crawford said: "I wish to say at once how charmed and deeply flattered we were to receive your ladyship's card, and Mrs Frankland's. We come to Bath as strangers and this was an attention we could not have anticipated. I would like to thank you for it now."

"And very prettily said," returned Lady Alicia. "In Bath we lead a very humdrum life. There is a certain every-day sameness about our life in Bath. The opportunity to welcome someone to dispose of that sameness—for however short a time—is one that we cannot allow to escape us. I hope you may be with us for some months?"

"For *six* months," said Miss Crawford, with a certain gravity. "It must depend upon my sister's health—or, to be more exact, it must depend on what the waters of Bath can do for her."

"I hope she may not be very ill?" said Mrs Frankland, gently.

"My sister is not ill precisely," said Miss Crawford, "but crippled I am afraid she is. To mount such a flight of stairs as these—and I perceive this house to be the twin of ours—is for her a quite unbearable labour which would leave her exhausted for the rest of the day. It is a happiness to be able to arrange the whole of her life on one level. She goes into the warm bath tomorrow and one must hope that this will afford her some relief."

"And we must hope so, too," said Lady Alicia. "You have travelled far?"

"From Norfolk only," said Miss Crawford. "My brother was so good as to lend us his carriage for our journey. Though when I say 'only' it is two hundred and twenty miles and, although we spent four days on the road, my sister is hardly yet recovered. She sends her deep regrets to you."

"We must hope to make her acquaintance later."

With the civilities over, the conversation became general. Elizabeth had the good fortune to sit next to Miss Crawford and found herself in contact with a lively mind, certain of itself and its opinions. She felt a great desire to know her better and, with this in mind, remarked to her: "My sister and I are here with our father and my husband. Our mother is only lately dead and we live very quietly. But I hope to engage Lady Alicia and Mrs Frankland for a dinner early next week. May I hope that you would be able to accompany them? How would your sister feel about that?"

"My sister must remain stationary for the present, I grieve to say, but for myself nothing could give me greater pleasure. I have, of course, no conveyance, but perhaps you live at no great distance?"

"We live about as far from here," said Elizabeth, smiling, "as it is possible to be while still in the same town. My sister and I have become great walkers, and I must recommend this sort of locomotion to yourself. Your kind neighbours, however, will certainly take you up. While they pay their afternoon calls on foot, if the weather permits it, they take out their carriage for a dinner."

Elizabeth gave her invitation when she and Catherine rose to go; but, after some discussion, "early next week" was found to be too far away and the day after the next was fixed on.

XV

A note was delivered to Elizabeth on the following morning as she and Catherine lingered over their breakfast.

This letter is to introduce Captain William Price, who stops at Bath in his way to Plymouth. He is the brother of my sister-in-law Fanny and is in every way a most interesting man. He is made Captain in recognition of his service with Admiral Wentworth, removing the French Emperor to St Helena and keeping him there! He has much to say and is of a most *amiable* disposition— pray invite him to dinner and spoil him unmercifully.

Your ever-loving Georgiana.

"Oh," said Elizabeth, getting up at once. "I hope he is still there."

In the hall she found the butler.

"This note," she said. "Who brought it?"

"The gentleman himself, madam. He did not wait."

"Then someone must go after him. Did you see in which direction he went?"

"He is putting up at the White Hart, madam, downhill all the way. I am sure that Thomas, or Robert, could certainly overtake him."

"Then pray send them off. Instruct them to say that, if he is not otherwise engaged, we shall be delighted if he will spend the whole day with us."

"It shall be done, madam, and on the instant."

Thus it was that, some fifteen minutes later, Captain Price, by no means out of breath, was ushered into the drawing-room upstairs. After introducing herself and Catherine, Elizabeth said directly: "You were not very kind, Captain Price, to give my poor footmen so much exercise so early in the day."

"I did them no harm at all, Mrs Darcy, *upon* my honour. I was walking as slowly as I know how—I doubt that they had to run more than a very few paces."

"That quite relieves my mind. We live very quietly here, as no doubt Georgiana will have told you—and gentlemen of the Navy seem to find acquaintance wherever they go."

"True enough—but not in my case, perhaps fortunately for me. I am quite a stranger in Bath and know of no one else."

"Then I hope you will consent to be included in our daily life and not stand on any ceremony. My father and my husband have ridden out, but I expect them back about noon. So pray sit down—and give us all the news from Mansfield."

"I am to say," said Captain Price, as solemnly as he could, "that it is to be a partridge. The goose was found to be too heavy—it cracked open its nest more than once and was found in pieces on the floor."

"Oh," said Elizabeth, after an astonished moment, "Georgiana's ceiling. I know she had reservations about the goose. But—the vegetation? Have the brambles met in the middle?"

"As to *brambles* I could not say. As a sailor my knowledge of botany may best be described as non-existent. But certainly, at one point only, the plants from one side are entwined with the plants from the other side—there are to be *two* hooks for the chandeliers, one at each end—and Sir Thomas thinks it the most remarkable thing he has ever seen."

"But can they *occupy* their house? The drawing-room I know they cannot, but do they still live entirely in their bedroom?"

"No, for on the other side of the house there is a room complete except for the ceiling—and there they are able to entertain. My sister Fanny," he added, almost as an afterthought, "thinks your sister Georgiana the greatest addition that the Mansfield family has ever received."

"We were sad not to see her at Georgiana's wedding. I hope the little girl goes on more prosperously?"

"Thank you, yes. She is, I believe, quite out of danger, but must, I suppose, always be delicate."

They were interrupted at this point by one of the nurse-maids, who came to say that they were quite ready for their morning walk and that the children awaited them below.

"I will go with them, dearest Lizzy," said Catherine at once. "You and Captain Price can have so much to talk about."

"Not at all," instantly responded Captain Price. "A morning walk in Bath, with children and nursemaids, would rank as a great novelty in my life. I must beg to be included."

"Then included you shall be," said Elizabeth very cordially. "You will excuse us while we find our bonnets."

They went towards the little glade where Elizabeth had sat with her father and, once more, she thought she saw Lady Elliot and her military escort disappearing into the wood. Captain Price distinguished himself by retrieving the hat of Jane Darcy, blown off by a sudden gust.

"A naval education, you see, is useful," he said, as he smilingly gave it back. "It enables one, upon occasion, to anticipate the wind."

Elizabeth, seeing her daughter quite overcome by this attention, thanked him as best she could, torn between amazement that he should think of doing such a thing and admiration of the speed with which he did it. They returned peacefully, without further incident, Elizabeth a little ahead with the children and Catherine a little behind with Captain Price.

Mr Bennet and Mr Darcy awaited them at home. A pleasant nuncheon followed. Captain Price returned to dine and, by the end of the evening their whole party was more than just well-disposed towards him, singling out for comment his common-sense, his good humour and his readiness to join in every aspect of their unremarkable daily existence. Catherine said very little, but there was a glow in her eyes which did not escape Elizabeth.

She half-remarked on this to her father.

"I am glad to be able to place them together at dinner to-morrow without any appearance of connivance."

"Oh," said Mr Bennet, "are you there? He asked my per-mission to pay his addresses to my daughter before I had been five minutes in the room. I could think of no objection and there seems to be none on Catherine's side."

"It would leave you quite alone," said Elizabeth, after a moment.

"In such a cause, one could not repine. I regret only that your mother is not here, since he is just the kind of man she always hoped would appear at Longbourn, riding a white horse."

Captain Price rode out with Mr Bennet and Mr Darcy the next morning, returning with them for a nuncheon.

"I find this habit of eating in the middle of the day a very agreeable one," he said to Elizabeth. "It is not yet in force at Mansfield, but I can see that it is my duty to suggest it."

"I should have thought that Georgiana—but I daresay her parties are given in the evening."

"I am a little surprised," he said pleasantly, after a moment, "to find that you and your sister have not yet ventured so far as the Pump Room. As I cannot feel it right to be in Bath without visiting it myself, perhaps I could offer to escort you, should you wish to undertake this perilous excursion—this very afternoon for instance?"

Elizabeth could only smile.

"You are perfectly right, Captain Price," she said. "We have lacked courage, I think, rather than opportunity; but with your protection, and my husband's, we should certainly be safe from any danger liable to be encountered in this very peaceful town."

Their visit passed off without incident. They dutifully drank a glass of water, pronounced by Elizabeth and Mr Darcy to be quite inferior to that available at Matlock. Captain Price said he hoped he would never develop an ailment that could be cured in such an unpleasant way; and Catherine smiled and said nothing.

They were seated at a table a little set back from the main stream of the crowd, and Elizabeth was shortly astonished to see an unmistakable Lady Elliot among it. It hardly seemed a suitable place to conduct a clandestine *amour* and she thought she had caught a glimpse of a military uniform at the same time. But she was very soon astonished even further, by the entrance of Sir Walter himself with Lady Elliot on his arm. They were followed quite closely by a woman so like Sir Walter in countenance that she could only be his daughter; and she was escorted by the man who had accompanied Lady Elliot into the wood at the top of the town.

They sat at a distance; and Elizabeth, rather anxious to avoid them, suggested that they walk slowly back up the hill, visiting a certain pastrycook's on the way. She was quite sure that Lady Alicia, or Mrs Frankland, would be able to tell her who the newcomers were. They made, she thought, a very handsome couple.

Their evening opened with a surprise. Lady Alicia presented Miss Crawford to Mr Bennet and Mr Darcy and Elizabeth presented Captain Price to her and Mrs Frankland; but, when Miss Crawford came to be introduced to Captain Price, he said at once: "I must claim prior acquaintance, Miss Crawford, though no doubt you have no memory of the scrubby midshipman that I then was. I can never forget that I owe my first promotion to your brother. May I hope that he is well?"

Miss Crawford, though visibly taken aback by this encounter, had recovered herself by the end of his speech.

"Yes, yes, indeed," she said, smiling only a little uncertainly. "*Captain* Price already, I understand. You must allow me to congratulate you most sincerely. My brother is well. May I hope the same of your sister?"

"My sister Fanny? Most certainly she is well, and is now the mother of two daughters."

"A wise choice of children," said Miss Crawford very definitely. "The labour of rearing boys can rarely be its own reward. Have you been recently to Mansfield?"

"I come from there directly—in my way to Plymouth."

"I must hope to have speech with you·later, to know how they all are."

There was something in Miss Crawford's tone which indicated to Elizabeth that this was precisely what she did not wish for, so she moved her in the direction of Catherine, who was between Mr Bennet and Mr Darcy. But as she did so, Miss Crawford said, in a low voice: "I had hoped to be free of

Mansfield in Bath. Pray, is there some connection with this family?"

"My husband's sister is married to Mr Tom Bertram."

"To Mr *Tom* Bertram?" said Miss Crawford, in amazement. "When last I heard of him he was dying of a putrid fever at Newmarket."

"He recovered, then, completely. But they have been married less than a year."

Her curiosity decidedly aroused, Elizabeth could only, with the deepest regret, settle Miss Crawford next to Catherine, her father and Mr Darcy, going over herself to assist Captain Price's conversation with Lady Alicia and Mrs Frankland.

He was, however, in no need of assistance.

"You escorted the Corsican Monster to St Helena?" said Lady Alicia, her hands actually raised in astonishment. "I hope you mean to tell me that he lives there in the greatest possible discomfort?"

"He is no friend at all of ours," added Mrs Frankland. "He took our husbands from us long before their time and those who impute greatness to him quite mistake the matter. However many Emperors he may have been, he caused the deaths of too many good men."

Captain Price drew up a chair so that he faced them on their sofa.

"I must regret to tell you, Madam, that the late Emperor is by no means chained to a wall and fed only on bread and water. Rather to the contrary, I believe. The yearly allowance to his household has just been raised to twelve thousand pounds."

"Twelve thousand pounds!" exclaimed Lady Alicia in horror. "And *all*, I have no doubt, expended in the kitchen."

"True indeed, Madam. When the French are not trying to conquer the world, they think only of their food."

"You do not mean to tell us, I hope," said Mrs Frankland, "that he is permitted to have his own chef?"

"He is, Madam, much as one must deplore it. He is regarded as both troublesome and dangerous, but it is considered that allowing him this little dignity may keep him from constantly plotting his escape."

"Surely escape from such a place must be impossible? Did you ever go upon the island?"

"I did and a very strange place I found it. The mountains are quite bare and very steep. No climbing them at all except by steps cut into them. The landing, too, is very awkward. One must wait upon a wave, and jump."

"But did the Monster do so?" demanded Lady Alicia.

"As he is undoubtedly upon the island, Madam, and there is no other way of landing, he must most certainly have done so."

They both laughed, quite loudly.

"A sight to behold, indeed," said Mrs Frankland. "That little plump Frenchman."

"But his prison?" pursued Lady Alicia. "I trust it *is* a prison? Where is *it*?"

"It is at a distance of some five miles from Jamestown, the only town. It stands by itself, a long, low house, not very large. It is thought to be easier to guard like that."

"Well, my dear Sir," said Lady Alicia, after a moment, "you have not quite convinced me that the Monster is living in misery, but at least we may be confident that there is no escaping from there."

"We mean to remain in mourning for our husbands," said Mrs Frankland, "until we hear that the Monster is dead. Then we shall go back into colours and perhaps—what do you think, Alicia?—we might even give a ball."

"I can only honour such an intention," said Captain Price. "I hope your wait may not be a long one. Though I think it only fair to warn you that the climate is healthy, if extremely damp."

To change the subject, Elizabeth said: "We ventured to visit the Pump Room this afternoon, Lady Alicia, escorted by my husband and by Captain Price. We found the waters quite unpalatable."

"Undrinkable," said Mrs Frankland, very firmly. "I would not recommend them to a friend, unless I never wished to see her again."

"We saw the Elliots there," went on Elizabeth innocently, "accompanied by a handsome couple, one of them undoubtedly Sir Walter's daughter."

"Yes," said Lady Alicia, "the eldest daughter, the one we do not much like. We prefer the second one. But whom was she with?"

"An army officer of about her own age."

"Oh," said Mrs Frankland, laughing, "it is such a ridiculous situation there. That would be Colonel Tilney, stepson to Sir Walter's daughter, who is of course step-daughter to Lady Elliot, the youngest of them all. But what," she said, turning to Lady Alicia, "can have happened that they should all be together?"

"You have opened up an interesting topic," said Lady Alicia. "In general, they do not speak."

Elizabeth suddenly found the situation to be most interesting.

XVI

When the ladies retired after dinner, Miss Crawford came straight to Elizabeth and said: "I come to you for sanctuary, Mrs Darcy. You will do me the great kindness to converse with me animatedly on any subject in the world but Mansfield Park. It is a place where I experienced great happiness and it is a place where I experienced lasting unhappiness and, of the two, the second quite overwhelms the first. I can hardly bear to hear it mentioned. But first you must allow me, in my condescending way, to congratulate you on your father."

Elizabeth smiled at this.

"I will accept your congratulations, Miss Crawford, however little I may deserve them. They should rather be offered to him."

"I think not, not entirely, that is to say. From the conversation at our end of the table I collected that he has only recently brought himself into the mode, as you might say. His mourning must have been purchased in London. His hair is cut in the latest fashion and altogether his appearance is such that I wonder he will admit to having a daughter of, indeed, a similar age to myself. I feel he did not do this on his own. Are there any more of you at home?"

"No more at home," said Elizabeth. "Only my sister Catherine is unmarried."

"And that will not be for very long," remarked Miss Crawford, wisely. "If you have never before seen a woman in love, let me direct your attention to your sister Catherine. While I do not much like to talk of Mansfield, I cannot but admit them as good people, as a family one would be lucky to marry into. But to return to your father: do you think he will marry again?"

"As to that, who can say? With my mother's death so recent. But I will tell *you* that I hope he may. We are five sisters. If

Catherine goes, he will be alone—but I am not even thinking about it yet."

"He is as good-looking a man of his age as I have ever seen—and you, if you will permit me to say so, bear him a strong resemblance."

"I had not thought of that before," said Elizabeth, by no means displeased. "The great beauty in our family is my elder sister Jane, but she, I think, took after our mother."

"Your father is certainly most fortunate to have two daughters who care for him so much, but I must not allow my sour tongue to run away with me on the subject of families. Pray, why did you bring him to Bath?"

"I fear," said Elizabeth, after a moment's consideration, "that it was largely because I had never been here myself. I wanted somewhere not too small, so that we did not depend too entirely on our own company; and then I found that my aunt was a schoolfriend of Mrs Frankland. It was she who found us this excellent house and who, with Lady Alicia, has made our stay here such a pleasure."

"It is rare to find sisters-in-*law* so comfortable with each other. My own sister—my own half-sister I should correctly say—and I have always been the greatest friends. We share a mother, a mother who died when I was only twelve, and my sister has been my greatest refuge ever since. I cannot say that Doctor Grant was a particular favourite of mine, so that when he died—of what I can, in complete confidence, call over-eating—my period of mourning was quite short. Our long search since then has been for somewhere that will relieve the pains in my sister's arms and legs. For us, this visit to Bath is in both senses a last resort."

"You have been to *all* the spas in England?" asked Elizabeth, in some surprise.

"Well, not perhaps to all of them, but we have been to Tunbridge Wells, Llandindrod Wells, Builth Wells and Tenbury Wells—anywhere, as you might say, that offers water to drink. But I think my sister needs to be *immersed*. We have been to Droitwich, where the arrangements can scarcely be described even as primitive, and to High Harrowgate, where they are hardly an improvement. And now we are here in Bath. We spent one miserable winter by the sea at Cromer and, if our stay here should not answer, I begin to feel that we are doomed to roam from one seaside place to another until we find somewhere that offers her some relief."

"You have never thought of Matlock?"

"No," said Miss Crawford, almost too quickly, "we have never thought of Matlock, though we did once consider Buxton, for a moment, that is to say, before deciding not to go there. Cheltenham my sister very much dislikes, though the reason escapes me just at present; and as for Islington and Sadler's Wells, you know, they are fallen so entirely into the clutches of the common herd that one quite risks one's life to go there."

"I can have nothing to offer against such a catalogue of experience," said Elizabeth, smiling, "not all of which, I hope, was less than pleasant. I can only say that my own few weeks at Matlock were of enormous benefit to me—and it was there that Georgiana met Tom Bertram."

A shadow seemed to pass across Miss Crawford's face when she said this, but it was gone so quickly that Elizabeth wondered if it had been there at all.

"I am glad to hear they are so happy," said Miss Crawford. "That is to say, you have not precisely told me how happy they are, but there is a certain satisfaction in your voice when you refer to them."

"I believe them to be extremely happy," said Elizabeth. "One may tell something from a letter. But we have yet to visit them there."

Mr Bennet now came over and asked Miss Crawford if they might continue the interesting discussion they had had at dinner. Elizabeth yielded her place to him and was pleased to see how agreeably they seemed to talk together. When the party had broken up, all four of their guests leaving in Lady Alicia's carriage, Elizabeth had just curiosity enough to ask her father what he had talked about with Miss Crawford.

"Well, perhaps it was not so very absorbing," he replied. "Miss Crawford has a brother in Norfolk who, it seems, is much addicted to the bottle, though she did not exactly *give* me this information. So much of the actual running of his estate is undertaken by her and this, I confess, did impress me. But she is a person of excellent manners who would never be at loss. So for one who is trying to learn to speak to young women who are *not* his daughters, it was a valuable exercise."

Elizabeth and Catherine were still on the stairs the next day, on the way down to breakfast in the morning-room, when Captain Price was admitted to the hall.

"I am recalled a bit before my time," he said, as he came in. "An express was there for me last night. I have come to take my leave."

"You have time, I hope," said Elizabeth, "to share at least a part of our breakfast." Turning to the butler, she said: "Lay a place for Captain Price;" and then, turning to Catherine, she went on: "Pray go on without me. I have remembered something I must say at once to Rebecca."

She did, in fact, go all the way upstairs, where Rebecca presided over the nursery. She lingered a little outside her own bedroom, recalling that Mr Darcy's actual proposal had taken only a matter of seconds, and congratulating herself that her presence of mind, inherited in this instance most probably from her mother, had not deserted her at such a time. After what she judged to be about ten minutes, she went downstairs again to find the butler still hovering in the hall. A look of great understanding passed between them.

"He has asked her, madam," said the butler, calmly. "It is quite safe to go in."

He opened the door a little way and said very loudly: "I will attend to it on the instant, madam."

And Elizabeth entered the room.

They were standing by the window, both her hands in both of his, and with a look of such delight on their faces that Elizabeth could hardly withhold her smile.

"Captain Price has asked me to marry him," said Catherine, coming over at once, "and, oh, I am *so* happy! Dearest Lizzy, of course you must be the first to know."

A hug and a kiss passed between them and Elizabeth offered her hand to Captain Price. Much to her surprise, however, he carried her hand to his lips and then bent and kissed her on both cheeks.

"Naval manners," he said, without apology. "I look forward with the greatest pleasure to becoming a member of your family." Then, after an instant of recollection: "When do you think your father will return? I must be off by noon."

"Not before eleven, I imagine," said Elizabeth. "We must have our champagne now."

"Then pray bring some up," said Catherine, actually laughing, to the butler; and when he had left them, she went on: "My mother could not object to our drinking champagne at breakfast in such a cause. Indeed, I feel her to be here with us, beaming with pride at the engagement of her fifth daughter. Perhaps," she said rather shyly to Captain Price, "your own mother might have some similar feelings?"

"No," said Captain Price, hesitating slightly, "I think not. She is not what one might call *active* in that respect. She was happy enough when my sister married Edmund Bertram, but my sister Susan's *understanding*—it is by no means a betrothal— is still unknown to her. My sister Betsy is as yet too young to think of such a thing and," he added, with a charming smile, "all the rest of us are boys."

The butler returned very soon with the champagne and laid a place for Captain Price, offering his good wishes as he did so. They drank a health to each other and then sat down at the table. Elizabeth was delighted to find how well the champagne accorded with the rest of her breakfast; the combination with a marmalade of quinces was especially agreeable. But before they had been seated long, she said: "We must be practical, however. My father would never countenance a wedding until we are out of mourning for my mother, and neither, I think, would we wish it. That will be in September. Does Captain Price know where he will be in September?"

"No," said Captain Price, "he does not. I think I should be hard put to it to discover a suitable lodging—be it in Plymouth or Portsmouth—by that time. But I travel now with an open mind, though I suppose my ultimate destination is already decided. I fear that Catherine will find, in common with every other naval wife, that she cannot plan much longer than six months ahead."

"It is a risk I accept," remarked Catherine. "I must hope to be placed in such a way that I can see you sometimes. I hope you may not be sent off to St Helena again?"

"I think not," said Captain Price. "In fact, I believe I may say, with confidence, that *we* shall not be sent there again, but there are other foreign stations. However," he went on, "if I may tell the Admiral that I am to be married, and in September, he may not post me too far off."

It now emerged that Captain Price had paid his shot at the White Hart and that a post-chaise was to meet him there at midday. A footman was despatched to change this order, so that he could leave from Upper Camden Place, staying with them until the last minute.

Cold meat and cheese were brought in to fortify him for his journey of close on a hundred and twenty miles, which he proposed to take without sleeping on the way; and Catherine had to content herself with sitting next to him and urging him to eat as much as possible, an instruction he seemed only too happy to obey.

If Mr Bennet and Mr Darcy were surprised by the festive atmosphere which hung over the ruins of the breakfast table when they returned at half past eleven, they concealed their feelings admirably. Captain Price applied at once to Mr Bennet, apparently by no means embarrassed at having to so do in public; and Mr Bennet gave his consent with no hesitation and with his broadest smile, offering his hand to Captain Price as he did so.

"I am only too pleased to welcome you to the illustrious band of my sons-in-law, my dear Sir. I know of no one in the country who can produce such a distinguished collection of young men—I may congratulate myself indeed, and," turning to Catherine, "I may congratulate you too, my dear child."

She came over to him and he kissed her, saying, with a lurking twinkle in his eye: "My mind is quite at rest at last, now that I know there is to be only one joker in the pack."

"As the senior member of the illustrious band," said Mr Darcy to Captain Price, also shaking his hand, "allow me too to welcome you to it. But I am reliably informed, and with great regret, that you are come to take your leave?"

"I am," said Captain Price, without preamble. "I must be off in twenty minutes."

A second bottle of champagne was sent for. Healths, good wishes, were exchanged all round. The last slice of cold meat was consumed by Captain Price. The post-chaise was at the door and he was escorted to it by Mr Bennet and Mr Darcy, leaving Elizabeth on the doorstep with Catherine who, tearfully smiling, could find nothing to say. As he drove off, Captain Price leaned out of the window and said, at the top of his voice: "I will send you my direction so soon as I know it myself."

XVII

The gentlemen returned slowly to the house. Elizabeth and Catherine went back thoughtfully into the hall, arriving at the same moment as the nursery party, prepared for their walk.

"An excellent idea, my dear Kitty, do you think?" said Elizabeth. "A walk might do us *all* good after such excitement."

They set off very shortly, in the direction of the woodland glade. The spring had begun in earnest and the leaves were larger every day.

It was not long before Lady Elliot and her escort could be seen approaching them, on the same pavement. There was no avoiding them and Elizabeth was curious to see how Lady Elliot would deal with the situation. There were no side roads, no little lanes and no secret alleys between them.

In the event, the gentlemen all stepped into the roadway and Lady Elliot, with a self-possession which Elizabeth could not but admire, said simply: "You must allow me to present Colonel Tilney, of Northanger Abbey, to you. He stays a few days with us in Bath."

After a suitable exchange of courtesies, Colonel Tilney said, very pleasantly and to Mr Bennet: "I believe, Sir, that there is a connection. Is not your daughter married to my sister-in-law's brother?"

As Mr Bennet did not immediately reply, Catherine said, after the pause of a very small moment: "Indeed she is, Sir. We had the pleasure of meeting your brother and his wife at my sister's wedding."

"Bless my soul," said Mr Bennet, rather hurriedly, "indeed we did. I recollect them perfectly."

Then the two parties disentangled themselves and everyone walked on. The episode had lasted about a minute.

Elizabeth now found her arm very firmly taken by Mr Darcy.

"I know not how it is, my love," he said to her, "but I scarcely seem to have any opportunity to talk to you these days. What did you think of Colonel Tilney?"

"Very handsome," said Elizabeth, "very dangerous. He has certainly an excellent set of teeth. And I regard our little encounter with some dismay."

"I am at a *total* disadvantage," said Mr Darcy.

Elizabeth tightened her grip on Mr Darcy's arm.

"Lady Elliot has called," she said. "I have left cards upon her but we have not met since that first dinner. I had hoped to escape from Bath without giving an evening party for her, but now I think I must."

"And is that so distasteful? I think I might enjoy observing Sir Walter observing your father, who has, after all, taken his advice, however indirectly."

"I recall that Lady Alicia said that, in general, the Elliots and the Tilneys did not speak."

"I can even enlighten you there. Mrs General Tilney—Elizabeth Elliot, that is to say—is of the opinion that she has the use of the family jewels for the rest of her life, or at least until the Colonel marries. The Colonel, however, does not think so and there is, besides, some argument about her jointure."

"But can they all live in the same house with such a dispute going on?"

"It is a large house, one can only remark."

"And I remember that Lady Alicia also told us that it is the women who do not speak, that indeed Sir Walter, in the first days of this marriage, was obliged to have breakfast with his daughter and dinner with his wife."

"He is a stronger man than I imagined," said Mr Darcy admiringly. "No doubt they are all in Bath to put these matters straight."

They walked on for a few minutes in easy silence, until the others were well out of earshot; but even then Mr Darcy spoke in his lowest voice.

"I have to commend the swiftness of decision and the single-mindedness of both your sister and our future brother-in-law," he said. "Their acquaintance has lasted for almost exactly forty-eight hours and yet they have pitchforked themselves into an engagement which seems to please everybody."

"The naval training," said Elizabeth, trying to sound as serious as possible, "must centre wholly upon instant decisions—things must be done before the wind changes. And in this case I am sure he felt he could not leave his vessel unsecured upon the beach without his flag upon it. For he could have no notion, you know, as to when he would be able to return to claim it."

"When did you begin to think that this might happen?"

"I think just after he had rescued Jane's hat from the bushes. A glance at Catherine told me all—and a glance at him then raised my hopes. I hope you have no gloomy feelings about the event?"

"None, my love," he said at once. "And this is what surprises me so. I am quite sure they will deal famously together."

It was a week before Captain Price's letter arrived, addressed to Mr Bennet. He was to be stationed at Plymouth for the summer, cruising between Ushant and Scilly, but might expect a different posting thereafter. He believed that, if a date could be set for his marriage in the middle of September, he would be able to attend it; and he gave the address of a lawyer in Portsmouth with whom Mr Bennet's attorney could deal.

This letter concentrated Elizabeth's thoughts. Charming though the spring was in Bath, she believed it to be even more charming at home; and she began to think about returning there before the end of May. Catherine had been able, without difficulty, to determine that the milliners and dressmakers of Bath were vastly superior to those of Meryton, and now proposed to purchase all her wedding clothes before going back to Longbourn. The Darcys therefore agreed to leave in the third week of May, leaving Mr Bennet and Catherine in possession until the end of the month.

Elizabeth had now to come to a conclusion about her evening party. She consulted Lady Alicia and Mrs Frankland. There was a small pause when Elizabeth had explained her position and then Lady Alicia said: "It was not very civil of Lady Elliot not even to ask you for an evening, particularly when you were so close. That was our idea in introducing you in the first place. But Lady Elliot, as the whole town knows, is notorious for the economy of her housekeeping."

"I have to say that she made plain her situation at the beginning of our acquaintance," said Elizabeth.

"Nevertheless," said Mrs Frankland, "she should have invited you. However, you must certainly invite *her* and Sir Walter, as this, if you do so soon enough, will mean that the Tilneys, Mrs General and the Colonel, would have to be included. We understand that they are here till the end of the month. And we would *all* like the chance to observe them from closer quarters."

"But do you think—?" asked Elizabeth.

"We think," said Lady Alicia, smiling rather sadly, "in fact, we *know*, and are amazed, if reports be correct, that Sir Walter himself should be so blind to the danger."

"Then, with them, and yourselves, and ourselves, and Miss Crawford—I have not yet met Mrs Grant. That would be enough for an evening party?"

"Certainly," said Lady Alicia, smiling more happily now. "A table of Whist for Sir Walter, a table of Speculation for the young ones, and Mr Bennet can sit a little apart and talk to Miss Crawford. There will be *some* music, a superb supper and it will in every way be a party to remember."

"My own idea exactly," said Elizabeth. Then, noticing a certain sparkle in Lady Alicia's eye, she said, smiling broadly: "That is to say—if your ladyship is quite serious?"

"My ladyship," said Lady Alicia very solemnly, "*never* makes jokes on serious subjects. It is the kind of party that I most enjoy and I find this prospect very alluring. The only flaw, of course, is that it is to be your farewell party. We shall miss you more than I can say."

"Then," said Elizabeth, "now is my moment. Mr Darcy and I would be so happy if you could find the time to visit us at Pemberley this summer. His sister will be with us in June—and

Mrs Gardiner," turning to Mrs Frankland. "May we hope that you can give us this pleasure?"

"Give *you* this pleasure?" exclaimed Mrs Frankland, after a short silence and without trying to conceal her surprise and delight. "Nothing in the world could give *us* more pleasure."

"It will transform the summer for us," said Lady Alicia. "We have never been to Derbyshire before. It is almost a foreign land to us."

"And after twenty-five years!" said Mrs Frankland gloatingly. "You will have to forgive me and Mrs Gardiner if we never stop talking!"

"I will do so, indeed," said Elizabeth, delighted in her turn. "But tell me—do you think Mrs Grant might come to our party if she were to be carried the whole way in a chair?"

After a moment Mrs Frankland said: "I cannot see why not. Your stairs are wide enough for two footmen to carry her up them—and report has it that she is a notable Whist player. By all means, ask her."

"I shall go next door at once, and do so."

The party took place ten days later, precisely as Lady Alicia had prescribed. Mrs Grant proved to be a cheerful lady, making light of her afflictions. She patiently and successfully partnered Sir Walter at Whist for the whole evening. Mrs General Tilney—wearing, in the opinion of Mrs Frankland, delivered in a low voice to Elizabeth, rather too many diamonds for a quiet evening party—overwhelmed them all with her graciousness.

"It is strange," went on Mrs Frankland, "that a woman who has been all her life a Baronet's daughter should consider that becoming a General's widow involves some access to grandeur. I think she was a little put out to find Alicia here. A penniless Earl may be penniless but he is also, *undoubtedly*, an earl."

Elizabeth joined in her laughter.

"I cannot wait to get you both together at Pemberley," she said. "The walls there have no ears."

"I will remind Alicia to *insist* on leading the way down to supper—a thing she *never* does in the ordinary way—but tonight she *shall*!"

The game of Speculation diverted the rest of the party very satisfactorily. Only Mr Bennet was left to observe the game and it was he who said to Elizabeth, as they began the move towards supper: "I thought Lady Elliot paid much too much for that knave in your last game. I hope it may not be a premonition—or a pre-vision."

A harpist sang ballads after supper, when the tea and coffee were brought in, and it was some time after midnight before the party showed any sign of wishing to break up.

The Elliots left first, their formal praise and appreciation of a most charming evening only just overcoming the deep regret that they felt at this being a last meeting. Mrs Grant's chairmen, summoned to the hall, proved to have been very well entertained below stairs. As they were about to set off, Mrs Grant let down her window and said, with a smile, to Elizabeth, who had followed her down: "It is not so far to the ground, after all. I expect I shall be quite safe—and the carriage, moreover, will be behind us."

Then, more seriously: "Thank you indeed, much more than I can say. My aches and pains for a time quite disappeared."

Elizabeth took a very kind farewell of Miss Crawford, hoping that they would meet again, and an even kinder one of Lady Alicia and Mrs Frankland, though *it* was spiced with the certain knowledge that they would soon meet again at Pemberley.

"I like Miss Crawford more and more," said Mr Bennet, as they went back to the drawing-room. "But I begin to think she may have left her heart at Mansfield Park, in the possession of Mr *Edmund* Bertram."

XVIII

Elizabeth left Bath with sincere regret and with no reservations. Their sojourn there had been answered in every respect, if not quite in the way she had intended. Her father seemed to be, at least, observing life again; her sister had found a husband; and they themselves had made true friends in Lady Alicia and Mrs Frankland. If her recollections had a shadow it was thrown by the fact that she had not felt able, on such a short acquaintance, to ask Miss Crawford for her correspondence. She had liked her very much, but reflected that, if she *were* to disappear when her six month tenancy in Laura Place expired, her neighbours next door would at least know where she had gone.

They called at Kympton on their homeward journey, to find Mary wreathed in smiles, smiles of surprise and smiles of delight, greeting them at the door with her son in her arms.

"I hoped you would come in on your way back," she said, "but you are two weeks before your time. I hope there is nothing wrong?"

"Nothing in the world," said Elizabeth. "My father is extremely well and Catherine better than I have ever seen her, buying her wedding clothes in Bath. You had my hurried note?"

"I had your hurried note, which told me very little. It must have been love at first sight?"

"On his side I think undoubtedly."

"Re-assuring to know that it happens outside the novel," remarked Mary. "But is not my son quite handsome? His name is Richard, after his grandfather Morland. I was ashamed to discover that I did not know my father's Christian name."

After a moment, Elizabeth said: "My mother always called him Mr Bennet. But Jane and I were very early of the opinion that it was Henry."

"It would be in our marriage contracts, I suppose."

"Indeed," said Elizabeth, laughing. "Neatly tied up with red ribbon and hidden away in Haggerston's office in London."

Refreshments were offered and accepted. The children went up to the nursery and Mr Morland retired to his study with Mr Darcy, wishing to consult him on some parish business.

"Well," said Mary, "now that we are alone, I have something quite pleasant to tell you. The man from Birmingham came last week."

"The man from Birmingham?" repeated Elizabeth in astonishment.

"The organ man from Birmingham—sent by the harpsichord people in Chesterfield."

"I remember," said Elizabeth, with a smile of relief. "I wrote to them before I went to Bath and asked them to deal with you."

"Which they did. They can supply an organ which will *exactly* fit the space in the north transept and there are to be two bellows—in case one should become perforated, you know—and eight pedals. And they will paint the pipes if we like."

"I hope the work is already in hand?"

"I did not quite like to commission it myself," said Mary, rather hesitantly. "It is to cost a hundred and seventy-five pounds."

"So I would have imagined," said Elizabeth, secretly amazed. "But do not be *too* dismayed. I will speak to my husband and Jane will speak to hers. Catherine, no doubt, will be spending all her money in Bath and you, I expect, on your house. But we shall find it—what colour did they mean to paint the pipes?"

"Crimson and gold," said Mary, "the gold to be a kind of Gothic trellis on the crimson."

"My mother would have liked that. Indeed it all sounds only too desirable. If Catherine is to be married in September, could the organ be installed some time in August? So that she and my father could come up for the dedication."

"You think of everything. Yes, indeed. I hope they will stay with me. And by then I may have learned to use the pedals—for I would wish to play it *well* that first time."

They received a rapturous welcome at Pemberley, Mrs Reynolds in particular saying how empty the house had been, but how pleased she was to see them in such excellent health and spirits. The children had grown, she thought; there had been no accidents or upsets in their absence—indeed the house was now in the most perfect order—but she trusted that they would be able to spend *all* the summer months at Pemberley.

Elizabeth smiled and put her mind at rest in this last respect, promising to fill the house with visitors as often as she could; and, in the evening, she found herself thinking that, although the view from the drawing-room in Upper Camden Place had been a handsome one, she much preferred the view from her own sitting-room.

They settled back very quickly into the pattern of their lives at Pemberley. Their neighbours called and she returned their calls. There was a new wallpaper in the nursery which she had chosen herself, and which she was now whole-heartedly able to approve. Georgiana's flower garden was full of promise, the lilacs, honesty and tulips in their first flower; but before Elizabeth could write to tell her this, a letter arrived from Georgiana herself.

Now that I am an old married woman—ten months tomorrow— I have to say how much I can appreciate the kindness and harmony that exists between you, my dearest Elizabeth, and my dearest brother. This I must partly ascribe to the excellence of character possessed by both parties, but the other part, I have to say, must surely be owing to the fact that you have married each other and *not* each other's brothers and sisters. I, of course, exclude myself from any censure here and hope that you will do so too. My troubles are due to my dearest Tom's appalling sister Julia and her insufferable, insupportable, *unbearable* husband, John Yates. He—the Onjohn—seems to have nothing whatever to recommend him. He is lazy, extravagant, patronising and *pointless*—I cannot see that he has any right to live at all. They exist entirely at the expense of other people—principally his own very reluctant brother and the luckless Sir Thomas Bertram—will go anywhere, and to anyone, for a square meal and talk to me, on the one hand as if I were some kind of unlettered rustic—"How very extraordinary that you should never have been to Brighton"—and on the other as if the whole future of the Bertram family depended on *me*. So what has provoked this outburst? (I feel *so* much better already!) The Honourable John and Mrs Julia find themselves temporarily without a home, being obliged to vacate their charming house in Charles Street as they were no longer able to pay the rent. So what does Sir Thomas do? He takes a house for them in *Brighton* for *three months* on the condition that my poor Tom will go with them—to keep an eye on them, Sir Thomas says, his problem being gambling and hers being drink, though Sir Thomas is not thought to know the latter. And whom do you think also has to go with them? Tom's unfortunate wife. I have simply no words to describe my feelings when this news was broken to me—I should think I stood stunned and speechless for a full minute, after which it all came pouring out. "Oh no, Sir Thomas, my duty to my husband I will accept and perform at all times," I said, "but this duty does not extend to acting nursemaid to his sister. I rather think you should accompany them yourself." "I cannot desert Lady Bertram, who never feels well by the sea." "Then surely Edmund and Fanny, and the little girls, might all benefit from such a change?" A silence. "I will propose the matter to Edmund," then said Sir Thomas, "but I regard it more as the responsibility of my son Tom, as being the elder brother." I left the room soon afterward, feeling much like a housemaid discovered in some dereliction of her duties, and did not go up to the Great House for two whole days, after which a polite note, enquiring after my health, you know, arrived from Lady Bertram. Well, I will not bore you any further. To put it simply, I had a small triumph. In the end Sir Thomas came to see me, apologised for ignoring my own wishes so completely—indeed I think it never occurred to him before that I might have any wishes—and he and Tom are to go with the Yateses in June and Edmund and Fanny are to take their place in July and August. I am thankful to think that I shall not be part of *that* household since Edmund grows more didactic by the hour—particularly on the subject of gambling— and Fanny, in her own sweet way, seems to disapprove of every- thing, both people and places. However, I truly think the sea air may benefit her daughters. So where does Georgiana go? She comes, my dearest Elizabeth, to Pemberley, for an extended stay, and should be with you on the first of June. Pray, pray do not put me off. I know I am guilty of taking you for granted whilst bridling when Sir Thomas does so to me, but my dearest Tom has said he has no wish to involve me in his family's under-current battles and has more or less ordered me away. For myself I need hardly say how much I long to see you both, and for the peace and quiet of Pemberley, and for a house entirely free of workmen—did Captain Price tell you about the partridge? We must have lost nearly half-a-dozen geese.

With my fondest love,
Georgiana.

Elizabeth replied immediately, saying only how much she looked forward to seeing her again, and sent it to the post, though her heart misgave her a little as she did so. She showed the letter to Mr Darcy as soon as he came in.

"Well," he said, when he had read it, "I think there is not too much cause for alarm. She and Tom appear to be still on the best of terms, and Sir Thomas Bertram is a man very much accustomed to having his own way. Georgiana is to be com-mended for stating her position so unequivocally to Sir Thomas. How extremely surprised he must have been. And we, after all, are the beneficiaries—it will be a pleasure to have Georgiana in the house again."

"It will," said Elizabeth. "She and my aunt Gardiner have always been great friends and I think Lady Alicia and Mrs Frankland will also like her very much. We shall all be able to go exploring together."

Georgiana, in the event, arrived three days before the first of June, escorted by her husband. Once more Elizabeth found herself thinking how well they looked together, and how amiable they seemed to be with each other; but Tom Bertram did not wait. He was to travel to Brighton within the week and he thought it better to return at once. After the briefest of nuncheons, he was off.

Georgiana shed a few tears as she waved him away, but she immediately turned to Elizabeth and said: "My tears are only because I love him so much. To be parted for four weeks is a new experience for us, but I know he thinks only of my happiness in seeking to spare me that visit to Brighton. We are pledged to write to each other *every day*, but," she added with a smile, which entirely banished the tears, "I do not expect him to honour it. For Tom the writing of even the shortest note is a quite intolerable labour. So now please show me to my nieces and let us all go together to the flower garden, since my dearest brother seems to be invisible."

"He has ridden in to Chesterfield on some kind of business," said Elizabeth. "I no longer enquire as so often he turns out to be planning some charming surprise for me. And if we had *known* you were to arrive today, he would not, of course, have done so."

"How I *almost* envy you, dear sister-in-law," said Georgiana, taking Elizabeth's arm as they went up the stairs. "I do not think my husband is as thoughtful as my brother, but I certainly have nothing to complain of. And, just as certainly, I had *quite* forgotten what a long way it is to the top of this house."

They were received with delight in the nursery and, very soon, they, with the two girls and the two nursemaids, were on their way to the flower garden. It was a clear, sunlit day and Elizabeth found herself thinking that Pemberley had never looked more beautiful, a sentiment echoed by Georgiana.

"I forget, sometimes," she said, "how perfect is this place, how lucky I have been to spend so many years here. But Mansfield is perfect, too, or it will be when everything there is as I want it. The two places are so totally unlike, you know, there is no comparing them. I keep them quite separate in my mind."

Elizabeth smiled at her and said: "I have the same feeling about Longbourn—it is a different kind of perfection. But, now that the children are a little ahead, let me tell you something very pleasing."

Georgiana merely looked a question.

"You could not have known," went on Elizabeth, with her warmest smile, "when you sent Captain Price to us in Bath, that he would find a permanent place in our family. He fell in love with my sister Catherine, and she with him, and they are to make a match of it."

"Oh," said Georgiana, clapping her hands together, "I will *not* pretend that it did *not* cross my mind—but to have it happen so *soon*? I hope your father is quite pleased?"

"I think him very pleased," returned Elizabeth. "It will leave him alone at Longbourn, but Catherine is entirely transformed and they will be married in September."

After walking a little, Elizabeth said, rather quietly: "We met another Mansfield connection while at Bath. A Miss Crawford, a Miss Crawford who, my father thinks, once lost her heart to Mr *Edmund* Bertram. Did you ever hear anything of this?"

"Well, no," said Georgiana, philosophically. "I expect she is part of what I think of as the Great Mansfield Mystery—and one day I shall get to the bottom of it. There was a Doctor Grant, a previous incumbent of Mansfield, who is occasionally mentioned. And I have observed that whenever he is, the subject is changed immediately."

"There was a Mrs Grant in Bath, in deepest mourning," said Elizabeth. "She is Miss Crawford's half-sister, but we saw her very little."

"And did you like her? Miss Crawford?"

"I did. Extremely. She has a confidence and a directness which might, I suppose, be mistaken for assurance. But, with a lively mind and a pretty face, that is not so likely. My father, I think, was very taken with her."

"She would hardly have done for Edmund if that is so," remarked Georgiana coolly. "He grows more like Sir Thomas every minute. My dearest Tom, I am only too deeply thankful to say, is as unlike his father as possible."

XIX

Rather more than two light-hearted, irresponsible weeks followed this conversation. The sun shone, the roses began to bloom, the water in the stream no longer made them gasp when they tested it with their toes. They had a picnic every day, sometimes in the glen, sometimes in the high woods, joined always by Mr Darcy at his most high-spirited, all formality forgotten.

Elizabeth drove the children, and the baskets of food, in the low phaeton, drawn by a pair of ponies, that had been hers ever since she married. The nursemaids, the grooms, the gardeners, the footmen, were nowhere to be seen. They could paddle, bowl Jane's hoop, play at battledore and shuttlecock, entirely unobserved.

"Perhaps it is a little late to be enjoying the boyhood that I never had," remarked Mr Darcy one day. "But at least I am now old enough to appreciate what it was that I missed."

The arrival of Mrs Gardiner by no means put an end to this. She took Elizabeth's place in the phaeton and Elizabeth walked with Mr Darcy to their meeting place. This was frequently a charming little meadow, just where the stream emerged from the wood, so that they could be in shade or sunshine as they chose.

"A place of quiet perfection," said Mrs Gardiner. "I do not know why anyone should ever want to leave England."

She had come alone, although she had persuaded Mr Gardiner to postpone his departure for India until the end of September.

"Wiser counsels have prevailed," she said. "Our information now is that the monsoon wind, as it is called, blows without stopping from May to September, with incessant rain, rendering all travel nearly impossible. The sea is rough and the roads, such as they are, impassable. But when this wind has gone, the sea is calm and the roads are dry and hard again—the dust and the insects are *then* the insupportable things. I can say to you that I wish very much that he did not mean to go, but at least I can congratulate myself that he now travels with three companions and enough letters of introduction to fill a trunk. But," she said, turning to Elizabeth, who was sitting beside her on the grass, "I have come here to *forget* that he is going upon this epic journey, at least for a few days. Tell me now about your stay in Bath and how you found my dear Mrs Frankland. What a meeting that will be, to be sure."

Elizabeth willingly complied with this request. When she had finished, Mrs Gardiner said: "This Miss Crawford sounds to be a person of some interest. I have heard about the Elliots, of course, from Mrs Frankland."

"I was never brave enough to ask about their families—and the subject did not directly arise. Has Mrs Frankland, or Lady Alicia, any children?"

"Two sons, both in the Army, and stationed abroad, and Lady Alicia two daughters, well-married but in the north. I am sure, indeed I *know*, that they were particularly pleased by your visit and your invitation. I fancy that money is not all that plentiful on their side—they keep a carriage but no horses. I would expect them to go into Yorkshire when they leave you, to see the daughters, you know. They were quite in raptures at being able to combine the visits."

The reason for Mr Darcy's visit to Chesterfield now became clear. Another low phaeton was delivered from the coachmakers there. It was higher than the one they already had, but not yet dangerously so, and it was to be drawn by a pair of Welsh ponies. Mrs Gardiner begged to be the first to drive it and she and Mrs Frankland set off nearly every day for their round of the park, confining their reminiscences, as Mrs Frankland smilingly said, only to people who would find them of interest.

Elizabeth was especially pleased to observe how instantly the ladies became friends with Georgiana and how quickly she came to like them. They made excursions to Chatsworth and Dovedale, Elizabeth and Mrs Gardiner delighted to find the latter, at least, unchanged from their visit six years before. Mrs

Gardiner left them for one whole day, to visit her old friends in Lambton; and, on the evening of Midsummer's Day itself, they held a party on the lawn for all their neighbours.

"An occasion to be remembered by everyone," said Lady Alicia, taking Elizabeth's arm as the last guest disappeared. "Never before have I witnessed the moon in just such a loving collusion with a harpist—and as for your red currant ice, I am sure it must be served every day in Heaven. It adds a great incentive, indeed. I have never been quite happy about ambrosia— I could never find a receipt that truly pleased me."

But the high point of their visit, and one that Elizabeth had put off until it was nearly at an end, was to be an expedition to the Druidical Circle on Hartle Moor.

Georgiana had been the first to speak of it.

"I have a particular wish to make a wish," she said to Elizabeth, as they sat together in the flower garden. "Mrs Reynolds tells me that there are two circles, one on Hartle Moor and the other, the Nine Ladies, on Stanton Moor. But the circle on Hartle Moor is easier to find—I believe one can drive to within a quarter of a mile of it. You must touch all the stones, you know, and make the same wish each time."

As Elizabeth, now certain that she was once more in the family way, was also conscious of a wish to make a wish, this expedition was most enthusiastically planned. They could go one way to the moor and return by another, making a most delightful and eventful circular tour.

They travelled in three carriages. Elizabeth and Mr Darcy, with the children and the two nursemaids, led the way. Georgiana and Mrs Gardiner came in the second, with Lady Alicia and Mrs Frankland; and the third contained their luncheon hampers and two footmen.

"A fine cavalcade," remarked Mr Darcy, "and everyone in it determined to make a wish. Once that news was general the difficulty was only to decide who was to be left behind. I hope there may not be too many disappointed hearts remaining at Pemberley—but perhaps, when we have learned the way, it may be possible to come again."

"We shall have to see how many of our wishes are answered," said Elizabeth, with a smile. "I have never before thought of making a request of a Druid."

"They do say," said Rebecca, the elder nursemaid, "as how nothing and no one can do you no harm if the Druids is your friends. But woe betide," she added darkly, "them as makes them enemies."

"Have you always known about the Druids, Rebecca?" asked Mr Darcy.

"I always have, but Jemima's grandma knew more about them than us. She had the spirit and could see the future."

"Yes," said Jemima, the other nursemaid. "She had the spirit and could see the future."

"Then we must be careful to make friends with the Druids," said Mr Darcy. "I hope they will accept us. At least we must do nothing to offend them."

It was a hot, clear day with just enough cloud to render the sun's rays bearable. At Rowsley they picked up the boy who was to guide them to the circle, known locally as Nine Stone Close; and by midday they had come as near to the stones as the carriages could take them. A walk of some four hundred yards, over what might be called rough pasture with patches of heath, presented itself to them.

There were three large upright stones and five much smaller ones. A dry stone wall separated the ninth, also large but on its side, from the rest. Some sheep lay huddled in the shade of the great uprights. A fresh breeze blew. They were at the highest point of the moor.

It did not take long to decide that this was no place for their picnic. There was neither shade for themselves nor water for their horses. A brief consultation with their youthful guide disclosed the fact that the road dipped off the moor about a mile further on, and that there was a spinney of small trees there, by the side of the stream. They would make their wishes and then drive on.

It was Jemima who led the way. She came to Elizabeth and, with a little curtsey, asked if she might do so.

"Because my grandma told me how it must be done and I hope I can remember."

A kind of stile was made, with two of the luncheon hampers, to cross the dry stone wall; and a footman stood by each one to help them over. Then, in a curiously solemn silence, they followed Jemima—Rebecca with Anne, Mr Darcy with Jane, Elizabeth, Georgiana, the three ladies and then the coachmen, the grooms and the two footmen. Only their guide remained behind. When questioned, he said simply: "I dursn't."

They made their wishes in silence. In silence they resumed their places and in silence they drove off. Not until they were seated in the spinney, which offered them a pleasant shade and which proved to be remarkably free from flies, did the conversation very slowly start again.

For this the excellent content of the picnic baskets was partly to blame. A certain concentration was required to eat, with a fork only, the delicious collation assembled on each plate. The ensuing silence could only be one of approval and Elizabeth accepted it as a high compliment. She was especially pleased to find that both the lemonade and the champagne were still most gratifyingly cold.

The afternoon passed quietly. By four o'clock the horses had been rested, fed and watered, one by one. The coachmen and the grooms had woken up, as had the children and the older members of the party. What remained of their feast was re-packed into the hampers and they were ready to return. Mrs Gardiner asked if she might take Elizabeth's place in the first carriage, as she wished to discover what Mr Darcy knew about India, and Elizabeth took her place in the second.

Their guide now left them, to begin his walk back, four miles across the moor. Amply recompensed by all the ladies, and by Mr Darcy, he said, with rather a red face, that he hoped he hadn't done wrong and trusted them not to tell Parson. His comment was discussed in the second carriage with some surprise, but great interest, until they found themselves actually driving through Matlock. As it was a Wednesday, which was not a market day, this was accomplished without delay.

They had left the town about a mile behind them, when Georgiana suddenly said, to Elizabeth: "Surely this is where we first came across my poor Tom, limping alongside his lame horse? I am sure that it was here."

"Yes," said Elizabeth. "I am sure it was."

"And," said Georgiana, "I recall that it was near a road coming in from *this* moorland, which I thought I would like to explore. It was a very dull day, I remember."

"Perhaps," said Mrs Frankland, who was sitting facing the horses, "*this* is the road that you spoke of? It does look, if I may coin a word, most explorable."

It was a dry, white road, disappearing round a fold in the hillside almost at once, but to be seen winding its way into the moorland at some distance.

"Yes, indeed, it is the one. Oh, Elizabeth, what do you think? But perhaps we had better wait until next year, for we cannot possibly do it today."

"I hope you mean to plant a tree at the spot where you first set eyes on your husband," said Lady Alicia sternly.

"Not a tree, I think," said Georgiana perfectly seriously. "A rose bush, perhaps, though they have thorns, of course. A *guelder* rose would be better. Yes, certainly—a guelder rose. But in fact I *had* set eyes on him before."

"And what shall we find at the end of such a road?" asked Mrs Frankland. "A Ruined Abbey? A Hermit's Cell? Another Druid Circle? I must hope for the former."

"It is more likely to be a stone quarry," said Elizabeth, prosaically, "or perhaps a waterfall. But there is no need to wait to discover. We are not so far from Pemberley and I, too, am intrigued to know where it goes. If you think we could all squeeze into one carriage, with Mr Darcy on horseback, we could arrange it for tomorrow."

The proposal was carried, with enthusiastic acclaim.

"And in *this* carriage," said Lady Alicia. "I think I have never travelled in one quite so beautifully sprung."

"It is my aunt's," said Elizabeth. "They are always one step ahead of us when it is a question of the latest fashion."

And so it came about, the following afternoon. The white road wound into the moorland for more than a mile, causing several remarks about the excellence of its surface. Then it began to go downhill very gently, leading to a handsome farmhouse. The white road finished there. A moorland track continued past the house.

A sense of disappointment invaded them all. Here was the most commonplace ending to their heated imaginings. But, the more they looked at it, the more romantic did the house become. It had a veranda and it was painted white. The outbuildings were behind it, a little higher up the hillside. A new plantation, scarcely five years old, rose above them. On the south side of the house a flower garden had been planted, now just coming into its fullest bloom; and, well beyond the house, a gate could be seen, leading into a considerable wood.

"This," said Mrs Gardiner, "is exactly the house of my dreams. If Mr Gardiner's mission to India prospers, I shall certainly make the owner an offer."

"But, my dearest aunt," said Elizabeth, quite hurt, "I hope that, whenever you are in Derbyshire, you will always stay with us."

"It is kind in you, I know, but with two daughters at the hoyden stage, and two sons with more energy than they know what to do with, I could not risk their destroying your house only too completely. And we should not be so very far away."

"It is a remarkable house," said Mr Darcy, "lived in by someone with no need to count their pennies. The white paint is a magnificent extravagance. But the house is by no means new, and that is a very respectable grange, from two hundred years ago, standing behind it. In my heart I cannot approve the paint. But we must all agree that it is very pretty."

"We think," said Lady Alicia, her mouth prim, "that this is the residence of a French Countess, hiding from the Monster."

"A lady novelist, perhaps," said Georgiana. "Madame d'Arblay—Mrs Radcliffe—Mary Shelley! Too pleasant, I think, for a Frankenstein—but certainly sufficiently remote!"

"Whoever she is," said Mrs Frankland, "her house is perfectly charming. And why do we all think that it is lived in by a woman alone? For I am sure we all do. And surely that is a rosemary bush beside the garden door?"

It was at this moment that the garden door opened, and a woman, tall and particularly elegant, stepped out into the flower garden. After looking about her a little, and observing their interested party, she put up her parasol and moved swiftly away into the wood.

"Most certainly not a farmer's daughter," said Mr Darcy.

"Perhaps a Countess after all," said Lady Alicia.

"Who buys her parasols in London," added Mrs Gardiner.

But Elizabeth and Georgiana knew better. Their eyes met. It was the younger of the two women who had argued so fiercely behind the screen on that first day at the Matlock Bath. They could not be mistaken. She had been walking away from them then; she was walking away from them now.

"And all we know," said Elizabeth to Georgiana in a very low voice, "is that her name is Maria."

"And that she has a very sharp tongue," added Georgiana. "One cannot but wonder why she chooses to live here."

"One cannot help wondering also," said Elizabeth in an even lower voice, "if her loft is still full of bandages."

Their laughter, instantly suppressed, went unheard.

"Well, my dear," said Mrs Frankland to Mrs Gardiner, "if you *do* buy it, and she *is* a French Countess, you may be quite sure that her kitchen will be full of *all* the latest contrivances."

XX

Their visitors left Pemberley on the following Monday, Mrs Gardiner to join her family at Cromer, and Lady Alicia and Mrs Frankland to visit one of the former's daughters near Beverley.

As they sat in the saloon after dinner that evening, Georgiana said: "Your visitors were perfectly delightful and I hope I may often meet them again, but I must make the most of this opportunity to tell you what is happening in Brighton. I had a letter from Tom today, the *first*. I have written every day but have only posted once a *week*. He has written every week but only posted once a month—so, do you wish to hear how they go on?"

"As you certainly wish to tell us," said Mr Darcy, with a smile, "I am sure we shall be quite happy to listen."

"I hope they may not have been too much at odds with each other," remarked Elizabeth. "I did not greatly care for the sound of Julia and the Onjohn. Sir Thomas I know only from your letters."

"Well," said Georgiana, "I will read you Tom's letter."

I am become a schoolboy again, dearest Georgiana, counting the days. Now there are seven. We leave here July the First and I trust to be with you by the Fifth or Sixth. Julia sulks, or scolds. Yates complains. Everyone is at fault but he. I ride out with him each morning. There are good gallops over the downs to the east of this place but there is no putting sense into Yates's head. The good luck is that all his debts are debts of honour (save that he has none) so we do not expect the bailiffs. But how can you settle debts when you have no money? My father does something, the Onjohn's brother something more and Yates accepts it all as if it were quite their privilege and pleasure to keep him on his worthless way. I have a stab of conscience there as he was *my* friend at the start. I am but too thankful to think that I shall be "home for the holidays" by the time Yates and Edmund begin to fight, and Julia with Fanny. My poor father is grown quite thin. I have missed you every day. Our cottage is peacefulness itself even with the workmen. Should I ever raise my voice to you, one word—Julia—will lower it again. Until very soon, my dearest love,

Your Tom.

A short silence followed. Then Mr Darcy said: "I have only to assure you, my dearest sister, that your money is perfectly safe. They cannot touch your principal without your—and without my—consent."

"I hope their house in Brighton is a large one," said Elizabeth. "I have heard that some of them are quite small. It would be too cruel if they could not get away from one another. And I cannot really feel that your Tom has in fact deserved this unpleasantness. The situation is hardly of his making."

"Indeed it is not," agreed Georgiana very warmly. "But how good it was in him to spare me all this—he must have known how it would be. I must just trust that these troubles may not have undermined his health."

She was entirely re-assured on this point when he arrived at Pemberley a few days later. He appeared very early in the afternoon, long before he was expected, and Elizabeth recalled that this had happened before. The horses were fresh; he himself was in no degree travel-worn, but he required no persuasion to remain with them for the night. Georgiana drove him round the park in the new phaeton and they were as pleased to see each other as they could possibly be.

They left very soon after breakfast the next day, in the expectation of reaching Mansfield Park comfortably by the evening. As they returned to the hall, having waved them away, Mr Darcy took Elizabeth's arm and said: "I love my sister. I love your aunt. Our friends from Bath are charming, elegant and entertaining. But let us now close our front gates, see no one and go nowhere for two weeks, or for so long as this perfection of summer weather lasts. Let us still have a picnic every day, but by ourselves. Let us forget that we have neighbours, abjure any responsibilities that have the temerity to raise their heads—in short, let us be ourselves by ourselves for as long as we may. It is the greatest luxury of all."

The weather lasted for ten days more and then changed dramatically, with a tremendous thunderstorm and tumultuous rain; but they had spent those ten days as they wished and were the more ready to face again their obligations.

These were by no means especially formidable. They drove to Kympton to see the start of the work necessary to install the organ; and began to consider what they were to give Catherine as a wedding present.

"There can be no dispute about that," said Mr Darcy very firmly. "Of course we must give her all her china and the china must come from Derby. Things are by no means the same there as they were ten years ago, but we can go to the warehouses in Chesterfield and Ashbourne and, if we have good luck, may find some old stock to give her without blushing."

Elizabeth had no quarrel with this. She was indeed more than content to find Mr Darcy so positive upon the point; but she was by no means prepared for his next words.

"And, while on the subject of wedding presents, my love," he said, with just a hint of uncertainty in his voice, "I have taken a liberty. I am never quite clear about *your* feelings for your sister Mary, but I would wish to make *mine* perfectly plain. Her work among the villagers, added to that of her husband, is slowly transforming Kympton into a happy, and much healthier, place. I am impressed by her, by them, and, as the highest mark of approbation that I can think of, I have directed that a forte-piano be delivered to them, or I should rather say to *her*, but as a wedding present so that they do not need to be too grateful."

He finished rather hurriedly, but Elizabeth could not find any words that seemed adequate. She went over to where he sat and took his hands in hers.

"You leave me speechless, as so often, with your generosity," she said. "I can only murmur my heartfelt, warmest thanks."

He carried her hands to his lips.

"I have a debt to pay, you know," he said, "to you and your remarkable family, that family which never ceases to surprise me. When I think of the proud, cold, shy, remote young man whom you met at Netherfield I marvel, sometimes, that you did not ignore me completely. You, and they, brought me to life—and brought life to me. That is a thing I can never forget." He looked up at her and smiled. "You will not scold me for doing this?"

Elizabeth felt suddenly very near to tears; but she managed to say: "I will not scold you for doing this."

They went first to the warehouse in Ashbourne, where they had the great good fortune to find a complete set of domestic china, commissioned more than ten years before but never collected. It was purchased instantly, with the best of good will on both sides, the owner of the warehouse even more delighted than they were themselves. It was delivered to Pemberley the next day.

The organ was completely installed at Kympton some three weeks before it was to be dedicated. Elizabeth and Mr Darcy drove over one afternoon, to see how it looked, and arrived some two hours after the delivery of the fortepiano.

"Your kindness *most truly* warms my heart," said Mary, as soon as she saw them. "Indeed, it *almost* overwhelms me. But I have decided *not* to be overpowered but to concentrate even more fiercely than before, so that I may learn to do the fullest justice both to your wonderful present and to the beautiful organ. I practise every day," she went on. "The pedals are something new to me, but I believe I shall have learned to use them before the inauguration."

The sole topic of discussion, for the rest of the afternoon, was the wording of the memorial tablet which had yet to be placed.

"We think it should be small enough to be on the front of the organ itself," said Mr Morland, "where everyone may see it; but not so small that it does no justice to her qualities. My own acquaintance with Mrs Bennet was a limited one," he continued, "but my principal memories of her must be of her welcoming kindness to me on all occasions and of her great good temper under much discomfort."

Elizabeth thought it better not to speak and was grateful to Mary for saying: "I think no one ever doubted her generosity. Certainly everyone in the village knew that soup, or bread, or both, were to be had from the back door whenever they were in trouble. But I hardly think that this is the occasion to say so. That is to say," she added with a smile, "there would scarcely be the space to do so."

"But we reserve the word 'generosity'," said Mr Darcy, also smiling. "We start simply by saying that this organ is the gift of the five daughters of your mother—whose name is perhaps no secret?"

"Catherine Mary," said Mary immediately. "My mother once told me I was so plain as a baby that they did not feel they could call me Catherine."

"There is certainly no space to record *that*," said Elizabeth. "She must have been particularly vexed to tell you such a thing."

"It was on a day when she found me reading instead of practising some music. She also told me, on that occasion, that no husbands were to be found in books."

Elizabeth was once again conscious of a desire not to speak, but Mr Darcy and Mr Morland both laughed.

"On behalf of *all* Mrs Bennet's sons-in-law," said Mr Darcy, "I would presume to say that no one could have been more welcoming once the engagement was assured—or more persevering in bringing it about, in Bingley's case at least."

He turned to Mr Morland.

"I think I am a principal beneficiary here," he said. "Mrs Bennet could not have known that, in striving so hard to secure the happiness of her daughter Jane, she was also securing *my* happiness and, I trust, that of her daughter Elizabeth."

"Yes," said Elizabeth, on safe ground at last, "and no. It came to her as a complete surprise."

"And yet," said Mary, "I hardly think that 'perseverance' would look well on a memorial tablet. It is too often attributed to those whose only attribute it was—where there is nothing else to say."

Her remark brought about a complete silence.

"That, however, is by no means the case," said Mr Morland, after a moment. "Is there not another word for 'perseverance'?"

"'Generous', 'virtuous'—what think you of 'assiduous'?" asked Mr Darcy. "Though it has by no means the complimentary sense of a hundred years ago."

"Let us begin at the beginning," said Mary, suddenly in charge. "'This organ is the gift of the five daughters of Catherine Mary Bennet, who died on—' Do we have the date exactly?"

"The thirty-first day of January," said Elizabeth, "though that is to be precisely ascertained."

"1820," said Mr Morland. "In the year of her age?"

There was another pause.

"My mother was born in the year 1775, at the time of the American Revolution," said Mary. "She once told me that her father, who had some sympathy with the colonists, wished to call her Carolina, only that her mother would not let him."

Elizabeth could not help laughing.

"I have often regretted that we hardly knew our grandmother Gardiner," she said. "I remember what she looked like but that not very well."

"I think, too," said Mary, "that our great Shakespeare has it quite wrong. There is everything in a name. If my mother had grown up being called Carolina she would have been quite different."

"In what way?" asked Mr Darcy. "Your theory is compelling, but I doubt that you could prove it."

"I could certainly not do *that*," said Mary, without a smile. "But she would have been a greater gadabout. You could not just sit at home if your name were Carolina."

"And would you, my dear," said Mr Morland very gently, "have been a different person had you been called Catherine instead of Mary?"

"I should think—undoubtedly."

"Then I must be very glad that you were not," said Mr Morland. "But let us return to the matter in hand."

After a small pause, and the use of some of his fingers, he said: "In the forty-fifth year of her age."

"Yes," said Mary. "Her birthday was in July."

"So," said Mr Morland, "are we agreed so far?"

"We are," said Mr Darcy, "for we are to this point only concerned with fact. But we have now to find a word to describe her as a wife. I think we cannot take refuge among the 'dearly beloveds' and 'greatly valueds' of convention. 'Esteemed' perhaps? 'Devoted'? 'Excellent'? This is not quite so easy."

"No," said Elizabeth, in warmest agreement. "It is not."

After a considerable silence, it was Mary who said: "I think we can spare ourselves this trouble and allow my father to take it on himself. He will put up his own memorial at Longbourn. The organ is from her family alone and we have only to state that she *was* his wife."

A smile seemed to settle on the room.

"A Daniel, my dear," said Mr Morland. "A Daniel come to judgment. So: 'She was the wife of—' Are we ever to know your father's name?"

"We only *think* it was Henry," said Elizabeth. "But I will write to demand it. In such a cause, you know, he could not withhold it."

"'Of Longbourn in the County of Hertford'," said Mr Darcy, "'and was—generous, virtuous—' I hope we may find a third word ending in '–ous'. 'Sedulous' I do not like, neither do I care for 'assiduous'."

"No, no, my love," said Elizabeth very quickly. "It is too brief, too almost a dismissal. We must say she was—there must be some other word for 'famous'."

"Yes," said Mary. "It must be 'renowned'."

"'*Renowned*'," said Mr Darcy, in deep appreciation. 'And was renowned for her generosity, her perseverance and—' What else?"

"'Her virtue'," said Elizabeth at once. "No one, not even Lady Lucas, ever doubted that. But I do not like the 'perseverance'."

"Do we think 'patience' might suit the case?" asked Mr Morland, after a short silence.

"'And was renowned for her generosity, her patience and her virtue'," intoned Mr Darcy. "It is not too solemn? Or far from the truth?"

"It is not at all far from the truth," remarked Mary, quite sharply, "though Lady Lucas aforementioned might not recognise it as my mother. But we may safely ignore her as I hope she will never come to Derbyshire."

Then, looking round and smiling: "I think it has a very pleasant ring."

"So," said Mr Morland, "perhaps we can agree? On 'her generosity, her patience and her virtue'."

"Yes," said Mr Darcy, after a moment. "I am sure we cannot improve on that."

"Yes," said Elizabeth, after another moment.

"Yes," said Mary, after a longer pause.

"Then," said Mr Morland, with the angelic smile which so entirely transformed him: "Amen."

XXI

Elizabeth received Mr Bennet's reply even before she had expected it.

As one gets older, one's secrets leak out. My mother's name was Hallam and my father gave it to me. He never used it as he could not forgive her for having died at my birth or me for having caused her death. On the rare occasions that we spoke he would call me "Sir", if he were in charity with me, "Sirrah" if he were not. My tutors always called me Bennet and it was Master Bennet from the servants and my nurse until I was old enough to be called Mister. But I have to concede that it will look handsome on a memorial tablet and I look forward almost eagerly to seeing the finished article. My cousin Collins informs me that Lady Catherine is doing very well by growing linseed. Not only do the stablemen require it but it is of use in the great manufactories of the north. He recommends that I put one of the south meadows down to it—though not of course until next year—and I may do so without mentioning the matter to him. Our correspondence is of little interest to me now; his earlier absurdities are disappointingly absent. But it seems to be of some importance to him as he clearly expects to occupy my shoes in the not-too-distant future. One feels him to be counting the days. I hope he may not be already plotting with my servants to poison me, but flatter myself that there is no one at Longbourn who does not prefer me to him.

Until we meet, gratifyingly soon, I remain,
Your loving Father.

The information was despatched at once to the brass engraver in Chesterfield, noted for the excellence of his work. He brought the completed tablet to Pemberley four days later; was praised and paid by Mr Darcy; and one of the grooms took it over to Kympton the next day. He brought back a note from Mary.

The tablet is extremely handsome, exactly the correct size and I think we have achieved the right wording. I still struggle with the pedals but I improve each day. I find that Haydn Sonatas played very slowly on the organ are impressive indeed and cannot believe that anyone would recognise them as such, or would object to them if they did. Certainly the Bishop of Derby, who offers to grace us with his presence, will not do so since he is of the old school who objects to the singing of psalms. I have assembled a lusty choir to confound him. But I am sure he has never heard of Haydn.

The Bingleys arrived at Pemberley the day before the organ was to be dedicated and Elizabeth decided that this was a perfect opportunity to take Jane for a drive in the new phaeton. Leaving their husbands and their children to entertain each other, they set off together within minutes of Jane's stepping into the hall.

"I think this an excellent notion," said Jane. "How very seldom do we have the chance to be alone and I have, besides, something quite interesting to tell you."

"That you are *also* in the family way?" said Elizabeth. "Since I am quite sure you are. Curious how we seem to increase at the same time. I hope he will be a son this time—ten days before Christmas."

"Well, you are right," said Jane, "though mine should be here a little earlier than that. But no—*my* news is about my lamentable sisters-in-law and I scarcely know where to begin."

"When last I heard, Caroline had what was described as 'bigger game in view'. You must tell me who that was—or, perhaps, who it is?"

"It was a Mr Rushworth," said Jane, "tall, quite handsome and rich enough for Caroline. But there was something odd about him. He had a mother who travelled everywhere with him and who would only permit him to meet women with dark hair. So Caroline was one of the first to put herself forward. But she found he had only two topics of conversation. The first was his property in Northamptonshire which, if I recollect rightly, was called Sotherton; and the second was a play he had once rehearsed but which was cancelled before the performance.

This play was called *Lovers' Vows* and he had had to learn two-and-forty speeches, or five-and-twenty, or six-and-thirty, I do not recall precisely. And what he liked to do, above everything else, was to recite them all over and over again."

"That would be hard on any listener who could not give him his cues," remarked Elizabeth. "Though I suppose it would make no difference to him if they were correct or not."

"No, you have it exactly—the other person had only to say *something* when he stopped speaking. But wait till I tell you where this entertainment was to have taken place."

"The Haymarket Theatre? Covent Garden? I hope it was somewhere not too remote as he had gone to so much trouble."

"At *Mansfield Park*," said Jane triumphantly. "Can you *imagine* such a thing?"

Elizabeth nearly dropped the reins but, recollecting herself before she did so, was able to say, as unconcernedly as possible: "Well, *it* is certainly in Northamptonshire." Then, after a small pause, she asked: "Do you know when this was supposed to have happened?"

"No, quite sadly I do not. Caroline was inclined to think some four or five years previously. I thought it did not sound like the Mansfield Park of today."

"It must be part of what Georgiana calls the Great Mansfield Mystery. But do I collect that Miss Bingley did not land this desirable person?"

"You do indeed, but through no fault of her own. Though between ourselves she was quite tired of *Lovers' Vows*, which, I believe, had not been seen on the London stage for twenty years. No. It was the Hand of Fate. She had to go into mourning."

"That was unkind of Fate," said Elizabeth unsympathetically. "But for whom? She had no parents."

"For her brother-in-law Mr Hurst, Louisa's invisible husband. He lived, more or less, at his club, at least after Caroline went to live with them—and he always sat in the same chair. And though I *know* this to be a piece of unfounded gossip, it was a friend of Bingley's who told *him* and of course he told *me*—he had been dead in his chair for *two days* before anyone noticed."

"I remember that time at Netherfield when you had your cold—he would lie on one of the sofas after dinner and *snore*," said Elizabeth. "One could not regret such a man."

"I am sure we do not," said Jane. "My dear Bingley, I am glad to say, said something *quite* unbecoming on the occasion and we, of course, were already in mourning for my mother."

"And Mr Rushworth went back to Sotherton?"

"And Mr Rushworth went back to Sotherton."

"Poor, poor Miss Bingley," said Elizabeth, in mock commiseration. "Now she must start all over again. And I," she added reflectively, "would be but too happy to see her locked up in matrimony. I do not like to see her always on the loose. For how long must one mourn a brother-in-law?"

"For three months, Louisa says, though she will remain for the full year. And meanwhile, you know, anything can happen. I am sure Northamptonshire is full of dark-haired women."

"I will write to Georgiana quite soon," promised Elizabeth. "I have never heard her even mention the name. If they are indeed in the same county it is strange that they do not visit."

There was enough of lasting interest in this conversation to keep Elizabeth's mind occupied whenever she had a moment's leisure; but for some reason, which she did not choose to examine, she did not burden Mr Darcy with any of it. They set off the next morning in the highest spirits, the Bingleys following the Darcys.

The Parsonage House at Kympton already bore substantial witness to the fact that it was lived in by someone very fond of gardening. The lawns were smooth and the gravel neat; the hedges were newly clipped and a round bed opposite the front door was full of flowers, larkspur, Canterbury Bells and snapdragons. An air of well-being lay over the whole, as though house and occupants lived together in the greatest harmony; and Elizabeth congratulated herself once more that she was, in part, responsible for Mary's present happiness.

They were received by Mary and Mr Morland at the door and by Catherine and Mr Bennet in the sitting-room, where they were followed immediately by the Bingleys. After all the bustle of arrival was over—for two of Mr Bennet's granddaughters were now old enough to offer him a curtsey—he drew Elizabeth a little aside and said: "This is a parade to do one good, indeed. Never before did I realise I had *four* such handsome daughters. Who would have thought that Mary would turn out to be so much of an advertisement for matrimony? Your poor Mother, I think, would scarcely recognise her. And as for her son—he is quite clearly born to be a Bishop. His wave of acknowledgement is already a kind of benediction."

Elizabeth laughed with him and said: "And we must rejoice in our turn at the possession of such a handsome father. I think I have never seen you look so well—and Catherine, too. I am most happy to find that you accord so pleasantly together."

"I must own myself mistaken in her," said Mr Bennet. "She presides more than adequately in your mother's place and I find her in every way a pleasure to be with."

"I am sorry to think she will be taken away from you so soon."

"Well, as to that, it was always to be expected, and young Captain Price is a son-in-law whom no one could disdain. But perhaps I can admit to you that I have now a new ambition. While I doubt I can live long enough to see Master Morland placed upon his episcopal throne, I have every intention to do so for at least another twenty years—if only to confound my cousin Collins."

A nuncheon was served in the dining-room and then they all walked through the village to the church. The service of dedication was quite short, performed gracefully by Mr Morland and the Bishop of Derby. Mary's choir sang the Magnificat and the congregation joined in the hymn "All People That On Earth Do Dwell".

After the blessing, Mary began to play them out with one of her Haydn Sonatas, one which it had taken her an entire summer to learn. Elizabeth could not quite avoid sharing a smile with both Jane and Catherine—for the sonata had pervaded the house at the time, day in and day out; but she was also delighted to hear how well it sounded on the organ and how completely

Mary had seemed to master the instrument. Her trouble was by no means in vain. The Bishop remained seated until the music ceased and then observed in a loud voice: "Upon my soul, Mr Morland, that is an excellent contrivance indeed. I shall expect to hear that your congregations are quite doubled."

On their return to the Parsonage—the Bishop being a guest elsewhere—the conversation centred on Catherine's approaching wedding, now little more than six weeks away. Both Jane and Elizabeth had been prepared to offer an elder daughter as a bridesmaid, but their offer was not to be made.

"Although we shall be out of mourning for my mother," said Catherine, "I think our ceremony should be as simple as possible. One bridesmaid, my dearest William's sister Susan, who comes with us to Torbay, is all I need—though I hope that all three of my sisters will be able to be present."

"Miss Susan Price is to live with you?" asked Elizabeth, her tone of voice by no means one of approval. "I had not realised that you were acquainted."

"We are not—yet," said Catherine. "But William will not always be on shore, you know. I think I shall be glad of her company and she, I know, will be glad of mine. For the Lieutenant to whom she is now engaged is fallen sick at the Cape and she would wish to be with him the moment he lands in England. And this might not so readily be contrived from Mansfield Park."

"And what has Lady Bertram to say to this?"

"That," said Catherine, with a little smile, "I cannot tell you, but I understand there is another niece in view, as well as two daughters-in-law."

"My dearest Georgiana being one of them," said Elizabeth quietly; then, pausing to reflect how comfortably she and Georgiana had always lived together, she said: "I am sorry if I spoke too sharply. I was not quite sure that you had been consulted."

"Oh, I was consulted," said Catherine, still smiling, "after a fashion, that is to say. I received a letter from Susan herself asking if she might come to live with us. She sounds to be an amiable girl, waiting to spread her own wings. I could not refuse such a request in any case, and am sure I shall not live to regret it. She will come to Longbourn with Mr Edmund Bertram, who is to support William—his wife Fanny will not leave her children. I hope to persuade Mr Morland to assist at the ceremony."

"You have thought it all through very well," said Elizabeth sincerely. "The only thing now to be mentioned is—who is to write to Lydia?"

"I have even done that," said Catherine, laughing. "But I have had no reply. Sometimes one cannot but wonder if those letters ever arrive. Perhaps I will write again *after* I am married—and send her my direction at Torbay."

Quite a short discussion decided that all Mr Bennet's grand-children should be left at Pemberley with their nursemaids, while their parents went to Longbourn. The decision was greeted with delight by all the little girls.

The Darcys' present to Catherine was contained in two enormous hampers, one of which they had brought with them. The Bingleys, too, had brought half their present, which was all glass, to be conveyed to Longbourn in Mr Bennet's carriage. Catherine, venturing to open just the top layer of both hampers, was overcome by the beauty of their contents and dissolved into tears on Mr Bingley's shoulder.

"It is too kind—I do not deserve it," was all that she could find to say.

Catherine's wedding took place on a mild and sunlit day at the end of September. Miss Susan Price proved to be both beautiful and agreeable, tall and fair, and she accompanied the three sisters up the aisle behind the bride and her father. Mr Bennet's neckcloth was white rather than black; his daughters, as though in collusion, were all in shades of blue. Captain William Price, in his dress uniform, was a magnificent sight indeed and made, with his cousin Edmund Bertram, as hand-some a pair, Elizabeth thought, as had the Bertram brothers at Georgiana's wedding.

The bridal couple did not linger. Captain Price's furlough was a short one and they left, with Miss Susan Price, immediately after a sumptuous wedding breakfast. Catherine, radiantly happy as a bride, nevertheless quitted Longbourn in tears, adjuring Mrs Hill to look after Mr Bennet, to give him only his favourite dishes and never to forget that he could not bear wool next to his skin. She waved to them until she was quite out of sight.

A curious silence settled on the house after their departure. It was as though the three remaining daughters began to feel the loneliness that was to be Mr Bennet's when they left him the next day. Jane and Mary were closeted a long time with Mrs Hill and Elizabeth took the opportunity to steal off, with Mr Darcy, in the direction of Oakham Mount.

"It is not quite the twenty-eighth of October, my love," she said, "but this year, for the first time, we shall not be here on that day. And I should miss our little ceremony if it were to be quite omitted."

"And I, too," replied Mr Darcy. "It makes me recall, without much pleasure, how intolerant I used to be. But I think I do not now offend in that respect very often?"

"Never at all, indeed. I would rather think that you are also *renowned*, but for your approachability and understanding. While our walk to Oakham makes me remember how blind I was, being short-sighted and hasty at the same time. But that is far behind us now. Weddings, I suppose, do always make one philosophical, though I believe today's has all the promise of a true and lasting one. They cannot, of course, be as happy as we are, because that is not a possibility for anyone else."

"True," he said, lifting her hand to his lips. "We are the happiest and most contented couple in the world. There cannot be a doubt of that."

They did not go beyond the stile.

Their journey home was accomplished without mishap, to find the children all in sparkling health; and they discussed, for a moment, their next meeting.

"But as," said Mary, "this Christmas is to be complicated by two happy events, perhaps I should invite my father to spend it with us. He will bring his own conveyance and we can drive over by the day."

The autumn proceeded calmly. In October some shooting parties were held at Pemberley and Mr Darcy left them occasionally to join the shooting parties of his neighbours. But the month was little more than three weeks old when a letter arrived from Catherine. Elizabeth was conscious of a certain alarm as she opened it, but she was speedily re-assured.

St Marychurch, October 19th

I write, dearest Lizzy, chiefly to say how comfortable and charming is the small house that my dear William has taken for us. It is called The Hermitage and is entered only by a door in a high blank wall; but inside is the prettiest imaginable little house, with long windows opening on to a lawn. We have three bedrooms, a cook, a maid and a mulberry tree and we see my dearest William, at the moment, every day. It is quite a ride to the harbour, but he says his horsemanship must benefit from the practice. But, as you might guess, I do not write *only* to share my happiness with you. I have now received from my sister Susan *the whole history* of Miss Crawford and the Bertrams and can hardly wait to let you hear it. So. You are to know that Miss Crawford and her brother once spent a summer at Mansfield with their sister Mrs Grant, wife of the incumbent at Mansfield. Sir Thomas was in the East Indies—or the West Indies—and it was decided to get up some dramatics to amuse Lady Bertram. Mr Tom Bertram was the great activator and *everybody* was to take part. Difficulties began at once. There were *two* Miss Bertrams but only one heroine. Mr Crawford was to be the hero. According to Susan's sister Fanny, who did not choose to join in, the whole of the first act was passed with the two main characters falling into each other's arms every two minutes and *this* act was rehearsed completely *every day*! Do not you wish you had been there, concealed behind some sofa, or a curtain? However, *this* Miss Bertram, whichever it was, was at the time engaged to a Mr Rushworth, a neighbour with a tiny part in the play. All was going well until Sir Thomas returned unexpectedly early and the whole project had to be given up. The appropriate Miss Bertram was married to Mr Rushworth and they went off, with the sister, to spend all his money at Brighton. The Crawfords remained at Mansfield. Now you are to understand that Fanny Price had been all her life in love with Mr Edmund Bertram. Mr

Crawford, having nothing else to do, laid siege to her, while Mr Edmund fell in love with—or more probably was dazzled by—Miss Crawford. So it was a miserable time for sister Fanny. But, to everyone's surprise, Mr Crawford declared himself. Fanny refused him and so was sent off in disgrace to her parents at Portsmouth, where she met Susan for the first time. (I should say that Fanny had been inmate at Mansfield since she was ten years old.) But Mrs Rushworth and Mr Crawford *met again* in London and resumed their former friendship, finally running away and *living together*. Indeed, according to Susan, they parted only when they had absolutely learnt to hate each other. Miss Crawford took her brother's part, which discomposed Mr Edmund Bertram to such an extent that he gave her up and returned to Mansfield. I am not clear as to *why* he was in London, but Susan thinks he was within a hair's breadth of offering for Miss Crawford. Meanwhile Mr Tom Bertram had fallen off his horse at Newmarket and his friends had left him there, in a high fever and cared for only by the servants. So *little* did they care for him, indeed, that he nearly lost his life, being rescued by his brother Edmund and brought back to Mansfield, quite at the last minute—just as Fanny returned from Portsmouth. Well, as we know, Fanny married Edmund; but what I have only just discovered is that Mrs Rushworth was *divorced* and banished—with a horrid old aunt, a sharp-tongued witch with a long thin nose, according to Susan—to somewhere in the north. She is never *spoken of* and even Fanny does not know where she lives! You will be as astonished by this relation as I was myself, but I have only space to say that Susan and I go every day to Babbacombe Down, in close bonnets and our oldest pelisses, and are as happy and as healthy as possible. Pray give my love to Mr Darcy and this brings much to you.

From your loving and most contented sister, Catherine.

Elizabeth was indeed so astonished by the contents of this letter that she read it over three times, before stowing it away at the back of a drawer in her writing desk. Although she recalled that Miss Crawford had once mentioned her brother, Elizabeth had not previously understood that he, too, was part of the Great Mansfield Mystery. She thought about it, from time to time, in the course of the next few months.

XXII

Elizabeth's son was born eleven days before Christmas, three weeks after his cousin Charles Bingley. He was a large and rather demanding baby, but Elizabeth was aware of a deep contentment which had been absent before. He lay in a cot beside her bed and she tried hard to admire his little, scarlet, screwed-up face. Mr Darcy was an early enthusiast.

"You may be safely assured, my dearest love, that he looks like you and me, his grandfather Bennet and all his aunts, of whom he has indeed a great number. The doctor, the midwife, everyone has convinced me that he is the finest child ever to be born—and, from where I now observe him, I have no difficulty in believing them. I have only to say, as I have said before—thank you." And then, after a moment and with deep feeling: "I can find no other word."

Elizabeth smiled a little at this.

"It is wise to decide that he looks like us all," she said. "It must shorten every future discussion. And as I am sure you have also decided what his names are to be, do please let me in on the secret."

"We must call him George, for my father, and perhaps Fitzwilliam, for his? I know you are not very fond of my name."

"It is not that, not that at all. It is just that one cannot call a small child Fitzwilliam without seeming to scold him."

"Then," he said, with one of his broadest smiles, "the choice is yours. And perhaps I now understand why my father and mother always sounded so serious when they called me by my name."

"I am too tired to think today, but I should warn you that when the Tsar of All the Russias was in London, five or six years ago, I fell quite in love with *his* name."

"Then—let that be your choice. Alexander George Fitzwilliam has a handsome sound, a certain unexceptionable grandeur. Not even Lady Catherine could find a fault there, I think."

Elizabeth, on the verge of falling asleep again, said only: "I am very glad to have a son called Alexander."

Mr Bennet and Mary were her first visitors, just over a week later. They called in on their way to the Bingleys, where they were to spend the night. They did not stay long, just long enough to admire the child and for Elizabeth to observe how comfortable they seemed to be in each other's company. But they returned on the following day, to dine and sleep at Pemberley; and after dinner Mary came to see her alone.

"I will not stay to tire you," she said, "but just to let you know that Jane is well and that she sends her best love. Her son, I think, is not as large as yours, but he, too, is very well and everyone is very pleased with him."

She sat down beside the fire and, by its light, Elizabeth thought she detected some concern in Mary's face. She said, very quietly: "If something troubles you, Mary, you must tell me what it is."

"Yes," said Mary, "I must, much as I dislike it. Miss Bingley is there with them and means to come over."

Elizabeth said nothing.

"It was my father who introduced us again," Mary went on. "'You remember my third daughter, of course,' he said, and then added, after the *smallest* pause—'Mrs Morland'. She did not recognise me at once—nobody does, you know—but when she did she said, in that *rallying* tone she has, 'I must congratulate you indeed. If *you* have found a husband I must suppose that *all* your sisters have done so.' So I thanked her as pleasantly as possible and told her that Catherine had married a naval captain three months ago and had gone to live at Torbay. And so she said that naval officers would have to do where other fare was lacking and that she believed Torbay to be extremely healthful. But then—and this I think upset us all, or rather Mr Bingley as well, for Jane was not present—she said to my father, with one of her *odious* smiles: "One can only admire the success of Mrs

Bennet's stratagems. I am surprised to find you still in mourning for her." And left the room! Could you *believe* that anyone could be so impolite?"

"Miss Bingley has a temper to control and does not always manage it," said Elizabeth. "Perhaps we should be grateful that she said nothing worse."

"Well, of course, Mr Bingley said what he could and my father passed it off, but I heard some raised voices later and so did Jane. So—when she asked me, I told her."

"There could be nothing there to surprise Jane," remarked Elizabeth. "It is Mr Bingley who calls his sister the fly in the ointment."

"So I thought I should perhaps warn you to prepare for her visit."

"I must hope to deny myself somehow," said Elizabeth. "Miss Bingley will never forgive me for having—as I suppose she thinks—stolen Mr Darcy from her. Though what symptoms of affection she could ever have seen on his side I am quite at a loss to know—and as I have now committed the ultimate sin of giving him a son, there can scarcely be a limit to her ill-will."

Elizabeth and Mr Darcy were alone when Miss Bingley came to call, at eleven o'clock on the morning of the day before Christmas. They could hear sounds outside the door which soon resolved themselves into the clearly spoken words of Miss Bingley: "Oh no, you may be quite easy. Mrs Darcy is my very old friend. I know exactly which is her room and she will be delighted to see me."

They had just time to compose themselves before she came in; and she had the grace to pause for a moment before she said: "Perhaps I do intrude. I had not expected that at this time of day."

"Not at all," said Mr Darcy, rising and at his most formal. "We have had this pleasure in view for some time. Pray come in and take a seat by the fire."

She came over and said, a little too enthusiastically: "But the child—the son and heir. I hope indeed that I may be permitted a glance at him?"

"You may certainly do so," said Mr Darcy. "Here he is, peacefully sleeping in his cot. We have made up our minds already that he resembles *all* his living relatives, so you may save yourself the labour of deciding whom he resembles most."

"I wish only to be assured," said Miss Bingley, with a beaming smile, "that he has inherited his mother's fine eyes. It is too provoking that they should be quite closed."

"My wife is more concerned, in fact, that our daughters should not inherit the Darcy nose."

"The Darcy nose!" exclaimed Miss Bingley. "I seem not to have heard of it before."

"My sister and I do not have it," said Mr Darcy, with a satisfaction bordering on relief. "But it was quite a general thing a hundred years ago. All the portraits from that time are painted from the front."

Miss Bingley sat down on the far side of the fire from Elizabeth, smiling firmly in her direction. After a moment her gaze became quite fixed and, after another moment, she found herself compelled to say: "But—my dear Mrs Darcy—do you always wear your jewellery in bed?"

"By no means all the time," replied Mr Darcy, as if to reassure her. "The necklace that you see came from the jeweller only this morning. It is my present to my wife—to thank her for my son. I had but clasped it round her neck for the first time when we had the happiness to see you entering the room."

"It is the most magnificent necklace I have ever seen," said Miss Bingley, very carefully.

"Yes," said Mr Darcy, very calmly. "I am having all the family diamonds re-set. My mother had a great many that she never wore and, as there are at present several jewellers in London of more than the first quality, it seemed foolish not to avail ourselves of their services. I am assured that all the stones are very fine indeed."

"Fate shines most kindly on the Bennet sisters, it seems," remarked Miss Bingley, with a kind of regret. "How long ago since we first met. How very different things were then." And then, addressing herself more particularly to Elizabeth, she said:

"I was so pleased to meet your sister—Mrs Morland—the other day. I remember so well her entertainments on the harpsichord. How long has she been married?"

"About eighteen months," replied Mr Darcy. "The living of Kympton, which was to have been George Wickham's had he entered the church, was vacant at that moment, so I was delighted to be able to present it to Morland—to enable them to marry, you understand; and I could not have found a more amiable, or a more reliable, incumbent."

"I am sure you hear frequently from Mrs Wickham," said Miss Bingley, her smile still fixed perfectly in place. "In what part of the country is she now living?"

"In Gibraltar," said Mr Darcy. "They have been there for more than two years. I was happy to assist in the purchase of the Captaincy that took them there."

"And Mr Bennet!" exclaimed Miss Bingley. "I declare I hardly recognised him. I should not say so, but it almost seems the state of widowhood quite suits him. Do you think he will marry again?"

"We are rather proud of Mr Bennet," said Mr Darcy reflectively. "He was obliged, you know, to purchase all his mourning new. No one had died in his family for thirty years—his own father, in fact. I fancy that my tailor entirely did him justice. For a man who has spent the last twenty-five years sitting in his library, his figure is a fine one."

"He must be quite solitary at Longbourn now that all his daughters are gone."

"He has some interesting neighbours, I am given to understand," said Mr Darcy, "and an excellent housekeeper. We are more than happy to see him here and Jane and your brother also. I think them very good friends indeed. The Morlands, too, where he stays at present. No doubt the new Mrs Price would be happy to see him, should he wish to venture so far."

"Indeed," said Miss Bingley. "I am quite charmed to hear that he has such a devoted family. But you know what they say about a single man being in the possession of a good fortune?"

She looked a little archly at Elizabeth.

"Your father cannot be more than fifty, I think, and he looks a good deal less. His property is worth two thousand a year, I seem to remember, and he is no longer encumbered with five daughters. But I suppose he will not come to London until the full term of his mourning is over?"

"Mr Bennet detests London," said Mr Darcy. "I suspect that anyone anxious to marry him would be well advised to seek him out, though with what probable success I would not like to guess. But now, I think, I must see you off. I cannot have Elizabeth tired out so early in the day."

Miss Bingley was forced to rise. Elizabeth smiled at her and said quietly: "Give my love to Jane and the children, if you please."

Mr Darcy opened the door and ushered Miss Bingley from the room, scarcely allowing her to utter her words of farewell. Elizabeth sighed and indulged in a few moments of enjoyable terror at the improbable spectre of Miss Bingley becoming her step-mother. The thought of it actually made her laugh and she was smiling when Mr Darcy returned, having seen Miss Bingley into her carriage.

"She has brought the Bingley presents for the children," he said, with a little grimace. "I suppose we have sent ours to them?"

"My father took them over."

"And could have brought back theirs. But I suppose a poor excuse is better than none."

Then, smiling down at her, he said: "What did you think of her parting shot?"

"I was doing so while you were away, with great pleasure. But what *did* please me was to hear her comments about my father. She was only *quite* satirical and I think he has a great deal to offer. Now that the cobwebs have gone."

"I am partial, I know," he said, sitting on the bed and taking her hand, "but it is my considered opinion that anyone who marries into the Bennet family is to be envied—to be welcomed, supported and envied—unless, of course," as he carried her hand to his lips, "they happen to be called Caroline Bingley. But not even she, I fancy, could mistake your father for such a fool. You need have no fear."

XXIII

It seemed to Elizabeth that the winter passed even more slowly than usual, enlivened only by a fall of snow at the end of January, which left them cut off from the village for more than a week; but Alexander beamed and flourished, the focus of everyone's adoring attention.

The end of February brought a letter from Mrs Gardiner.

> You will be interested to hear that your father has returned to Longbourn from Bath, since I cannot suppose that he informed anyone of this journey. My dear Mrs Frankland is inclined to think he had an interest in meeting Miss Crawford again, but she and Mrs Grant are gone off to Norfolk to put into order a Dower House on their brother's estate, where they propose to live together. They moved into the house you occupied yourselves some time after you left it, so Mrs Frankland saw very little of them; but, reading between the lines, as the saying has it, the assumption is that Mr Crawford is become addicted to the bottle and they fear that a fall out riding might well be fatal. Mr Gardiner writes that he intends to take ship, from Goa to Suez, at the beginning of May. He hopes to be with me by the end of June. The tone of his letter is entirely cheerful and I trust that the results of this long absence will be of value in the end. So the purpose of this letter, my dearest Lizzy, is to ask if I may visit you in May instead of June? With all the uncertainties incumbent on a journey of such length, I would wish to be at home the moment he arrives.

Elizabeth at once began a correspondence with Lady Alicia and Mrs Frankland, inviting them to Pemberley in the third week in May. A rapturous acceptance was returned and Elizabeth's own delight was further increased by a letter from Georgiana.

> At last, my dearest Elizabeth, I can inform you quite certainly that I am in the family way and expect to be confined in October.

Sir Thomas has decreed that Tom and I should spend the whole summer at Brighton—Julia and the Onjohn being banished, to a cottage near Dawlish away from *all* temptation, though I collect, from what I am *not* told, that his debts are in a way to be settled—so I am to have what Tom calls my "holiday from the Bertrams" in May. May I come to you for the last two weeks? I will come alone. My dearest Tom will take my place dancing attendance on his mother. I long to see my nephew and hope I am to provide you with one myself. I am well, but not as well as I would like.

No sooner, however, had all the arrangements been made, for the whole party to arrive together on the eighteenth of May, than Mrs Frankland wrote again.

A most delightful rumour, my dear Mrs Darcy, is now current in Bath, to the effect that the Corsican Monster has a bad cough, has taken to his bed and is confidently expected *never to get out of it*! However unfounded this may be, we are accepting it as a fact and wait only for the announcement that makes it quite certain. Indeed it may already have taken place, since St Helena is a long way off and even such momentous news travels slowly. Alicia and I are now closeted with our dressmakers in this expectation. We intend to put off our widows' weeds at the moment of confirmation and give a rout party, if not a ball. So I write simply to bespeak your indulgence and allow us to put off our visit to you until July. Nothing less than this longed-for event could occasion such a request, but we believe you will entirely enter into our feelings. Indeed it will give us a chance to visit you in such a flutter of pinks and blues that you may hardly recognise us! To compensate a little for our absence, I have to tell you that Lady Elliot and Colonel Tilney are gone off together, taking with them all the (undisputed!) family jewels. They are thought to be in Italy. Sir Walter and his daughter Mrs Tilney—whom one is sometimes at pains to remember is the Colonel's step-mother and not his wife—remain in shocked silence on top of their hill and have not been seen in these lower regions for more than a month. Their feelings one can only imagine but, as *you* may imagine, Bath is full of wisely wagging heads and unwisely wagging tongues.

Elizabeth, in her reply, said only that she much looked forward to seeing them in July, but added: "About Lady Elliot I find there is really nothing to say. I feel for her children although, if my own nurserymaids are to be believed, she was seen so seldom in her nurseries that they may scarcely be aware of her absence."

The month of April, a particularly brilliant one, passed quickly; and, two days before Georgiana and Mrs Gardiner were due, Mr Bennet arrived for one of his unexpected visits to Pemberley.

"I come from Mary," he remarked as he greeted Elizabeth. "I go on to Jane. Never was an old man so indulged by his daughters."

"We will ignore the word 'old', my dear Father," said Elizabeth. "I am *rejoiced* to find you looking so well. I trust your neighbours may have rendered the winter bearable for you? I never think of Longbourn as a *large* house—but when I think of you living in it all alone it seems to increase in size as I go from room to room."

"My neighbours have been more than attentive. A single man is of value in the country where tables are to be made up. But what I cannot now do is to invite women to the house— since nothing in the world will persuade me to ask your aunt Philips or, at worst, Lady Lucas—to preside at my table; and I find the masculine conversation of our worthy neighbours more than a little tedious. However, we have had some fine shooting parties and Mrs Hill has followed your mother's traditions most excellently. But you, my dearest child—how are you? I am glad to have a grandson called Alexander. His Greek namesake was not without some faults of character but one could hardly fault his energy—or even his initiative."

"He is a handsome child," said Elizabeth fondly. "The whole household dotes upon him."

With the arrival of Mrs Gardiner and Georgiana, the pace of their lives increased. Mr Bennet and Mr Darcy rode out every morning. The ladies drove in the park, or walked with the children in the flower garden. Two evening parties were held, for their more favourite neighbours, and the first week of the visit disappeared.

As they waited to be joined by the gentlemen one evening, Georgiana said: "Elizabeth, I have a very urgent request to make—I hope it may not be too difficult. But I have a great need to return to the Druidical Circle. I am not superstitious, I think, not more so than is quite reasonable, that is to say, but I was aware when we were there last summer of a certain power around those stones. I believe we all felt it. And as my wish has now been granted, in part at least, I believe it would be civil to go back there and return my thanks."

"An excellent idea," said Mrs Gardiner approvingly. "I, too, owe some gratitude to the Druids and it would be, if nothing else, a charming day's outing."

"And as I also have had my wish granted," said Elizabeth, smiling, "I think we cannot do better than go tomorrow. In one carriage. My father, I think, may be a little sceptical of our purpose, but he has learned from long practice to be patient with feminine foibles."

Mr Bennet, however, merely expressed a great interest to see the circle and they set off the next morning immediately after breakfast, the two gentlemen on horseback. They no longer needed to be guided to the place and they reached it without mishap in the very early afternoon, in high sunshine and with a stiff breeze blowing.

Jemima, consulted once again, had said that she knew only that to make a wish you went round to the left, but to thank the Druids you went round to the right. She was still waiting, she said, for her wish to be granted.

Elizabeth and Mr Darcy went together, now able to admit to each other that they had made the same wish—for a son. Mrs Gardiner and Georgiana followed them and one of the grooms, who had been with them last time; but, their thanks given, Mrs Gardiner and Georgiana went round again, the other way, to make a further wish. They were followed by the footman and, to Elizabeth's surprise and secret amusement, by Mr Bennet.

"I have long had an interest in the Druids," he said when he returned. "I do not doubt their power and would be the last person to wish to affront them. Our pagan activities are the business of nobody else," he added with a smile, "so there can be no need to discuss them."

They had to descend completely from the moor to find a sheltered spot in which to picnic; and they did not linger, for it was not precisely warm. As they began their journey homewards, it was Mrs Gardiner's turn to make a request, to go again to the white farmhouse she had so admired last year. The wind had dropped by the time they reached it and, as the ground seemed to be quite dry, the ladies agreed to take a walk along the road in front of them.

Elizabeth got out of the carriage first, but Mrs Gardiner, following her, missed her footing on the step and fell heavily to the ground. She said, in alarm:

"My hip. My knee. My *ankle*."

She then fainted entirely away.

Elizabeth was with her in an instant, cradling her head in her lap; and Mr Darcy, interpreting the situation at once, went off with the groom to ask for help at the farmhouse.

It was not long in coming. A disused door was found in one of the wash-houses and on this, supported by several cushions from the carriage, Mrs Gardiner was carried down by the groom, the footman and two manservants from the house. Mr Darcy and Mr Bennet, sensing that they could be of no further use at that moment, went off to Matlock to bring back a surgeon.

Elizabeth and Georgiana walked down together, Elizabeth by no means displeased to think that she might, at last, be going to meet the lady of the house; and grateful that the accident had occurred where such a deal of help was so readily at hand. They followed the invalid party to the front door.

If Elizabeth was surprised by the degree of comfort in the hall—for a log fire glowed cheerfully in a large fireplace and the stone-flagged floor was covered by thick woollen rugs—she was still more astonished by the charm and tranquillity of the bedroom which led out of it.

Mrs Gardiner was placed on a modern tester bed, with curtains of starched muslin and a handsome chintz, and was immediately attended by a comely, matronly woman and a maidservant. Elizabeth mentioned what Mrs Gardiner had said about her hip, her knee and her ankle; and the woman replied that, in that case, they must try to keep her lying as still as possible. She had not yet recovered from her faint.

They removed her bonnet and her outer garments with a most remarkable dexterity; and the woman, after feeling the areas mentioned, was able to say, with satisfaction: "I think nothing is broken."

They then concentrated on reviving Mrs Gardiner, with *sal volatile* and a vinaigrette, mopping her forehead with lavender water, leaving Elizabeth and Georgiana with nothing to do.

When Mrs Gardiner returned to consciousness, the maid-servant went off to bring some tea. Mrs Gardiner was told, quite firmly, to lie still and she did so, Elizabeth taking her hand and saying, very gently: "You are in the kindest care, my dear aunt, and in your favourite house. It cannot be long before the surgeon comes."

Mrs Gardiner returned the pressure of her hand, but said only: "So clumsy. So stupid. So *careless*."

She lay quite still, with her eyes closed, but when the tea arrived, which it very quickly did, she was able to sit up and drink it, Elizabeth holding the cup to her lips.

"We cause you a great deal of trouble," said Elizabeth apologetically, to the two women. "I must thank you most sincerely for your prompt and considerate actions."

"As to that, madam," came the smiling reply, "it was nothing more than any Christian would have done. And as the surgeon may be some time coming, you may like to sit with my lady in the parlour."

Mrs Gardiner, her eyes still closed, murmured: "Yes, my love. Go and offer our regrets for all this upset."

The maidservant led them across the hall, opening the door for them, into a charming room looking southwards on to the garden. A handsome woman, very fair, her hair arranged in quite the latest fashion, rose to greet them.

"You must forgive me for remaining a little aloof," she said. "Bridget has been dressing blains and bruises since before

I was a child, and I thought it better to let her do so in her own excellent way. I hope her patient may be somewhat recovered?"

Elizabeth and Georgiana had halted together in the middle of the room.

"Thank you, yes," said Elizabeth. "She has been able to drink a little tea."

Then, after a moment: "I am Mrs Darcy and this is my husband's sister, Mrs Bertram. Mrs Gardiner, our invalid, is my aunt and I am more grateful to you than I can say for your help and hospitality."

As she spoke, a very quick smile passed over the face of their hostess, adding a certain sparkle, even a slightly malicious sparkle, to her eyes. Georgiana did not speak. She seemed to be consulting within herself.

"Yes, I know who you are," was the reply. "Your carriage, your party, were recognised last year. The maid who showed you in is the daughter of one of your gardeners at Pemberley and I am more than just happy to meet you. But now—it is for me to tell who I am."

She paused for an instant before turning to Georgiana. Then she said, almost abruptly: "I am the sister of your husband Tom, and it has always been a great grief to me that we have never been allowed to meet."

"You are the other sister!" exclaimed Georgiana at once. "I thought of Julia as soon as I saw you—but, on closer inspection, you do not after all look very like her."

"I am glad to hear that. I hear she is grown very peevish."

"Then," said Georgiana, going up to her and offering both her hands. "How do you do? Maria."

"You know my name? I though it was never uttered within the family."

"Your sister," said Georgiana, "is by no means as circumspect as your brothers and your father. She was at the Great House for some time last year and one cannot help overhearing. But," she went on, turning to Elizabeth, "I never thought of that until this moment."

"Then let us all sit down," said Maria. "Your presence here gives me the *greatest* pleasure."

A long silence followed. Elizabeth thought Maria even a little moved by Georgiana's calm acceptance of her, but it showed only for a moment. She could not think what to say first and Georgiana seemed similarly undecided. In the end, it was Maria who spoke.

"I must suppose you know my history?"

"No," said Georgiana immediately. "That is to say, not in any detail. To me you are part of the Great Mansfield Mystery—one I never expected to solve."

"Perhaps," said Elizabeth, almost diffidently, "I am better informed than Georgiana. One of my sisters is married to Captain William Price and they have taken his sister Susan to live with them."

She looked very directly at Maria.

"So I have had your history from them, but I hardly think it need concern us here. We find you in this charming house, coming generously to our rescue—the present and future can be all that matter, particularly as I understand that the history you refer to is, in its way, quite ancient?"

"I have lived here for five years," said Maria, "and either you are very kind or else you have some very advanced views."

"My father was never one to be tied by convention," said Elizabeth, smiling, "and so far as I have any views at all, I would expect them to have been influenced by his. But if a Queen may be sued for divorce, I believe much of the odium to be removed; and, if nothing else has emerged from that quite disgraceful episode last year, it is that there are always faults on both sides."

"I cannot accept that here, however," said Maria candidly. "My behaviour was thoughtless and unpardonable. Mr Rushworth had no fault beyond being himself."

"I believe Mr Rushworth is to be found in London, courting only women with dark hair," said Elizabeth lightly. "It is a prohibition placed upon him by his mother. And, now that I have met you, of course I understand why."

But Maria did not laugh.

"His mother!" she exclaimed. "How she detested me indeed. I sometimes think that, had she not been at hand, our whole episode would have vanished. You are lucky, I think," she said to Elizabeth, "to be without a mother-in-law, but," turning to Georgiana, "I am most anxious to learn how my sister-in-law fares with hers."

"Lady Bertram and I are the greatest friends," said Georgiana, calmly. "I could wish that she had learned to be alone at some time in her life, since either I or Fanny are obliged to be with her always. She will not hear of having a companion and, I have to say, Sir Thomas and Edmund are very good about sitting with her when they have nothing else to do. But that, of course, is not very often."

"I think that quite outrageous," said Maria, very warmly. "Could not Miss Lee, our governess, be brought back to live there? They always dealt extremely well together."

"Well," said Georgiana, with a disarming smile, "perhaps it is not so very bad. Your mother is rarely settled on her sofa much before midday. We have tea and little cakes towards three o'clock and at four she retires to rest—to recruit her energies, you know, in order to sit through dinner."

"Welcome, welcome, Georgiana," said Maria delightedly. "Tom has always told me that you were a person after my own heart—not to be thought of at the same time as Fanny or John Yates."

"Do you see him often?" enquired Georgiana.

"Not so often since he married," said Maria, "but I can hardly reproach you for that. He and Edmund stayed with me the night before your wedding and he was on a visit to me when you met him first, when his horse had cast a shoe."

"So you are his mysterious friend in Matlock!" exclaimed Georgiana. "I might never have met him otherwise."

"But we had seen him before, at the Pump Room in Matlock," said Elizabeth, "and we thought him very handsome."

"At the Pump Room," remarked Maria. "Was he alone?"

"He was. He stood to one side as we passed."

"Then that must have been when he went to escort my aunt to Buxton where, I am thankful to say, she remains to this day. I have put your aunt in my aunt's room," she said to Elizabeth. "I hope there may be no lingering echoes."

Then, looking out of the window, she said: "A cavalcade of gentlemen, I perceive. I only hope they have brought the right surgeon."

"They were given very precise instructions by one of the men who carried Mrs Gardiner down," said Elizabeth.

"Poor man," said Maria. "He went himself for the doctor often enough when my aunt was in residence."

She got up and said: "I think you should remain here. We must not crowd your aunt. I will send the gentlemen in to join you."

"My husband," said Elizabeth, "and my father, Mr Bennet."

Maria bowed a little in recognition of this; and left them alone in the room.

XXIV

S he also left a complete silence behind her.

Elizabeth had never shared the contents of Catherine's letter. The full details of the Great Mansfield Mystery scarcely concerned her family and the responsibility to inform Georgiana, if she were to be informed, rested solely with Tom Bertram. As he had not chosen, or had been strictly forbidden, to do so, Elizabeth now found herself in the position of having to explain to Georgiana, as briefly as possible, the hidden facts of the case. She tried to summon the courage to speak.

Georgiana was similarly silent. It was impossible to guess what she was thinking and, to Elizabeth's considerable relief, it was she who spoke first.

"I think I am disposed to be offended," she said, but quite pleasantly. "Why could not the Bertrams trust me with the knowledge of Maria's existence? Particularly when, as it happens, she lives quite close to Pemberley."

Elizabeth gathered her strength.

"I have never quite liked to tell you this. It came in a letter from my sister Catherine and I did not think it wise to put it in a letter to you."

Georgiana gave her her fullest attention.

"You have heard me mention Miss Crawford, whom we met in Bath?"

"Yes, indeed, and whom you liked very much."

"It was her brother who ran off with Maria shortly after she was married to Mr Rushworth. They lived together until they could bear it no longer."

"Poor Maria," said Georgiana sympathetically. "I suppose Mr Rushworth divorced her?"

"Yes," said Elizabeth, "and, so far as I can see, that is what they wish to keep secret."

"By hiding her away and never mentioning her? I seem to scent a great deal of Sir Thomas in this. Dark secrets have a way of emerging into the daylight at the most inconvenient moments, as this one has certainly done. But I do not see that we should drop her acquaintance now that we have made it."

The silence which this remark occasioned was broken by the entrance of the gentlemen.

"I am glad to have one small mystery cleared up," said Mr Darcy as he came in, and addressing himself to Elizabeth. "You may recall the mine disaster at Ashover Colliery two years ago? And I found that, wherever I tried to offer help, a certain Mrs Bertram had offered it before me? We are now in that Mrs Bertram's house, and as it is so far from civilisation it is perhaps not surprising that I have never been able to trace her."

"She is my dearest Tom's sister," said Georgiana, without further ado. "The one they never mention. And her married name is Rushworth."

"She lives apart from her husband?"

"Her marriage has been dissolved."

"You mean that she is divorced?"

"I mean that she is divorced and has lived in this remote place for the last five years."

"I see," said Mr Darcy, and fell silent.

"Twenty years ago," said Mr Bennet, consideringly, "or even ten, we might have recoiled in horror at meeting such a person. I might indeed have forbidden you, my daughter, to mix with her for fear of the contamination that she offered. Now I think merely that such an attitude is perfectly absurd. Here is a beautiful woman engaged, apparently in good works, doing harm to no one, directly benefiting a member of our family—I think that the dictates of society, in this case, may all be safely ignored."

"And yet," said Mr Darcy, "I have to confess that my enthusiasm for Georgiana's marriage might have been a little dimmed had I been aware of this situation."

"And rightly so," agreed Mr Bennet, "in the first instance—until some explanation were offered. What I think reprehensible here is that no mention of this lady has ever been made to

Georgiana, who is married to one as close to her as a brother. So that she now finds herself in a position which could be extremely painful—one which, if we allow it, could be most embarrassing to us all."

He stopped for a moment and then said, in a rather softer voice: "We shall do better to say nothing. If she chooses to be called Mrs Bertram, then let us call her Mrs Bertram. We are, after all, about to be placed most seriously in her debt."

When the doctor was ready to leave, Elizabeth went through to her aunt's room to receive his instructions, although they were, in fact, delivered to Mrs Bertram. Mrs Gardiner was shocked, and badly bruised. Her ankle was sprained, but there was likely to be no lasting damage. She was to drink, and to sleep, as much as possible. She was to be kept warm and quiet, but on no account was she to be moved in less than four days.

When he had gone, Elizabeth turned to Mrs Bertram and said: "We trespass indeed upon your good nature and I feel, in my heart, that you will allow us to do nothing to assist you. But I will come tomorrow, if I may, and bring whatever provisions my housekeeper recommends in the way of invalid foods. And these, if you do not need them, you may put straight into your store cupboard without saying a word to me!"

Mrs Bertram smiled.

"You may do so, certainly, and with my very good will. I shall not permit a *contest* between your housekeeper and mine, but you may be sure that Mrs Gardiner will be given every attention we can think of. Indeed," she added, almost absently, "if your aunt were not in such a deal of pain, I would welcome the diversion."

They had plenty of time to think about this episode as they drove back to Pemberley. Elizabeth and Georgiana sat side by side in silence, and their silence, on the one topic which engrossed them all, was to continue throughout the evening. Only as she was falling asleep did Elizabeth recall that that house was full of bandages, and the recollection actually made her smile. Mrs Gardiner had indeed chosen the scene of her accident well.

Elizabeth and Georgiana set off shortly after breakfast the next day, taking with them Mrs Gardiner's clothes, her maid and a hamper containing everything considered necessary by Mrs Reynolds for the sustenance of an invalid. Just as they were leaving, they were joined by Mr Bennet.

"I will come with you," he said. "Mrs Gardiner is, after all, my sister-in-law. I wonder if that may be considered a closer relationship than an aunt?"

"Whether it is or not," said Elizabeth, "we shall be delighted to have you with us."

Their silence, on the one burning topic, continued, rendered the more necessary by the presence of Mrs Gardiner's maid. She was an old friend, however, whom Elizabeth had known since she was a girl, and innocent, innocuous conversation with her was easy. When they arrived, Mrs Gardiner was found to be much improved.

"Indeed," she said to them at once, "I cannot recall that I ever was so spoilt. If you should choose to fall ill, or fall over, I should rather say, be sure to do it where there are only women in the house. And what is more, my dearest Lizzy," she went on, lowering her voice though Bridget was no longer in the room, "they do everything for me in such a way that makes me feel that *they* are beholden to *me*—for giving them something to do!"

She turned a little, to face Georgiana, but with a lurking smile.

"And I hope you mean to tell me, my dear Mrs Bertram, how it comes about that I find myself in the care of another Mrs Bertram?"

Georgiana's answering smile was not a very strong one.

"I had expected your question, of course," she said, "but am nevertheless in some distress to answer it. Perhaps it is simplest to say that she was in truth a *Miss* Bertram—the elder of my husband's two sisters."

"So," said Mrs Gardiner, suddenly more alert, "have we happened upon an interesting scandal? I would have no wish to wound my charming hostess by making some ignorant comment."

"Of course you would not," said Georgiana, with a rather more confident smile. "She was divorced some five years ago and has lived here in retirement ever since. What I find much more disturbing than that is the fact that her own family has never so much as mentioned her existence, or her name, to me."

"How little one knows of real life, after all," remarked Mrs Gardiner, a moment later. "From what one hears one might suppose a divorced woman to be instantly recognisable—by some fault of behaviour, or some immediate lapse in taste—as though they had a red mark on the forehead, one might say. And yet this one is the kindest, handsomest, most considerate person in the world, looking after me as though she had known me all her life. I cannot feel that this is quite as it should be."

"I am sure we should all agree with that," began Elizabeth, but any further discussion was halted by the entrance of Mrs Bertram herself. She had been talking to Mr Bennet in the hall and he followed her into the room. The conversation at once became general and cakes and wine were shortly brought in.

"It is some time since I had so much company in my house," said Mrs Bertram. "I cannot allow the occasion to pass without at least a *small* celebration. Do, pray, do justice to these beautiful little cakes."

She handed the cakes herself. She asked Mr Bennet to pour the wine and he did so with more skill than Elizabeth had expected.

"We find our invalid marvellously improved," remarked Elizabeth, as she accepted a glass of wine. "And I am sure that, if cakes and wine are a part of your treatment, one cannot be altogether surprised."

"I believe in making my patients as cheerful as possible," said Mrs Bertram. "After the dreadful catastrophe in the coal pits at Ashover, we nursed some of the men here—and I found that a pint of porter every day worked more wonders than anything the surgeons were able to suggest. So perhaps it is to be recommended quite seriously."

"Did they stay with you for long?" asked Elizabeth, her curiosity completely aroused.

"Not as long as I could have wished. We had, of course, only the less grievously hurt—those who could be moved as far as this. But, as soon as they were able to travel, they left. I sometimes thought they found the obligation too much."

"That was very good in you—Maria," said Georgiana, hesitating a little before the last word. "It must have kept you very busy—it must have taken all your time. I trust the results gave you the fullest satisfaction?"

"Well, I lack employment undoubtedly," said Mrs Bertram. "With my house and my garden just as I like them, this is not always so easy to find. But on that occasion the only regret one could have was—that one could do so very little."

Mr Bennet hardly spoke while they were in the house; but as soon as they were in the carriage, having promised to return on the following day, he said, with an undeniable edge to his voice: "And now, my dear Lizzy, you may tell me all about this Mrs Bertram, as Georgiana informs me that you know the whole tale. Why has she chosen to bury herself thus, under the brow of Matlock Moor?"

As briefly as she could, Elizabeth did so, having prefaced her recital by saying that she knew only what she had learned from Catherine. Georgiana, too, listened most attentively, but Mr Bennet was the first to speak when Elizabeth finished.

"So this Mr Crawford seems to be the cause of all the trouble. And why, may I ask, did he not marry her? That is behaviour that no one can approve. It takes two to run away, as you may remember."

"I understood they could not like one another well enough to live together any longer," said Elizabeth, "after they had done so for some time."

"It does not quite suit my sense of justice that Mrs Rushworth—as I must suppose her to be—should be called upon to quit society in this way," said Mr Bennet. "We may be perfectly certain that neither of the men in the case felt any obligation to do so. And indeed *who* has decreed that she should have to absent herself from her family, from the circle in which she grew up? I suspect the existence of a pompous, or an overbearing, father."

"Well, as to that," said Georgiana, in rather positive tones, "no one, I think, ever suggested to Sir Thomas that he could be mistaken until I came upon the scene myself. And even I have never dared to do that. I have once or twice been forced to let him know that I have an opinion of my own and, to do him justice, he has, in the end, accepted this. But you must remember that I am in no way dependent upon him. Maria, I imagine, still is."

"And there *I* imagine," said Elizabeth, "is the heart of the problem."

"The errors of a foolish youth are not to be following you all your life," remarked Mr Bennet, almost reminiscently. "Sometimes, indeed, the results cannot be avoided—you make a thoughtless marriage or you choose the wrong profession. But that does not apply in this case. However, I have no experience of this kind of thing. Lydia's little escapade at least ended with the *appearance* of regularity."

"And mine," said Georgiana, without a smile, "ended before it began. How thankful I must be to say so, too." Then, turning to Mr Bennet, she said, almost shyly: "Perhaps I might ask you, Sir, for some advice? As to how to treat this matter when I return to Mansfield?"

"An excellent question," responded Mr Bennet thoughtfully, "and I am by no means certain of my answer. What I think *is* certain is that you must share the problem with your husband. Do not reproach him, or Sir Thomas, or anyone else. I am at one with you in considering that you should have been informed, once your marriage was accomplished, at least. But no good comes of recrimination. You will find, I have no doubt," he continued, a smile in his voice, "that their efforts were made on *your* behalf—to avoid contact, contamination—even contagion, I might suppose them to say. Where I am in no doubt is that you should now do what you can to restore this lady to her family. If you have no objection, if your husband has no objection, why should you not invite her to stay with you? You have a house of your own?"

"My own thought precisely," said Georgiana at once, "and how pleased I am to hear you say so. Sir Thomas, as I understand it now, believed that to receive her again at Mansfield would be to offer an affront to the neighbourhood—but I think she can come and go away again without that neighbourhood being conscious of it."

"And yet," said Elizabeth, doubtfully, "I cannot but wonder if, in her circumstances, I would *wish* to return? Some very hard things must have been said."

"No doubt," said Mr Bennet, "no doubt at all. But *I* seem to recall, my dear Lizzy, that when Lydia's father declined to receive her and her newly-acquired husband at Longbourn, it was you and Jane who persuaded him to change his mind."

"It was," said Elizabeth, cordially, "but I cannot feel that the two situations have much in common—except as being between a father and his daughter."

"Nevertheless," said Mr Bennet, rather more seriously, "my advice to Georgiana stands. I believe she will do well to make as little comment as possible."

Elizabeth and Georgiana drove over again on the next day and once more Mr Bennet came with them. Mrs Gardiner was found to be sitting up in her bedroom, having taken a few steps round the room, supported both by Bridget and her maid. Once again, Mrs Bertram came in with cakes and wine, but this time, as Georgiana was to leave on the following day, they went off to talk together. When, a little while later, Mr Bennet left the room, Elizabeth seized the opportunity to say to Mrs Gardiner:

"I know one should not gossip with the servants, but Bridget can no longer be looked upon as anything but a true friend in need. I wish to know as much of Mr Crawford as you can discover from her. I believe her to have been at Mansfield all the while the great drama—that ended with her coming here—was playing. I would like to hear another account of it."

"There will be no difficulty about that," returned Mrs Gardiner. "I have more than once had to prevent her from telling me the whole, so eager is she to exonerate her mistress. But why should you suddenly be so interested in him?"

"Partly, I think, because I am acquainted with his sisters, who are now gone off to Norfolk to look after him; and partly because I wish to know what kind of man can discard a woman like Mrs Bertram, who seems to be a person of more than usual worth."

"It has crossed my mind as well," said Mrs Gardiner, "to wonder how she precipitated herself into her present situation. But I did not like to enquire too closely. I will, however, see what I can discover, as artlessly as I am able."

XXV

Once more Elizabeth and Mr Bennet asked if they might return the next day, and once more this was smilingly taken for granted. Georgiana took a sad leave of Mrs Gardiner, to whom she had become very attached, and a fond farewell was said by both the Mrs Bertrams.

Georgiana remained silent until they reached the turnpike road and then, almost vehemently, she exclaimed: "I hate to leave her there. It is the *waste*, my dearest Elizabeth, an excellent person thrown away by a censorious society—it is this waste that I deplore. But she seems strangely content. I asked her if I might invite her to Mansfield and she quite astonished me by saying it was the last place in the world where she ever wished to go—the obstacle being, not Sir Thomas as I had thought, but her sister-in-law Fanny."

"That puts a new complexion on the matter," said Mr Bennet. "What cause can they have had to quarrel?"

"It may be of very long standing," said Georgiana. "Fanny was brought up at Mansfield as a poor cousin—her mother is sister to Lady Bertram. There is no knowing what little frictions there may have been in such a long time."

"I have been wondering myself what I could do to restore her somewhat to society," said Elizabeth.

"There cannot be two opinions there," said Mr Bennet very firmly. "You may continue to visit *her*, particularly if Darcy goes too. But it will not do to invite her to dine with you. There would be too many questions to ask—too many conjectures to arise. I would suppose her to be quite conscious of this herself. She could have scraped acquaintance with you on her brother's marriage, but she did not do so. I think one might admire that."

This opinion was reinforced by Mr Darcy's. Elizabeth opened the subject with him when they were alone that night.

"Your father is right, my love. While we can receive her here privately, should her brother happen to be visiting, for instance, or Georgiana herself, we cannot impose her on our friends and neighbours. A woman alone must always be suspect, however unjust that must be. Why did she send her aunt away?"

Elizabeth, remembering the extreme bitterness of the conversation she had overheard in the Pump Room at Matlock, said only: "Because she is the most disagreeable woman in the world and Catherine's letter confirms this."

"*Catherine's* letter? You have never told me about that."

"I have never known just what to do about it," said Elizabeth hesitantly, and after quite a long pause. "At the time it seemed to concern no one in our family, not even Georgiana, since she was never to meet—Maria. That anything of this sort was to happen, you may imagine, was very far from being in my mind."

She went over to the desk and took out the letter.

"I think you must read it for yourself. You must forgive me for not sharing it with you before, but I could see no purpose in burdening you with what seemed to be—knowledge that had no bearing on our lives."

He took the letter and settled down to read it. Elizabeth waited, in some apprehension, to discover how he would feel at never having been shown the letter before; but her alarms were groundless.

"You were quite right to keep all this to yourself," were Mr Darcy's first words, when he came to the end. "I cannot offer you the *smallest* reproach—indeed I am glad to have been spared this until now. It changes nothing, of course. Merely, we are now in possession of *all* the details and will be better informed as to what *not* to mention."

"There seems to be an enormous difference between the Maria in that letter and the Mrs Bertram we have met."

"Does Georgiana know all this?"

"Yes, and my father, too. Georgiana, I believe, is principally disappointed that the Bertrams have never trusted her with what must be called their secret. But my father has advised her not to complain about this—indeed to say as little about it as possible."

"He is a wise man, your father. We are all most fortunate to have him."

Georgiana left the next day, after an earlier breakfast than usual.

"I am quite in a turmoil, inside," was her last remark to Elizabeth, "but at least I shall have the chance to talk it over with my dearest Tom before I say a *word* to anyone else."

Elizabeth and Mr Bennet drove over again in the afternoon, to find Mrs Gardiner dressed and waiting for them in the sitting-room with Mrs Bertram.

"You find me here," she said as they came in, "a monument to the nursing skills of Mrs Bertram herself and her wonderful Bridget. Never could two people have taken such excellent care of a stranger, though a stranger I certainly am no longer. I believe I am now well enough to come to Pemberley tomorrow and, perhaps, to return to London the next day. Though I have to say," she went on, smiling at Mrs Bertram, "I do so with no little regret. Your house is as delightful as I thought when first I saw it. Its loneliness is one of its chief charms."

"And on my side," said Mrs Bertram, "I can only half-regret— if one can do such a thing—that our skills produced such excellent results so soon. We should have been happy to nurse you for much longer."

Once more the cakes and wine came in; once more the conversation turned on amiable, general topics. Elizabeth was aware of a feeling of sadness that this would be the last visit for some time and debated within herself exactly what she was to say in farewell.

"You will allow me to visit you again, I hope," was all she said as she was leaving, "when there is no sick aunt in the case. I can never thank you enough for your kindness to her. And perhaps, in July, when some friends from Bath are with us, I may bring them to see you? They much admired your house last year."

"I shall be more than delighted to see you, and them, whenever you choose to call," replied Mrs Bertram.

She and Elizabeth exchanged a kiss. Mr Bennet kissed her hand and they drove off very cheerfully, with many smiles and much waving.

"That was well-done of you, Elizabeth," said Mr Bennet, after a short while. "I should not have liked her to feel that you had only been making use of her."

"So far as that goes, I wish very much that I could do more. It is a strange aspect of our society that, while women are the principal objectors to divorced ladies being received in *mixed* company, they see no objection to such a person being visited at home, so long as it is only by other women."

"And is that really so, my dear?" said Mr Bennet, in very real astonishment. "Women have always their little secrets, but no doubt you are, as usual, right."

"In any case, as Georgiana's sister-in-law, no matter how disgraced, she has a claim to our acquaintance and I have every intention of continuing it."

Mrs Gardiner arrived at Pemberley the following morning, while Mr Bennet was out riding with Mr Darcy.

"So we can have a comfortable gossip together," said Mrs Gardiner, "somewhere *downstairs*, if you please, and I will tell you all about Mr Crawford."

Elizabeth led the way to the morning-room, which was particularly pleasant at that time of year, and they seated themselves where they could look on to the park.

"Difficult to know just where to begin," said Mrs Gardiner, immediately, "but the whole crux of the matter seems to have been that Mr Crawford was very handsome."

"Perhaps," said Elizabeth, with half a smile, "we should have guessed that."

"Bridget said that all the maids at Mansfield were in love with him, though she did not specifically include herself. He was dark, and very well made, and not too tall and an excellent dancer. He had dark eyes, too—which *smouldered*, I expect—*and*, which is probably the explanation of everything, the longest eyelashes that Bridget has ever seen."

"Perhaps," said Elizabeth, extending her half-smile, "we should have guessed that, too."

"Quite how Bridget who, as I understand, was in the still-room at that time, ever came close enough to observe that, she did not tell me. But, however, having conquered both the Miss Bertrams, as one might say, he then laid siege to Miss Price—the niece—as soon as Mrs Rushworth was married. And she, if you can believe this, refused him."

"Yes," said Elizabeth, "I *can* believe it. Georgiana tells me that she is a lady of unimpeachable morals, of an almost uncomfortable rectitude, and if she saw him flirting with *both* the Miss Bertrams, she would certainly not have accepted him. But did he actually propose to her?"

"That, alas, my informant did not tell me, and there, in fact, my information ends. The great drama, as you call it, unfolded entirely in London, or on the river at Twickenham, to be precise. Only when it was all over, and the servants at Mansfield were asked to make up a household for Maria, did Bridget offer her services. She had known her, and loved her, ever since she was a small girl—and she says she has never regretted it."

"Fortunate, fortunate Maria—what a debt she must owe to Bridget. But while, my dearest aunt, all this information is of the greatest interest—and I must thank you for obtaining it—I do not quite see what it alters."

"It alters nothing, of course. Merely it presents Maria, as it is rather easier to call her, as a volatile girl, capable of a great, if mistaken—I think one *can* truthfully call it passion in this case. She would not be the first woman in the world to be seduced by long eyelashes and to find herself abandoned at last. Though Bridget did hint to me that it was *she* who left *him*, unable to endure it any longer."

"So we may position Mr Crawford as the villain of the piece, as I suppose we must wish to do, with perfect confidence, and without distorting the truth too far? At least I now know, even more completely, what I must never mention."

Mrs Gardiner left for London on the following day and, two days later, Mr Bennet went on his visit to Jane. He said he would probably not call in on his way back, being of a mind to travel south by another route, getting him to Longbourn in a single day.

As she waved good-bye to him, Elizabeth realised that she had had very little private conversation with her father; but she was glad to assume, from his handsome and cheerful appearance, that he was extremely well and by no means disheartened by his solitary life at Longbourn.

A letter from Georgiana arrived less than a week after her departure.

As you could never guess how The News was received here I will just tell you—I quite expected to have put a fox into the henhouse, as it were, but not at all. My dearest Tom simply *roared with laughter*. "Oh my poor Father," he said, "he will have a seizure, or a stroke, or a spasm at the very least. I will tell him very carefully myself." And he must have done so for Sir Thomas said, when next I saw him, in his *grandest* manner: "While I much regret the contact you have recently made, after all our efforts to prevent it, I am gratified to learn than my daughter behaved so correctly in her dealings with your sister-in-law's aunt. I shall certainly inform her of this." But it was Lady Bertram who amazed me most. She suddenly became *alive*. What was she wearing? How doing her hair? What colour were the chairs in her drawing-room? What did she give us to eat? Were there any flowers in her garden? Did I not think Maria the most beautiful girl I had ever seen? Where had she put the cushions that she, Lady B., had embroidered for her? How did the Mansfield furniture look in its new surroundings? (I had to guess the answer to that) and so on. She questioned me for more than three-quarters of an hour, smiling and nodding and *paying attention*. I was quite unnerved. And then Baddeley, the butler, you know, said very quietly to me as I left—"I should be much obliged, madam, if I could inform the Servants Hall that Miss Maria is not only alive but in excellent health." So I assured him that she was, extremely excellent. Only Edmund and Fanny did not say much. I am having to strengthen all my most Christian feelings in order to be civil to them—who should be, of course, far more Christian than I am. I find myself sighing with relief that I shall not see them for nearly two months—we go to Brighton tomorrow and I will send my direction when I get there. But I could not wait to tell you this!

> With fondest love,
> Georgiana.

And underneath she had added: "Pray let my brother read this. He will be as astonished as I was."

Mr Darcy, shown the letter, smiled and said only: "Time is a great healer, indeed. Even Sir Thomas appears to be melting a little. I wonder how much he knows of her life here. I find that it was she who made provision for warmer clothes for the children in the orphanage at Matlock—and also for their more plentiful food."

The month of June was always a favourite one at Pemberley. Elizabeth took the fullest advantage of it, driving every day in the park with her children, meeting Mr Darcy by arrangement in the course of his morning ride, when he would take one of his daughters up in front of him. It was not yet warm enough to spend the whole day out of doors and they usually returned to the house in the early afternoon to give the children a chance to rest before going out again at about four o'clock.

It was on coming back from one of these morning excursions that Elizabeth recognised the carriage drawn up at the front door as belonging to her father; and she was further informed by the butler that he was waiting for her upstairs in her own sitting-room. Stifling her anxieties, and controlling as well as she could the wild conjectures which immediately darted through her head, she made her way there with as little delay as possible. She found him standing by the window, staring out of it.

She was unable to decide on his mood when first she saw him. He looked particularly upright and assured as he turned round, but at the same time there was a suggestion of something in his manner that she could only recognise as uncertainty.

"A charming surprise," she said at once, "but I hope there may not be something wrong?"

"Nothing at all," he said, coming over to her, "but there *is* something I wish to disclose to you."

Elizabeth sat down on her favourite sofa. Mr Bennet remained standing.

"I will not prolong your alarms," he said, very seriously. "I passed only four days with Jane. The last two weeks I have spent in Matlock, going every day to visit Maria Rushworth, with the intention of offering her my hand. Yesterday I obtained her promise, but—as I think you might imagine—there is a condition, and it is this condition that I am come here to discuss."

Elizabeth could immediately think of nothing to say and did not speak. Mr Bennet went on: "You say nothing. It is not altogether unexpected."

Then, turning directly to face her, he said very quietly and with no hesitancy in his voice: "The condition is that our marriage has your full and unreserved approval."

Elizabeth, determined not to remain silent, said, on impulse: "Yes, yes, of course. I think so." And then could go no further.

"You have reservations," said Mr Bennet. "I cannot pretend to be surprised."

Forcing herself to speak, Elizabeth said, as warmly as she could: "All that I—that I and my sisters—could possibly want for you, my dear Father, is your complete and uninterrupted happiness. That your life with my mother was by no means ideal I have known for a long time. To Maria herself, as we know her, there can be no objection beyond the one—that she has been divorced by her husband. I fear that this may be a stigma that there is no removing."

"As I thought," said Mr Bennet, with some satisfaction. "Exactly as I thought. As you might guess, we have talked of little else this last few days."

He walked over to the window again and, standing with his back to her, said, almost as though he were talking to himself: "Probably I am one of Nature's own recluses at bottom. Although, as your mother once said, we dine with four-and-twenty families, it was chiefly on your account that we did so; and very often, as I dressed for yet another noisy party, I wondered how inconsolable I would be if all such occasions were to become a thing of the past—and you may not be too astonished to hear that I thought I could do without them altogether."

He turned towards her again.

"We face, at worst, a total ostracism. This she has endured uncomplainingly for five years, busying herself on other people's behalf in what one must describe as a most exemplary fashion. If we are to live at Longbourn for the rest of our lives, without being visited by our neighbours, how dreadful, I have to ask myself, will this punishment be?"

Elizabeth could only smile.

"I can quite see that you would not be entirely overset if you were never to see Lady Lucas again—or, I suppose, her son-in-law," she said.

"The thought that Mr Collins will cut the connection entirely I regard as one of the more desirable aspects of the situation. But, to be very serious, my dearest child, Maria's fears are centred on my daughters. If they will not accept her, her promise is withdrawn."

Elizabeth sat very still for a moment, marshalling her thoughts and surprising herself when she discovered what they were.

"Your daughters are all married," she said, "and may be supposed to be immersed in their own lives, in every case at a distance from Longbourn. Four of them are known to be concerned that you should not be lonely for your remaining years, which a second marriage would certainly prevent. You choose a charming, beautiful woman, well-born and courageous, who, one must assume, is anxious to share your life with you. But I, too, have a condition. I must hear, from Maria's own lips, her reasons for marrying you. I would not like to think that she does so only to remove herself from a way of life that has suddenly become intolerable."

"Ah, my dearest Lizzy, exactly what I thought you would say—exactly, too, what Maria thought you would say."

"Our only concern, my dearest Father, as I have said, is for your happiness. If Maria is to be the source of that happiness, all we can do is to rejoice."

"She has given me this letter for you," said Mr Bennet, taking it out of his pocket and giving it to her. "Perhaps you should read it now."

It was very short.

I will not compromise you with your neighbours by drawing up unannounced at Pemberley. But see you alone I must. Pray come to visit me, if you are able, this very afternoon.

"Yes," said Elizabeth, at once. "I will go, this very afternoon."

As she got up her father, looking suddenly much younger and more handsome, said to her: "No fool like an old fool, if you like, once again dazzled by youth and beauty, and smitten, no doubt, with midsummer madness into the bargain. But I think myself a great deal more clever than Sir Walter Elliot—and I have already been to thank the Druids for acting so swiftly."

"Then let us hope," said Elizabeth, "that they will continue to smile upon you."

XXVI

It was Bridget who greeted Elizabeth at the door. Maria rose at once when she entered the sitting-room, and came forward with arms outstretched.

"You have come," she said, "you have come, just as your father said you would."

Once more they exchanged a kiss, but Elizabeth was very conscious, this time, of the restraint between them. They sat down opposite each other, on separate sofas, and a long silence followed. Elizabeth would have liked to begin, but every avenue of approach seemed to be blocked. In the end, it was Maria who said: "Your father, I am thankful to find, is fifteen years younger than mine and about as unlike him as possible. While it would not be true to say that I was interested in him from the first moment, it was not long before I found his solicitousness for Mrs Gardiner, for instance, very engaging, and his comfortable relations with you and your husband very remarkable. I will admit, however, that by the time you all went away, I had ceased to regard him as a father and had begun to look upon him as a man. But his appearance here a week later was completely unexpected by me."

"So I would suppose," said Elizabeth. "I love my father and am not surprised when other people do so, too. But the two people who lie between us, at this moment, are Mr Rushworth and Mr Crawford. You have to explain to me—and I make no apology for demanding this—what your feelings were for them and why, in the end, they foundered so completely."

Maria made a gesture with her right hand, though whether it were one of impatience, or one of desperation, Elizabeth was unable to decide. After a long moment, Maria rose and walked over to the window. Looking out if it, with her back to Elizabeth, she said: "Yes, you have the right to know that, much though it pains me to have to tell you. But I will ask you to remember, all the time, that there is almost no resemblance between the Maria of those days and the Maria that you see before you. I have *learned*."

She returned to her seat on the sofa and clasped her hands very tightly together.

"I was at fault all the way through," she said steadily. "I should never have flirted with Mr Crawford, during our acting days at Mansfield. I should certainly never have married Mr Rushworth. Within a week of our wedding I found I could scarcely bear the sight of him."

She looked towards Elizabeth and said, in a voice nearly devoid of expression: "It was a moment of despair that I can never forget—to realise that I was tied for ever to this man, whose touch quite simply made me cringe, and whose mental processes I could unravel only with a monumental patience that I did not then possess. I believe, now, that if we had started at Sotherton—his house, not far from Mansfield—I should have found enough to occupy me there. But we did not. We went from Brighton to London, and there," she went on, with a small sigh, "a little gleam of hope emerged. I found that many fashionable couples led entirely separate lives, but this, of course, would not have suited Mr Rushworth. I was his wife and where I went, he followed. It was indeed a sentence for life."

She sat up and shook her shoulders. She re-arranged her skirt.

"So that when Mr Crawford re-appeared, he was in the nature of a rescuer. I sincerely believed that, if I ran off with him, we could eventually be married."

This time she rose completely and continued talking as she walked up and down, sometimes pausing to make a point with her hand, sometimes appearing to steady herself on the back of a chair. Elizabeth sat quietly; mesmerised; transfixed.

"I think you know what happened. At Everingham, his house in Norfolk, I found that there was much to be done, but we could agree upon nothing. It was a simple clash of titans, of two selfish people who had always had too much of their own way—who were *unable*, as I now realise, to make allowances for other people, or their opinions. We argued constantly. We fought. We slept in different parts of the house. And, of course, nobody came to see us. But in the end it all collapsed very suddenly. At the height of one of his rages, which were very terrifying things, he shouted at me that I had nothing to offer him—that the person he really wanted was my cousin Fanny and that I had divided him from her."

There was a long, long pause. Then Maria went on: "My cousin is a pretty girl—that is to say, I have not seen her since she was my bridesmaid. But she was pretty, in a quiet, unremarkable way. It was, of course, quite wrong to bring her up as we did, believing ourselves superior to her, as in every moral way she was superior to us. She was of fixed and firm opinions. When we tried to persuade her to join our play, one would have thought we were trying to push her on to the stage at Drury Lane itself, so nervous and frightened did she become. She prevailed, however—and in the result we did not perform that play at all. But to be told that Mr Crawford—whom by now I had come to distrust and dislike—preferred her to me was something that my pride could not stand. It was another moment of despair— the first of many, very many."

She was speaking more quietly now.

"I spent that summer in rooms at Sheringham, without a maid. I could not go to Mansfield, I certainly could not go to Sotherton, though both my father and Edmund tried to persuade me to do so. It was there that Bridget came to me, to comfort me and cosset me, and she has been with me ever since. I could say I owe my life to her. I certainly cannot imagine it without her."

She came over and sat down again, clasping her hands as before.

"So—what are my feelings for your father? For that is really what you want to know. If one can love a person gently, without too much interference from the passions, I love him—I *esteem* him. Nothing he has ever said has upset me, and we have talked a great deal. His courtship has been consideration itself. His age is of no matter to me, though it seems to concern him. I am sure he can give me the children that I want. He is, I think, extremely handsome, his eyes especially, those eyes that I see looking at me now, from either side of your nose—there is nothing to offend, but everything to admire, to respond to—to cherish. You need have no fear. He offers me a new life—I hope to give him one. While I may be thought to have deserted two husbands, I shall never do that to him. He comes to me as a refuge. He accepts my past, the stigma that must always come with me. What else can I do but devote the rest of my life to him?"

And she began, quite silently, to cry, the tears falling softly down her cheeks. She did not sob, but sat completely still, making no attempt to stop those tears. After perhaps a minute, which seemed a very long one to Elizabeth, she wiped her face with her handkerchief and said, with a pale smile: "There. It is over. I am better now."

Elizabeth, too, had sat quite still, examining her innermost feelings as closely as she dared. She had wanted her father to marry again. She had expected a widow, or perhaps a girl with several seasons behind her, plain, grateful and serviceable. Instead, she was faced by a young, competent and beautiful woman, who promised to devote her life to that father. There could no longer be any doubt as to her course of action. Gathering herself together, therefore, she said, very calmly: "You have told me what I wished to hear and I believe you. On our side, you will have the full support of my husband and my sister Jane's. Mary's husband is a parson and we can only expect a shake of the head from him. Your own cousin William I would suppose to offer you his endorsement in this or any other situation? And my other sister Lydia and her husband are so remote as to be quite irrelevant."

In her turn, Elizabeth walked over to the window before coming back to face Maria.

"So—we make a bargain. We give you our approval in every aspect in return for your promise to make my father's life a long and happy one, even should you find yourselves ignored by the countryside. Above all, you must promise me never, under any circumstances, to leave him on his own."

She could not have uttered another word, so great did she find the emotion of the moment; but, to her immense relief, Maria instantly replied: "You have my promise. Indeed, it is easily given. I believe I may come to love your father very deeply."

"Then," said Elizabeth, going over to the sofa and offering both her hands, "welcome—Maria."

Elizabeth had plenty of time to consider all the implications of the events of the day as she travelled back to Pemberley. While she was by no means sure that her permission, had it been withheld, would have prevented the marriage, she was certain that the sanction she had now given would ensure that it took place. A very small part of the responsibility for it was therefore hers and an army of doubts assailed her. There was only one person in the world with whom she could discuss what she had done and she was particularly glad to see him waiting for her at the top of the steps when, at last, she arrived. It had seemed a very long way, each mile the length of three.

As he handed her out of the carriage himself, Mr Darcy said to her, in a low voice: "I saw your father today, quite by chance. If it is not *precisely* what we hoped for, it is a situation full of promise."

"I hope only that I may have done right," said Elizabeth anxiously. "Let us go somewhere where you can re-assure me completely."

"And that I am sure I can do."

Upstairs in her own sitting-room, they sat down together on the sofa. Elizabeth placed her hands between his and went through the adventures of the day in a voice which by no means expressed the agitation that she felt inside. Mr Darcy encouraged her all the way through, smiling and occasionally squeezing her hands. When she had finished he said, very firmly: "She rings true, at all points, as do you, my dearest love. If she had set out to ensnare him it would be another matter. But that seems not to have entered her head. The initiative has been entirely with your father. He comes into her life rather as a knight errant and appears to know exactly what their position will be—I truly honour him. A younger man would not, I think, have been quite so intrepid."

"But—you do not blame me? You think they may deal comfortably together? I could not endure the thought that any future unhappiness could be in any way owing to me."

"As to that, I believe you may be perfectly easy. Your father does not aspire to any great social heights. He is a country gentleman, very well regarded in his own neighbourhood. If this second marriage were the result of some wild and recent scandal—in which they were both involved—perhaps there would be talk. But a five-year-old divorce can really touch no one in his circle. It does not have to be denied. It does not have to be advertised. Maria may come to Longbourn, already married, the elder daughter of Sir Thomas Bertram. It must be put in the *Gazette*, of course. How many of your father's neighbours read it, do you think?"

"I should think—none of them. But *all* their wives."

"Then—we must be a little militant there. By giving your father our *fullest* support, those wives may not ask too many questions. If Longbourn comes to life again—it must be very silent now, with you all gone—if Maria's dinners are as good as your mother's, only the most strait-laced of their neighbours will refuse to call. It is when such couples are seen to be avoided by their families that the questions begin to be asked."

"I must hope you will be proved correct. I am glad to think how frequently you are."

"I believe Sir Thomas to have been most unwise to banish his daughter in this unforgiving way, though I do not think Maria thinks so. Now that I have enquired about her everywhere, I find her name most fragrant, particularly in and around Matlock. We may find that your father, to use a vulgar phrase, has pulled out the largest plum in the pudding."

Comfortable again, Elizabeth was able to do justice to her dinner; and she was further re-assured by a visit from Mr Bennet the next morning.

After thanking her, with a slightly satirical gleam in his eye, for her consent to his marriage, he said: "We shall be married in Scotland. The Scotch have an altogether more human attitude to human frailty. I will not go cap-in-hand to some self-important little bishop, to be dragged through every layer of embarrassment before having the Special Licence graciously bestowed upon me. By staying for three weeks in Scotland it can conveniently be brought about there. I go now to astonish Sir Thomas—I hope only that I may not drive him into an apoplexy—even though I do not require his permission. But, particularly in cases like these, one must be civil at all points. And then to London to the lawyers, to Longbourn again and off at once to Edinburgh. I hope we may be married by the end of July."

"I trust, Sir," said Mr Darcy, "that you will permit me, and Bingley if not otherwise engaged, to stand supporter at your wedding?"

His question silenced Mr Bennet for a moment. Then, clearly moved, he said rather gruffly: "Yes, yes, of course, I had not thought." After a small pause, and with a smile, he added: "That would indeed be the kindest thing you could do."

"I have often thought of visiting the Athens of the North."

"I must admit I never have," said Mr Bennet, "but I hope we may not be very disappointed. I fear at least, even at this time of the year, that it may not be as warm as it is in Athens."

XXVII

Events now moved at commendable speed.

Within the week, Mr Bennet wrote from Longbourn to say that, once his initial mixture of stupefaction and disbelief had been soothed away, Sir Thomas Bertram had offered nothing but the most eager compliance. Mr Rushworth had returned Maria's dowry to Sir Thomas "as he was by no means required to do. I understand that he, Rushworth, wished to make the break as complete as possible and presume he took his pound of flesh from Crawford." Sir Thomas had travelled with him to London; the contracts were signed and he, Mr Bennet, could embark on his journey northwards on the following day.

Elizabeth now went once or twice a week to see Maria, sometimes accompanied by Mr Darcy; but on one notable occasion she took her sister Mary with her, at the latter's very strongly expressed insistence.

"I must suppose," said Mary, "that I am the only one of my father's daughters to have read *The Wrongs of Woman* by the late Mary Wollstonecraft. Quite what it was doing in my father's library I cannot imagine and I am sure he had never read it himself. But as it is, of course, unfinished I then went on to read her *Vindication of the Rights of Woman*—and this made a *lasting* impression on me. So I find it quite enlivening," she continued enthusiastically, "to be part of a situation where there are wrongs and rights in a case between a man and a woman. Not that, from what you tell me, Maria seems to have been anything but entirely at fault from beginning to end, but, as my dear Mr Morland said to me only yesterday—we must never forget that Christ came into the world to save sinners."

"But I hope," said Elizabeth, at heart truly relieved to hear her say this, "that you will not view Maria only as a sinner. She is, by any standard, a sinner come to repentance. I believe her to have paid back to society, in the last five years, many times over what it might have demanded in reparation."

"I have a secret admiration, you know," said Mary, with a small smile, "for women who actually do follow their hearts, as I suppose her to have done, the once at least. I remember one summer at Longbourn I dreamed quite constantly of running off with Captain Denny—do you remember him? We were to settle in a cottage in the Lake District and I was to support him with my pen."

"I do remember him," said Elizabeth, concealing her surprise. "Indeed it was he, I rather fancy, who brought George Wickham into our lives."

"Then—the less said about him the better. Though I have to say that I recall him as having been extremely handsome."

Their visit passed off well. Elizabeth was constantly astonished by the continued flowering of her sister, whose behaviour on the occasion was beyond reproach. She admired, without affectation, everything she saw; was as pleasant as possible to Maria; and was in every way the perfect companion.

"Of course," said Mary to Maria, "I think my husband would have married you, had you managed to obtain a licence from the bishop. But I think the present arrangement is the better one. It has all the appearance of a great romance, without any of the usual drawbacks. I only wish I could come with you. But perhaps your own family will be there?"

"At the moment, my father only," replied Maria. "My new situation has cast them all into further turmoil. My brother Edmund refuses to countenance my marriage and will certainly not attend it. My brother Tom is in Brighton and my mother would as soon consider crossing to France as journeying to Edinburgh. Not that, in fact, I would wish her to be there. I shall go with my faithful Bridget. If my father will support me, that is enough."

"I am sorry to find your brother Edmund so unyielding," said Elizabeth.

"He will remember me in his prayers," said Maria, without smiling.

"With what in mind, I wonder?" demanded Mary. "Mr Morland is of the opinion, and I *quite* agree with him, that one should not bombard the Almighty with impertinent requests. That is to say, one should phrase them differently to prevent any tedium developing on high, you know. What further salvation can your brother wish for you?"

"That," said Maria, almost too solemnly, "he does *not* tell me."

"If God did indeed create the human race," said Mary, "His sense of humour—I can never decide. Is it to be admired—or deplored?"

"I think," said Elizabeth, straight-faced, "without any doubt— the former."

"I agree," said Mary, "though Mr Morland, on particularly troublesome occasions, does have his reservations. But," she went on, turning to Maria, "he also says that one must never confuse Christ with His Church. He feels able, therefore, to send you his blessing and his highest hopes for the future."

For which Maria, very seriously, thanked her.

The news of the death of the Emperor Napoleon became general early in July, and a letter came very promptly from Mrs Frankland.

> It is true—it is *true*—the Monster is gone! Our rout party is arranged for the fourteenth of July, which falls this year quite conveniently on a Saturday, and we hope that the irony of this may not be lost on the Monster himself, wherever he finds himself now. Our ball must end at midnight, of course, but that is *not* a matter of regret to *us*! May we then come on a week later, to arrive, should it suit you, the twenty-fourth of July, on our way to my nieces in Yorkshire? Alicia and I are quite astounded by how differently we look in colours—and, indeed, how differently we feel. We have confessed to each other that this was the wish that we made at your Druidical Circle, and we are slightly shame-faced to have had it granted so soon. But I convince myself that this desirable event would have come to pass in any case, and without assistance from such a quarter!

Mr Bennet wrote again, this time from Edinburgh, to say that the marriage ceremony was fixed for the fourteenth day of August.

He had found extremely comfortable lodgings for himself, at Number 14 India Street, and some more, for Sir Thomas and Maria, at Number 24. The air in Edinburgh was both invigorating and healthful. He had discovered a particularly excellent print shop, which sold ravishing views both of the New Town and the Old City, which he would certainly purchase and bring down. He was, in short, in the highest of spirits and Elizabeth's own rose accordingly.

Maria, in some doubt as to whether she, too, had to spend three weeks in Scotland, set off with Bridget as soon as the date of her wedding became known, to eliminate, in her own words, all possibility of error. Elizabeth was surprised to find how much she missed driving over to see her.

She had not felt it necessary to write to Georgiana on the subject of Maria's wedding, since the Mansfield family would have been certain to inform her. She was, therefore, all the more delighted to receive a letter from her two days after Maria had left for Edinburgh.

Strange, strange happenings, dearest Elizabeth, but supported by me with the *warmest* enthusiasm. May I not become aunt to your half-brothers or sisters? It would amuse me to become *your* aunt as well, but that, I think, we cannot accomplish. I am so, so pleased. I like your father extremely and can scarcely believe Maria's good luck—he will give her home, happiness and respectability—more, in a sense, than she had any right to expect (there I seem to detect the fell, the baleful, influence of the *other* Bertram men). But I think them very well-suited and wish them all the good fortune in the world. My dearest Tom goes with his father to the ceremony, since Edmund declines to do so. I think I may remain alone for ten days in Brighton without being abducted or dying of boredom. But I really have no words to describe Edmund's behaviour. Sir Thomas came straight from London to tell us about it and even he, for all that he is for ever on the side of the good, the worthy and the upright, permitted himself a very small word of criticism. Does he, Edmund, I wonder, never listen to his own sermons? I am suddenly grown very *large*—and still October is three months off.

Her letter was followed by one from Mrs Gardiner, announcing the return of her husband.

> He came accompanied by more boxes, chests and trunks than he could find room for in his own warehouse—but he is *well*. So many times I have feared his succumbing to some dreadful fever but he assures me that he was never better in his life. He says he has laid the foundation of a great fortune and, now that I have him back *alive*, I am prepared to rejoice as loudly as he likes.

Then there was a space, a new date, and:

> I am speechless. Your father informs me in a letter three lines long that he is to marry Maria Bertram—and in *Scotland*! I must have been sitting here staring at those last words for a full five minutes and the result of my musings is to ask—am I responsible for this event? I am sure it could not have happened had I not fallen as I did. So the next questions are—Should I feel guilty? Am I accessory? Or should I be congratulating myself as a divinely skilled matchmaker? I am quite astonished to find myself inclining towards the last of these. Here are two, shall we say, *solitary* people joining together to the immense benefit of each other. Mr Gardiner said to me, soon after your mother died, that he hoped your father would marry again, if only to prevent him becoming a total recluse, as his father was before him. So that is now avoided. Longbourn will have an excellent new mistress, if one is to judge by the charm and comfort of her moorland retreat, and perhaps they may both have a family to live for. As far as the fact of her previous marriage goes, I do not know what to say—the less said the better, I fancy. Indeed, there is no reason why it should ever become known in Hertfordshire and we must just trust that this will be the case. This must be all for the present, dearest Lizzy. I find I am still a little breathless.

The month of July slipped by, swiftly and in a blaze of hot sunshine. Their own Open Day, on the nineteenth of that month, took place on the same day as the Coronation of the King. This event passed almost unnoticed in Derbyshire and it was not until the next day, when the London papers arrived, that it became a topic of discussion at Pemberley.

"Our new monarch," observed Mr Darcy, rather dryly, "seems determined to set no pattern of gentlemanly behaviour for us, his humble subjects. To close the door of the Abbey in his wife's face—for wife she remains in spite of his efforts—is an action quite unworthy of any Christian, let alone the Head of the Church, as I must suppose him also to be. Though, perhaps, the alternative is equally unalluring. Had she obtained entrance, only to find no bishop willing to place a crown upon *her* head—*what* an uproar there would have been! Possibly he was wise—though I have to say I think him very lucky to have avoided an out-and-out riot."

"It must be many, many years," remarked Elizabeth, "since the people of this country paid any attention to the goings-on at Court. Which, I think, I now regret. The Court's attitude to adultery, if not precisely to divorce, is there for all to see."

"You are still not happy about this marriage, my love? What principally disturbs you?"

"I fear they may be dropped by many people close to Longbourn."

"If Maria can establish herself ahead of her reputation, there should be no difficulty. It may never follow her, but it is a possibility that we should be very unwise to discount. And I do not, in any case, deny her ability to outface them all, even should your direst imaginings come to be realised."

"But you would not like a divorced woman to marry into your family?"

"No, I suppose, I would not, though the two cases are hardly similar. Your father is a mature, established man, his means as independent as his mind. He is subject to no patronage. He is second to no one in his circle. He has no relatives except his daughters, who support him. If anyone can override such a situation, he most certainly can. And consider also what Maria brings him—health, beauty, a grateful heart and, if I am not very much mistaken, a handsome fortune. Should your father have a second family, they will be off to an excellent start."

Elizabeth tried hard to convince herself, but she said only: "I must learn not to be so faint-hearted."

XXVIII

Mr Darcy's opinions were echoed by Lady Alicia and Mrs Frankland. They arrived, as arranged, on the twenty-fourth of July. They were smiling, cheerful and delighted to be back, both looking quite ten years younger out of their widows' weeds.

"Your father is not a young man," said Lady Alicia, "not a probationer on his preferment. If his new wife is as young and beautiful as you tell us, his old friends will merely be envious—and the younger ones as well, for that matter. They will be more likely to come and stare than to stay away."

"Unless, of course," amended Mrs Frankland," she is going to put all the wives *entirely* in the shade. Then, perhaps, there might be cause for alarm. But we wish them well in any event. We like your father very much, although perhaps this is the moment to admit," she added, with her charming smile, "that we did not think Miss Crawford would have filled the bill at all."

They stayed two weeks and left with Mr Darcy, on his way to Edinburgh. They were all to spend a night with the Bingleys and then to travel together as far as York.

The days now passed slowly for Elizabeth. The weather was kind and she spent every day in the park with her children; but Mr Darcy did not come back until the end of the third week in August. He was full of enthusiasm for the northern capital and the degree of comfort he had found on his journeys. The inns had been everywhere excellent and the lodgings in Edinburgh beyond criticism. Elizabeth barely repressed the thought that he and Mr Bingley seemed to have much enjoyed their return to bachelor existence.

"Your father was quite right, I think, to keep the party small. It was a simple, straight-forward service, unlike our own but not too different. Tom and Sir Thomas supported the bride as impressively as anyone could wish. I hope we may have done the same by the bridegroom. It was an austere, elegant church in the Canongate of the Old Town, and they are to honeymoon in the Waverley country, to the west. Your father seems very taken with Scotland," said Mr Darcy, adding with a smile, "although, to use his own words, he had never before given a thought to that country in the whole course of his life."

"And how did he look?"

"As handsome and as healthy as any bridegroom I ever saw, by no means old enough to be the father of five married daughters. Maria I thought to be looking magnificently well and, though I fancy there must be twenty years between them, this did not at all appear to be the case."

In October, their shooting parties began and, before that month was two weeks old, Georgiana, in the words of Tom Bertram, "was safely delivered of a fine boy." The jubilations at Mansfield were tremendous and Elizabeth and Mr Darcy joined in them all, in spirit; but it was not until the beginning of the next month that Elizabeth received the letter she was really waiting for, and even then it did not entirely satisfy her.

Longbourn, November 8th

With deepest shame, my dear Elizabeth, do I inscribe this date. I am compelled to state also that I know it to be the right one, since I have had to consult an almanac in order to make sure. Pray, pray forgive this disgraceful, long silence and believe only that the wish to write has never been lacking, but only the leisure and tranquillity to do so. So let me begin by saying that, if ever I had any reservations about this marriage—and in the far recesses of my own heart, you will concede that there must have been *some*—they have all, all been done away with. The revolution in my life brought by the last six months is equalled only by the six months that ended in my flight to Matlock. But where *that* revolution left me stranded, static, regretting with my whole heart what I had lost, what I had done, *this* one leaves me breathless and speechless, joyously computing what I have gained. My husband is the kindest, most smiling, most ironical, most humorous, the wryest and most compassionate man in the world. He forms a stark contrast to Mr Crawford, who did not at all understand what it was to be human—or perhaps I should more truthfully say, what it was to be a woman—and Mr Rushworth, who barely merits inclusion as a human being. Our honeymoon was a joy from start to finish. My arrival at Longbourn, though for the first time, contrived to be a homecoming. I am already in love with this house. I shall change it very little, you may believe me. And in the last six weeks I have been, I state in all humility but with a *little* pride, much in the nature of a raree-show. Our delighted butler tells me—and I am sure he knows—that no one of any consequence (if I may employ his rather *consequential* phrase) within a circle of twenty miles has failed to come *and have a look*. And we have—and you will certainly appreciate this—returned *all* those bride visits. Perhaps, after all, I have some reason for not writing before. But I am charmed by the servants, who smile and take care of me. Bridget and Mrs Hill appear to be the greatest friends (an area of some anxiety before) and the butler is already as much a friend as my dear Baddeley at Mansfield, always a great supporter and encourager. Only *one* little patch of gloom—as of course there must be *one*—in the person of your gardener. No matter how hard I try, I cannot regard him as mine. I wish him to make a flower garden on that piece of ground between the dining-room window and the paddock. But every objection is placed in the way. No doubt he thinks of it simply as a great deal of unnecessary work, but it was I who tended my flowers in Matlock and I who will do so again at Longbourn. Perhaps he has not quite understood this. I believe your mother did not at all enjoy gardening? However, I am loud in praise of The Boy, other appellation unknown, who is a most notable Digger. I have to mention also a delightful surprise of ten days ago, when a set of magnificent curtains for the drawing-room arrived, ordered *eighteen months ago*, by your sister Jane. They are a kind of amber, warm and elegant, quite the right colour for the room. I mean to repeat it by covering the old sofa below your grandfather's portrait—on which no one, to my husband's knowledge, has ever actually sat—in the same material. On which housewifely note I close. A tenant has been found for the house at Matlock, a young woman with two very young children, but not a widow. The agent thinks she is hiding from her husband

and, if she is so, she has certainly chosen the right place. I do not, in my turn, *choose* to subscribe myself as "your loving step-mother", but only as Your most loving Maria.

Elizabeth read and re-read this letter. Nowhere did there seem to be any mention of Maria's own health and neither was there any reference to Georgiana's baby. She sat down, therefore, and wrote to Maria by return. The hint was taken.

Longbourn, November 21st

Why, I wonder, did no one at Mansfield think of informing *me* that Georgiana's son was safely born? You observe that I am sufficiently displeased *not* to refer to this child as Tom's son. They must be overjoyed and I hope and trust that Georgiana is perfectly well again. Which gives me the space to disclose that I too am increasing, with the expectation of being delivered in May. I must have conceived on my wedding night. I hope that, with the faint mystery attached to this marriage—although we have told them *nothing*—the child will consent to be late rather than early. I have received charming letters from three of your sisters and think that perhaps the time is come to inform them all, and the Gardiners, too. They are to be here at Christmas and we shall go to them after those festivities are over—to go to the theatre and have supper somewhere afterwards and behave in general like foreign visitors. Your father—as I sometimes think of him when he is being, very rarely, disobliging—has no enthusiasm for this outing, but as it is twenty years since *he* went to a theatre, and at least seven since I did so myself, I do not mean to let anything stand in the way. I propose also to move into the room that was yours and Jane's, before this child is born. It is quite the best room in the house and would overlook my flower garden, should it ever happen to be made. So I indulge at present in a most favourable occupation—choosing wallpaper.

Perfectly satisfied now, Elizabeth showed this letter to Mr Darcy and then settled down to enjoy the preparations for Christmas. The house was filled, by the Bingleys, who stayed for a fortnight, and by the Morlands, who came for a week. Mr Morland did not like to leave his parishioners for longer than that.

The snow fell immediately after the New Year and lay until the middle of February. Elizabeth began to feel anxious for news from Longbourn but, when it came, it was a letter from her father.

Longbourn, February 22nd

I enclose, my dearest Lizzy, a letter from your erstwhile suitor, William Collins, which you may show to Darcy and then put into the fire with my goodwill. It seems that he believes, and hopes, that Maria and I are not legally married and I wonder what I have ever done to make him think me such a fool.

Mr Collins's letter was very clear.

Sir, I can hardly express the horror I experienced today, on receiving a letter from Sir William Lucas. Sir William, on a visit to St. James's to compliment our new monarch, there encountered a certain Mr Rushworth, who informed him, among other things, that the present Mrs Bennet is a former wife of his. While undoubtedly a daughter of Sir Thomas Bertram, in my opinion, and in the sight of God, her second marriage must be regarded as bigamous until the decease of Mr Rushworth. I understand, furthermore, that her divorce was necessitated by an ugly scandal, with her at its centre. As I cannot allow myself, or Mrs Collins, or my daughters, to associate themselves with such a person, I must demand that all communication should cease henceforth between us.

I remain, Sir, Wm. Collins.

Elizabeth showed both these letters to Mr Darcy and they enjoyed a quiet laugh together. She put the letters in the fire but, at the back of her mind, lay the uncomfortable conviction that the fact of Maria's previous marriage must by now, through the agency of the Lucases, be common knowledge around Longbourn. She awaited the next letters from Longbourn with a little trepidation, but the first one, from Maria, was very short.

I am become so huge that I now live upstairs entirely. Either I am with child of an elephant or I am about to give birth to an army. My husband eats his meals up here with me—I am now happily ensconced in *your* bedroom—and Hill and Bridget vie with one another as to who shall take the greater care of me. If anything should happen, dearest Elizabeth, I wish it known that I have never been so happy.

Elizabeth replied as soothingly as she could to this letter, unable to feel any real anxiety. Maria, she knew, had been attended throughout by a surgeon from Hatfield, who had never indicated that there was any cause for alarm. It was, however, to be the last letter from Maria for some time.

A brilliant April had followed a reluctant March. A damp and sullen May went slowly by. Not until the fifteenth of that month, to Elizabeth's great relief, did an express arrive from Longbourn.

> My superb Maria yesterday was delivered of two fine sons, seven and six pounds in weight. All are thriving. She wishes them to be called Henry, for my father, and Thomas for hers. She desires her best love to you and Darcy. We hope to have them christened in six weeks time and depend upon your presence then. I have informed Mansfield and all your sisters save Lydia. Meanwhile, believe that everyone is well and in particular,
>
> Your loving and *exultant* Father.
>
> Have not informed Collins. He may read it in Lady Catherine's *Gazette*.

It took a very short time to assimilate the import of this letter.

There were now *two* heirs to Longbourn.

Elizabeth smiled; kissed the letter; and handed it to Mr Darcy.